Cracking Open
a Coffin

GWENDOLINE BUTLER

Cracking Open a Coffin

St. Martin's Press
New York

Library of Congress Cataloging-in-Publication Data

Butler, Gwendoline.
Cracking open a coffin / Gwendoline Butler.
p.   cm.
"A Thomas Dunne book."
ISBN 0-312-09777-8 (hardcover)
1. Coffin, John (Fictitious character)—Fiction.   2. Police—England—Fiction.   I. Title.
PR6052.U813C7   1993
823'.914—dc20   93-25501
CIP

First published in Great Britain by HarperCollins Publishers

First U.S. Edition: September 1993

10 9 8 7 6 5 4 3 2 1

Letter to John Coffin from Professor Lessingham, The Institute of Mental Health, Bury Hill.

'I am coming to the opinion that there are certain types of killers who might be called periodic serial killers in as much as they will only kill when the victim offers exactly what is required. So there may be long gaps in the cycle.

'In these cases there is a symbiotic relationship between killer and victim: they move towards each other.

'The rules as to the victim, manner of killing, disposal of the body have to be kept . . . But even the most dedicated of serial killers will be frustrated by circumstances, something the killer did not take into account, or could not control. There will always be cases out of pattern, that do not conform.'

CHAPTER 1

A day in early autumn

One day in early autumn the neighbourhood newspaper, *Second City News*, carried a special supplement on the university, then celebrating its fifth birthday and welcoming that year's intake of students. As well as a large photograph of the head of the university, Sir Thomas Blackhall, there was a page of photographs in colour of some of the students.

Students at tutorials, seen in a booklined room, are neatly posed around their tutor. One of them is reading an essay, the others listen.

Students at lectures, observing the lecturer write an equation on a large board spread across the wall behind him. He does it with some electronic device that he does not understand because he would prefer old-fashioned chalk. Once he failed, unknowingly, to use it correctly, so that nothing appeared on the board, and then, absent-mindedly back in the days of chalk, he turned round and wiped what wasn't there clean away with the back of his sleeve. This brought down the house.

Students in the library, heads bent over their books. Because this is not Oxford (where the habit was abandoned years ago) and because the university is so young, it is the fancy here for all the students to wear shortish academic gowns.

Students at parties, at their summer ball. A crowded scene with many outsiders, among whom John Coffin might have recognized one of his own officers if he had looked more closely. Later, he was to regret this. The girls wear long dresses and the lads wear black ties and dinner jackets. There is even a couple where the girl wears what looks like a Christian LaCroix crinoline and the boy wears tails.

A golden pair, thinks John Coffin, head of the Second City Police, and he remembers his own youth was so far

7

from golden. A line underneath says: *Amy and Martin*. Well, good luck Amy and Martin, he thinks.

Tutorials, academic gowns, formal evening clothes, the new university is building its traditions. Unfortunately, it looks as if murder might be one of them.

John Coffin took the *Second City News* regularly and it happened that he had seen this photograph while sitting in the sun by the river. Not far from where he lived in his home in an old church was a small park which overlooked the Thames. It was an ancient, rundown little park, all that remained of the grounds of a mediæval bishop's palace. A stretch of old stone walling, probably all that was left of the old place, ran along the river for a few yards and this was where Coffin sat.

In the first place he liked the wall, in the crevices of which yellow and white weeds flowered in the autumn, and secondly there was a smell to it that reminded him of his childhood.

It was communicating something to him, that smell. Opening up a window through which he could peer at the past.

He had grown up by the river. This river, just as dirty and travelworn by the centuries, but winding through a different part of London. South, where the river takes a deep curve and looks up to the hills of Kent.

It had not been a happy childhood. More or less orphaned (although mother, as it turned out, was still alive but missing), brought up first by a grandmother and an aunt, and then by the aunt alone, and finally fostered out to one family after another.

There were a lot of memories of that childhood that were thrashing around in his mind, some he was busily engaged in repressing but others were getting through.

He remembered sitting by the river, aged ten. He was fishing with a bit of string, a hook, and a tin can for the fish. But inside he was dreaming of himself in an open motorcar with a princess beside him. She was faceless but definitely royal.

The beginning of sex, he supposed. Late, by current standards.

Well, he eventually got the motorcar, although not the bright red open speedster of his dream, but never the princess. Although he had had several shots at it.

And that brought him back to Stella. Darling, beloved, infuriating Stella to whom he had never been totally faithful nor totally unfaithful either.

Which was where you had to think about it, because Stella was angry with him. She had opened her eyes wide and said: 'To hell with you.'

They hadn't met for a few days now. They would meet again and things would be patched up, neither was prepared for a decisive break.

There was another aspect to the problem of Stella, and he had a letter in his pocket, highly personal and very unwelcome, and one which caused him fury but which would have to be addressed.

And all the time he was thinking about Stella and the golden pair of students, he was conscious of dry bones moving at the back of his mind. So that of all the people presently concerned with the murders, he was the least surprised.

CHAPTER 2

October. The first two days

A girl's sweater, striped blue and white, lay on the edge of the River Thames near where Herring Creek and Leadworks Wharf looked across the water to each other. It was stained and muddy. On the front was an initial which might have been a D or a C but some small river creature had nibbled away at. No one had noticed the sweater yet, but it ought to be found soon.

*

9

'The trouble with opera is the singers,' said Philippa Darbyshire gloomily. She shook her head so that the slightly greying fair curls bobbed around her face; she was large but pretty and enjoying her middle years more than she would admit to her women friends. She had banned the word menopause, women didn't have it now, you had hormone replacement. A smile lightened her face. 'It would really be better without them.'

'But not nearly so much like opera,' suggested John Coffin. The two of them were seated in the bar of St Luke's Theatre late on the chill October morning. This theatre was the creation of his talented sister, Lætitia Bingham, who had taken a derelict church in the old docklands beyond the Tower of London and turned it into a theatre with a theatre workshop attached. The main theatre was due to be opened officially this summer by the Queen, but of course it had long since been opened and running unofficially, operating at a handsome profit. Recession, it seemed, was not hurting the theatre.

John Coffin, Chief Commander of the Second City of London police force, lived in one of the three apartments which had also been formed from the old St Luke's Church. He had come through a difficult three years since his appointment to this new command and the lines around his eyes had deepened and the once dark hair was neatly silvered at the temples. He had fought his way up the career ladder to the top and now wondered whether and when he would fall off.

But he liked heights. He had a flat in the tower of the old church with a fine view across his troublesome bailiwick. Hard by, in another apartment, lived the actress Stella Pinero, the love of his life or the bane of it, depending how their relationship was going.

He was waiting for her now. Stella had been playing in a West End revival of *Mourning Becomes Electra*. It had not gone very well, although she personally had had delightful reviews, and she was now back at St Luke's Theatre of which she was Director and guardian spirit. It had been created around her.

10

Philippa had seized on him with the joy of one who needed to talk, beginning with a brisk: 'I suppose you're waiting for Stella? She came in, said you were late and went out again.'

I wasn't late, Coffin thought sadly. I'm never late. Or if I am, it isn't my fault. What he was, was not there much. As a serving police officer of high rank, he had a crowded life. But Stella herself was often absent and her excuses were nebulous and vague.

'But she left you Bob,' Philippa had added.

'I know.' Bob, a mongrel of loving disposition, had already pressed his head on Coffin's foot. You are my friend and half-owner, the pressure said, and now I can look after you and you can look after me. 'Move over, Bob.' Coffin tried to lift his left foot which was going numb. Bob growled. He believed fiercely in physical contact. Coffin patted his head which was rough and wiry, he knew that there would now be gingery hairs all over shoe and trouser leg. 'Good dog,' he said.

He sipped his coffee and looked at Philippa, whom he liked and admired and somewhat feared: she seemed capable of everything, and had once persuaded him to take part in a play production. But he would have nothing to do with singing. Not even as a goblin.

His mind moved back to his own purely personal and private problem. Several weeks ago he had had a telephone call. A man who did not announce himself.

The call came through in the early morning, at home, in his sitting-room, which outraged him even more. This place was his sanctuary, his refuge.

'Copper, watch your back. They're gunning for you. Better get your answers ready.'

It was repeated several times.

'Copper, watch your back. Watch your back. Watch your back.'

He had slammed the telephone down without answering it, shrugged and gone back to drinking his coffee. Not exactly forgotten it, but taking not much notice of it, either. He was used to the odd mad call.

11

A week later to the very day, to the hour almost, came another call. Someone who knows when I drink my morning coffee, he had thought wryly. Same message, not exactly word for word but close enough.

Some days later he came to find a message on his answering machine. More of the same. He thought he recognized the slight cough that prefaced the advice.

But it was different this time.

'This is a message from a friend: tidy up your private life or you will be in trouble. Serious trouble. No joking.'

He turned the machine back, slowly and carefully.

The letter came several days later, as he had always supposed it would, and it was now festering inside him like a bad boil.

His unknown caller had had good information. All this was at the back of his mind while he listened to Philippa.

Philippa was still going on about singers: 'Oh, we have to have them, but off stage, that's the place for them. Where we can't see them. Just their voices. On stage we would have actors, dancers, who would look right. Singers have the wrong shape. They can't help it, they need it to produce the voice, but we shouldn't have to look at them trying to be Tosca or Mimi. Not to mention Siegfried and Brunnhilde.' Mrs Darbyshire gave a feeling shudder. 'And the Valkyries . . . Overweight, all of them. How can you dress them as warriors, I ask you?'

Coffin looked his sympathy and tried again to shift Bob from his foot. Bob sank deeper down.

'And I'm having such trouble with the students from the university. Such sharp little critics. Must think things through, they say. Just sing, I say.'

Coffin offered sympathy again. 'You'll manage.' In his experience of the ladies of Feather Street, of whom Philippa was one, they managed all they wanted. Even this production of extracts from The Ring would work out.

'I think it's university life. They're spoilt, those kids.'

'They have their troubles,' he said softly.

He knew something she didn't.

He knew that two students were missing. A boy and a

12

girl. Whether together or otherwise was not yet clear. They had last been seen standing by her car.

Gone two days. Not long, but in the circumstances, long enough.

In the new university there were three residential blocks in which the students had rooms. The rooms were tiny, but each had its own bathroom and tiny slip of a kitchen. This was not so much for ease of student living as because in the long vacation there was much lucrative letting for conferences.

The three blocks were named after benefactors, they were Armitage, Barclay and Gladstone. Each block had its own character, or was thought to have, and which was perhaps self-perpetuating: Barclay was rowdy and thus attracted the drinkers and the rugger players; Gladstone was near the library and the science buildings, so the industrious and the scientists settled there; Armitage was the fashionable and social block, the smartest place to live, and it attracted as well as the party-goers, the drama and music students.

The missing students had lived in Armitage. Their group of friends there were among the first to be worried by their disappearance.

In Angela Kirk's room a small meeting was taking place.

'It's horrible.' This was Mick Frost, tall and thin.

'Don't exaggerate, Mick, we don't know that anything's happened.' Beenie was a year older than Mick and inclined to slow him down.

'We know what's been happening,' said Mick. 'We've seen, we've known the state she was in even if we haven't talked about it.'

'It wasn't easy to talk about it. That sort of thing isn't easy to talk about, and anyway part of it was us guessing.'

'Pretty clear,' said Mick. 'Pretty clear. Sex and violence.'

Angela said: 'Don't talk like that.'

'Mick's right,' said Beenie from the floor where she was stretched out. 'We should have done something . . . After all, there was Virginia last year.'

'We don't know about Virginia.' Angela again.

13

'I think we do,' said Mick.

Beenie shifted uneasily. 'OK, OK, so let's do something.'

'I'm frightened,' said Angela. 'I don't want to go that way.' She was scared and yet excited.

'Oh, come on,'

'No, I tell you, it's evil, talking like this.' The word dropped into the room, cold and hard.

Angela bent her head to let a long fall of shining blonde hair cover her face. She stretched her thin white arms and imagined them with blue bruises and saw herself as victim.

It can't happen to me, she thought. If I keep quiet perhaps it will all go away . . . Beenie's all right, she's brown and tall and strong. She crossed her arms across her chest, protecting herself.

Aloud, against her will, she heard herself say: 'We owe Amy something. I could go down to Star Court, offer to help.' It was as if she wanted to be a victim, that was what she had chosen and it would do.

'Don't let her, Beenie,' said Mick. 'Stop her.'

Beenie shrugged.

There was silence in the room.

'I've got to go,' said Mick, standing up. 'I've got to audition for some creepy amateur performance of Wagner.'

'Why do you go, then?' asked Beenie.

'Sucking up to our dear Professor,' said Mick with a ravishing smile. 'Also, we get paid, not much but something and if you are aiming at a professional singer's career (and I might be) you have to learn to take the money where you can find it.'

At the door, he turned and said: 'While I am singing Wagner, look after yourself, Angie. Wagner, here I come.'

The Friends of St Luke's Theatre, a group of local ladies important in Coffin's life for all sorts of reasons, who put on an amateur performance once a year, were attempting an opera. Not the whole opera, just a scene or two. The choice bits, as they said. They had considered *Rosenkavalier*, *The Marriage of Figaro*, and *La Bohème* (a strong lobby for this last opera), but they were long-time supporters of the

14

rights of women and the Ride of the Valkyries seemed just to fill the bill.

There was an added motive: they had a vibrant dramatic soprano among their ranks, Lydia Tullock, and Lydia was also rich. Others among them had good voices. So they had joined up with the Spinnergate Choral Society and the very strong Music Department of the local university, the University of the Second City, to launch their production.

Mrs Darbyshire was the designer for costumes and sets for this ambitious enterprise; in her youth she had been an assistant to Motley and then gone on to work for Douglas Duguid. She had retired to marry Harold and bring up her family in their Victorian house in Feather Street, but now in middle age she had gone back to work, and had been hired by the Friends of St Luke's. Of course, she was a Friend herself, but she was a professional, as she pointed out fiercely when they suggested she should do the job for nothing, and women must be paid. She would have done it for nothing, she loved her work, but standards had to be maintained. Also, Lydia was rich and could afford anything and Philippa was poor, but she had her problems and was being vocal about them.

'Our Siegfried now, Turnwall Taylor, he's a lovely man, I have nothing against him personally, but he is frankly fat. Imagine dressing him up in brown leather togs and getting him to woo Brunnhilde. She's outsize too, and every one of the Valkyries has a weight problem.'

She sighed heavily. 'You never get everything. I remember saying to Larry once what a lovely Wotan, King of the Gods, he would make. He had the majesty, you see, but he hadn't the voice.'

She probably had known Lord Olivier, Coffin thought, or at least met him. Philippa did not lie, but she had the trick, familiar to him from his theatrical friends, of slight exaggeration.

'He'd have brought in the customers. Bums on seats, we need that, money is so short, and opera *costs*. I hoped to get more out of the university, but . . .' She shook her head.

'Money's short all round,' said John Coffin. He had

15

budget problems himself. In the few years that he had been Head of the Force in the Second City of London, he had never had enough resources to do all that was required in the turbulent area for which he was responsible. The old villages of Spinnergate, Swinehouse, Leathergate and Easthythe that were bound together in his Second City were expensive to police.

'But they have been very generous with help, the Drama Department there, so vital, isn't it? And such a vigorous Music Department.' The Music Department was providing the orchestra, musical director and conductor as well as a few singers to audition. Philippa Darbyshire was half in love with the conductor, a beautiful young man, some sixteen years her junior and none the worse for that, she thought.

My goodness, she said to her inner self, how times have changed. My mother wouldn't have dreamt of letting herself be attracted to a man so much younger than herself, wouldn't have admitted the possibility, but I'm not only admitting it, I'm enjoying it.

She even enjoyed the fact it was not reciprocated. It might have been awkward indeed if it had been, for Harold might not have liked it. Well, wouldn't have done. Harold was her husband. Once a banker, now enjoying early retirement, he was doing a course at the nearby university. Not in drama or anything dangerous like that, thank goodness, she thought (she was the one allowed temptation, not Harold), but in fine art.

The university had been put together out of a Polytechnic and College of Advanced Technology, when it was decreed that the new Second City of London must have its own university.

This Second City had several great hospitals, one of which had a history going back to a monastic foundation of the thirteenth century, three museums, two art galleries and an assortment of old and new industries. It was represented in the House of Commons by two MPs and in the House of Lords had one recently ennobled peer who bravely called himself Lord Brown of Swinehouse.

16

Many of the old warehouses of the former docklands had been converted into smart apartment blocks, but old streets and grimy old housing estates still supported the old poor who eyed their new rich neighbours without love.

It was no easy area to police, with violence never far below the surface and always threatening to break out. A large garage attacked only yesterday. A few days ago a robbery with savage violence in a shop in the Tube station in Spinnergate, two badly injured, a crime that was still being investigated, no leads.

On the two large housing estates which were separated by a railway line and a belt of expensive upper-class apartments, gangs formed, fought each other, and the police too if they could, then melted away as fresh and younger outfits took their place. The Dreamers, once the most powerful group, had gone into decline when several members had been sent to prison and another couple had married, which as far as active gang life went came to the same thing. This had left the field to their rivals, who called themselves The Planters after the Planter estate where most of them lived. But somehow, without the competition, The Planters too had gone into decline. With no one to fight, what was the point to being? There was a short-lived revival of Dreamers Two, but it failed to inspire. Either the police were getting quicker to stamp out trouble-makers or the gangs were getting weaker. Who could say?

At the moment there were no big gangs, but Coffin had heard stories of a new one forming itself around a female leader. He believed it.

He had not met her yet, but no doubt he would if she became powerful enough. He had heard she was called Our General.

Such was the Second City where John Coffin held the Queen's Peace and in which he lived.

'You can't think,' said Philippa, 'how hard it is to find women warriors who can sing.'

Wonder if I should suggest she tries Our General, thought Coffin.

'I'm not sure if I like the Valkyrie concept anyway,' said

17

Philippa. Under the influence of the Drama Department, whether she admitted it or not, she had started to intellectualize her reactions to plots and story lines. 'I mean, I don't know any.'

They exist, thought Coffin.

Philippa finished her coffee, looked regretfully at a plate of chocolate croissants, but she mustn't, she really mustn't, that last inch on her hips since she had given up being a vegetarian was one inch too many, and got to her feet. 'I must be off. Got an appointment with the Head of Drama at the university, he's going to help me find some extra Nibelungs. I could do with some really short, dwarflike men with good voices.' The Head of Drama was a handsome man too, she was looking forward to the half-hour together. She picked up her bags, Philippa always travelled with a full complement of shoulder-bags, clutch bags and the odd plastic carrier. Her mood was good in spite of the difficulties with the Valkyries. She would see her beautiful young musician, he had promised to be there, bringing a few young male singers to audition. It was wonderful how a family growing up and leaving home emancipated you. I am a New Woman, she announced to herself.

'I'll hang on a bit longer,' said Coffin. He watched her departure with indulgence and a touch of sympathy; he could guess her motives. There was one thing about being a policeman: you often knew more about your friends and neighbours than they guessed. He knew about the young conductor, Marcus Deit. He even knew more about Marcus than she did, but that would be telling. 'Goodbye.' He was glad to sit thinking.

'They have been gone two days. This is day two and we are into day three, and nothing, not a word. With students, you never know, just gone off, you say to yourself. But she's my child, my child.' He could hear the man's voice, rough with worry. 'And her car has been found.'

John Coffin would not normally have been concerned with the story of the missing students. Or not so soon. The Chief Commander of the Second City Force had access to all information about what was going on in his difficult and lively territory. He was responsible for all and was meant to know all. That was the theory. As with the Queen, all important documentation came his way for signature but it took time. Reports were filtered through subordinates, prepared and then presented on his desk. His secretaries might do a bit of selection here too, he was protected and had to keep a wary eye on that protection. He knew that things were kept from him.

So he had developed the habit of just dropping in on departments. Of prowling round and asking questions. The CID inevitably got a lot of his attention. He couldn't give up the habit; once a detective, always a detective. Also inevitably, this interest did not meet with the total approval of the CID teams, and although obliged to grin and bear it, they had ways of getting their feelings across.

Coffin had noted with amusement and understanding the tactics of Chief Superintendent Paul Lane and the wily manœuvring of Chief Inspector Archie Young. Young's tricks were cleverer but Paul Lane got away with more: experience did tell, Coffin had told himself wryly while furthering the recent promotions of both men. The nominal head of the CID was Harry Coleridge, but he was a quiet, efficient administrator who would soon be retiring.

Jockeying for Coleridge's position was already going on, but John Coffin was considering bringing in an outsider. What about a woman? Was there one? Yes, there was, he knew a name. Keep quiet, he told himself, and watch events. He had learnt politics, willy-nilly, in his job.

But in the matter of the missing students he had not had to go out and ask: he had been dragged in on Day Two of their disappearance. In person.

He got a notebook out of his pocket and put a photograph of the missing girl on the table before him.

There she was: small, dark-haired, not really pretty but interesting, a good face. Amy Dean, nineteen years, with a birthday coming up next week if she was still alive to enjoy it.

She had been snapped against a background which he

19

recognized as the University Senate and Library, she was sitting on the steps in the sunlight with a bag of books at her side and the columns of the portico showing behind her.

The older buildings of the university were undistinguished, having been taken over from the earlier establishments from which it had been put together. Utility was all they aimed at, but the new blocks had higher artistic ambitions.

A grant from Whitehall, a subsidy from the Corporation of the Second City (which was fully alive to the prestige of its own university) and several private donations, had enabled a competition to be held to produce the best design.

The winner of the competition, which had been fierce and bitter, was a young American architect who had survived the battle between modernist architects, neo-modern architects, post-modern architects, classicists and the neoclassical men, and come out with what his critics called 'nostalgia' architecture. His building was pretty and much loved by the students. Oddly, since the whole was built of pale stone and wide open, the new building had not suffered the ravages of graffiti writers or vandals. Perhaps it really was too nice to touch.

A telephone call from the Rector's office had got through to Coffin yesterday; he was on his own in his office, working late.

'Tom Blackhall here.' The Rector of the University (this was his preferred title as opposed to Vice Chancellor or Principal) had a pleasant, deep voice. He was Sir Thomas, recently knighted, but to John Coffin he said Tom, they were two heads of mini-states meeting on equal terms. John and Tom.

Then he got down to it, with the briskness that he was famous for displaying: Would John come round, there was something he wanted to consult Coffin about?

Coffin was cautious. 'I'm just finishing off a piece of work.'

'I'd appreciate it.'

It was important, then. A small prickle of apprehension

20

started at the back of his neck and ran down his spine.

Students, trouble.

Once the words had been synonymous, but that had been some time ago, all had been peace lately, students were keeping an eye on their future, jobs and income alike. There hadn't been a student riot, march or sit-in for years now, so perhaps they were due for one.

But no, the anxiety he had picked up in Tom Blackhall's voice had sounded personal. Like someone threatened with a terrible illness.

'I'll walk round.'

'Let me send a car.' The university had several official cars, Coffin had one himself, which he avoided as much as possible, preferring to walk or drive himself.

'Rather walk.' His security code name was WALKER.

'My house then, not the office. You know where it is?'

'Yes.' You asked me there not six months ago, to a dinner-party where your wife was, for once, present. You've plainly forgotten.

'Come straight in, then, I'll leave the door unlocked. My study's on the left.'

In the days when he had been a uniformed copper on the beat, at the very beginning of his career, he had thought wistfully about those of his contemporaries whom he knew to be at their university studies. In those days he had thought of dons and students as living civilized, intellectual days, engaged in reading, studying, passing their days in a solid manner, then drinking fine wine at college dinners while engaged in good conversation. Nothing trivial, nothing mean.

He knew better now. University life as life in an ivory tower did not exist, had possibly never existed except perhaps for a few people in one or two places for a short time in the settled period between the wars. Now the centres of learning were centres of hard, competitive work, with as much rivalry and edging for position as anywhere else. And they had to fight for money with all those other institutions like the arts, the hospitals, and the police.

Mind you, they were doughty fighters and Sir Tom one

21

of the best. Coffin had learnt to respect the way he and his like operated.

He had walked fast through the streets, enjoying the air and the movement. Soon, he saw the stone archway of the university buildings ahead of him.

As he came through the archway a motorbike shot past, just missing him. The rider was a girl wearing black leather and a black crash helmet. She had a lean, muscular face without much expression, but he was almost sure she had known how near she had come to hitting him and was enjoying it. Damn you, he thought, as he walked on.

Tom Blackhall had come forward with hand outstretched as Coffin walked into the room. 'Glad you could make it. Decent of you to come.'

There was another man in the room, looking out of the window, his back to the door. He swung round at that moment, and Coffin took a step backwards in time.

For a second he could not speak, this was a face from the buried part of his life, his unhappy, married, struggling youth. This man had walked a beat with him, been a partner, but left the Force, and been heard of as from a distance as a very successful business man. He had vague memories of hearing of a marriage that had failed. Well, that made two of them, he thought.

'Jem, Jem Dean.'

'That's me all right. I use James more now, but I'll answer to Jim.' Jem was dead and buried, it seemed, no doubt wisely. Change your name, change your status.

They looked at each other, seeing reflected in their eyes that past they had shared, not all of it good. Jim Dean moved his thin, rather beautiful hands in a way Coffin remembered. Wonder what habit I've still got that he recalls, Coffin thought. What empty shell hangs on me?

'Still the same old way of coming into a room,' said Dean, answering him. 'As if you were going to conquer it.'

'Rubbish.' But he was aware of being gently flattered. That was another thing he remembered about the man: he could smooth the waters. He had pale blue eyes that seemed to whiten and widen as he spoke: yet one more memory.

22

He wore spectacles now and that shrouded the eyes a bit. He'd gone grey, but the crest of hair was still as strong and curly as ever. Well cut now, as was the dark blue suit. Shirt by Turnbull and Asser, tie by Hermès, gloves by Hermès.

Suddenly, Dean tore away the spectacles to show the pain in his eyes. 'That's my kid that's missing, my girl.' The eyes were wider and paler than ever.

Tom Blackhall put a hand on his arm. 'Steady on, Jim. I'm in this too, remember.'

He turned to John Coffin: 'Two students of this university are missing. One of them is Jim's daughter, Amy.' He paused for a moment, then went on: 'We informed the local police after the first day. This may have been a bit quick, but you may remember that we had a student murdered on campus last year and this has made us extra careful.'

'I remember.' Coffin also recalled, and with some bitterness, that it was one of the police failures, they had never caught the killer. Or not yet; but the file was not closed.

'The police told us it was a bit too soon to do much, these being two young adults who might have taken themselves off for their own reasons.' He paused again. 'I think they did something, ran a few checks, but not much.'

'I'll find out.'

The Rector ignored this and went on as if he hadn't heard. 'They must have sent out some sort of alert, because today I got a 'phone call telling me that Amy's car had been found, empty. Across the river in Rotherhithe.'

Not my area, thought Coffin automatically. That's the Met.

'No sign of her. But her handbag was in it and her coat.'

Jim Dean made a noise like a groan.

'That looked bad,' said Sir Thomas. 'Even to them.'

We don't come well out of this, thought Coffin. 'What about the other student?' he said. 'Any sign of him?'

'My son,' said Sir Thomas, his voice suddenly heavy. 'Martin. There was a relationship there, but I don't know much about it. No sign of him either, but his wallet was found in the car. We don't know if they started out together,

23

or when they parted, if they did, but on that evidence they were together at one point.'

There was silence in the room.

'Whichever way you look at it,' said Sir Thomas, 'it doesn't look good.'

Coffin said slowly: 'They still could be somewhere, anywhere, together or not. In spite of the way you feel, two days is very little time, and people do turn up.'

'Three days, nearly three days,' Jim Dean spoke sharply. 'That's too long.' He reached into his pocket to pull out a small photograph. Black and white, not new, a little battered as if it had been carried around. 'That's my Amy. Look at her.'

Coffin looked. 'Can I take this away?'

'Not that photograph, I'll give you another . . .' He reached in his pocket. 'Have you got a child? No, of course, I heard, tragic . . . I want her found, she's got to be found. Your lot can do it. You and I know how it goes, you can see they make a push.' Coffin saw his eyes were bloodshot. 'It's day two, into day three, and she's my child. I want her found.'

Sir Tom said: 'That goes for me too, I want my son found.'

Coffin turned towards the door. 'I'll see things get started.'

'I'll walk you across the campus, the gate may be locked now.'

At the gate, which was closed, a security man stood. The Rector nodded and got out a key. 'I'll do this, Bill, thank you.'

'Right, sir.' The man stood back, but he studied John Coffin's face as if he meant to remember it.

With the key in his hand, the Rector said: 'Dean thinks my boy has killed his daughter. I don't believe Martin did it. That's another reason I wanted you here. Dean wasn't so keen.'

He put on a good act then if that's so, but Coffin did not say this aloud. 'Thank you for telling me.'

He walked back through the streets to the big new police

24

buildings in Spinnergate. Not much of a walk but an interesting one, with plenty to observe. He passed the Great Eastern Dock, once the place where furs and timber from Russia and the Baltic arrived and now a wall of new apartments, well lit up on this autumn evening. On his right was the new hospital, an ambulance going in and another speeding out with all lights flashing.

He walked on, there was the Old Leadworks Art Gallery, said to be prospering in spite of the recession. Past Rope Alley, scene of a notorious killing of a girl, avoiding the turn to Feather Street and the junction which led to St Luke's Mansions where he lived himself, walking fast to the unpretentious but efficient blocks of his own headquarters where he would find someone on call in the CID rooms.

And they would certainly know he was on the way, the message would have been flashed ahead that WALKER was coming.

It came back to him with a shock then that he had seen Dean not so long ago without taking in who it was. A figure in a pub (the Lamb and Lion, much patronized by his Force), talking to a face he knew. Yes, Harry Coleridge. Not one of his admirers. Dean had left with a laugh, slapping Coleridge on the arm and calling, 'Keep me in touch with the barnyard.' Just a flash of memory but it was interesting. Yes, that was the authentic Dean touch, friendly, bantering but sharp.

He was still studying the photograph of Amy Dean, a sensitive face but possibly a troubled one, and weighing up the interview with the two fathers last night, while waiting for Stella to arrive. He was thinking too about that earlier case of the death of a student around which there had hung an unpleasant smell as of people not telling all they knew; he had called for the file on this before leaving his office last night. One of the good things about his now automated life was that he could summon material on his screen at any hour of the night or day. No waiting about as in the old days.

On the screen he had read the details: Virginia Scott, twentyish, a third-year student of sociology, her body had been found outside the departmental library, partly concealed from view by bushes.

She had been badly beaten up, and had died from shock. The post-mortem had turned up the news that there were old bruises as well as new on her body. No one had been charged, but there were rumours she had been beaten up by her boyfriend. The name of the student was Martin Blackhall. Nothing could be proved against him. She had had other boyfriends, in and out of the university, and she liked older men.

He was mulling this over and drinking his now tepid coffee when Stella Pinero walked into the bar.

Bob got up, nearly heaving over the table the better to let off a stream of happy barks and embrace his beloved mistress.

'Down, Bob.'

Stella Pinero kissed John on his cheek and patted Bob's head, all one lovely flow of motion that only an actress could have achieved. Coffin felt that if she had patted his head and kissed Bob it would have looked as elegant and meant as much. Kisses were not tokens of affection to Stella but a sign that she knew you were there and could speak later. Her turn first. Relations between them were still strained.

He knew better than to deliver more than a modest peck back nor to praise her appearance although she looked lovely, she had cut her hair short and tinted it red for a part she was rehearsing on TV and it suited her. He suspected she had known it would or a wig would have been ordered for the television series. A flourish of Guerlain came with her. Over the years he had learnt with some amusement that she wore Mitsouko with jeans and Chamade with skirts: it was a Mitsouko day.

With her was a tall, thin figure draped in what looked like rags and tatters until you saw the rags were of jewel-like colours and glittered here and there with gold thread. Then you realized you were looking at a carefully put together composition. A turban of soft chiffon scarves framed a thin face with huge brown eyes.

26

A striking face, so bony and yet so strong that it was hard to say if it was beautiful or ugly, it could be both.

Coffin stood up.

'This is Josephine,' said Stella, as if this explained everything: her late appearance, and the slight fluster in her manner now. 'She knows you, of course.'

Josephine held out a long, thin hand, heavy with rich jewels, every one of them false.

'She wants to talk to you, she has something to tell you.'

'You don't know me, no need to pretend,' said Josephine, 'no one knows me now.' Her voice was deep and sweet with the remains of strong cockney accent overlaid with something transatlantic. 'I was in New York and San Francisco far too long, but I've come back to my roots now.'

Life with Stella had trained his nose to scents. He knew a Chanel from a Dior, and he detected Josephine's: oddly enough, she was wearing pine disinfectant.

Not a doctor, he thought, and definitely not a nurse. She was tall, he was tall himself and her eyes were level with his; Stella only came up to her shoulder. She appeared to be very thin, but with every movement she made he was becoming aware that inside that flutter of draperies was a body that knew how to move.

As well as the pine disinfectant he had caught the whiff of distinction which, like decay, has its own particular smell. Josephine was or had been Someone, but who? Stella acted as if he ought to know.

'Josephine works at Star Court House,' said Stella.

'Ah.' Coffin knew Star Court House, it was well known as a home for battered wives and children. He walked past it occasionally, just to see how it went on, but one did not enter unless invited. Not if you were a man and especially if you were a police officer. No one had so far asked him to Star Court House. 'You do good work, but you've had your troubles.' There were outbursts of violence in and around Star Court House at intervals; it attracted the very physicality it dealt with.

'Haven't had nearly so many incidents since one of the local gangs took us under their protection . . . No, since

"Our General" started looking after us, we've felt safer.'

'Oh, she's down there, is she?' Star Court was well south in his district, right down the bottom of Swine's Hill and near the river. He hadn't known Our General's territory stretched so far, he had placed her in Spinnergate, that was gangland.

'Been a real good friend. We owe her.'

Certainly interesting, he thought, but he was stepping carefully, because Star Court House did not welcome police interference, and he was surprised to be invoked. 'Shall we all have a drink?' He could see Max, who ran the bar, eyeing them hopefully. 'Or we could have lunch, Stella?' He managed to keep reproach out of his voice, because the arrangement had been a picnic lunch together.

Stella raised an eyebrow at Josephine, who shook her head so that the chiffons moved and waved about her head.

'I have to get back. I promised. We're short of help today. There's a court case and that always drains us.' Then she gave a smile. 'On the other hand, a cup of Max's coffee would be nice.'

Behind the bar, Max, a well-known local figure and owner of the nearby delicatessen (but this was recession and you needed as many jobs as possible), heard and started moving the cups. 'Espresso, Miss Josephine, as usual?'

So he knew her, Coffin thought, but Max knew everyone. Still, it was his own job also to know everyone, how had he missed Josephine?

Josephine sat down but did not wait for the coffee before beginning. 'I'm a volunteer worker at the hostel, most of us are, the hostel can't afford much trained staff. We all muck in. It works mostly . . .' She paused. 'We had a girl, a student from the university who came in one day a week, she helped in the office, typed letters, saw that bills got filed if not paid, that sort of thing. She cooked if necessary, we all do everything . . . She's gone . . . We're worried about her, we think she's missing and might be dead, and the girls, that is all of us who work there or live there, have sent me round to say.'

'What was the name of this girl?'

'Amy Dean, Amy to us.'

The coffee arrived and Max, who had certainly heard every word spoken because he always did, set the cups down carefully.

'I know about Amy Dean,' said Coffin.

'Ah, I suppose that's something. We thought the police were being shifty. So what are you doing?'

'Action's being taken, you can count on that.'

'That's good, isn't it?' said Stella, leaning forward eagerly, as if Coffin was her pet and deserved a pat on the head. Like Bob.

'Because it's the second time.' Josephine picked up her cup. 'Another girl who helped at the centre was killed. Last year. She was murdered. And we don't like it.' She drained her coffee. 'We think that's two too many.'

Coffin absorbed what she had said, then he said: 'One would be.'

'I agree there.'

'But Amy could turn up any minute.' Only, like Josephine, he did not think she was going to.

Josephine was silent. 'No,' she said.

'But thanks for telling me.'

Josephine drew her flutter of clothes around her, touched Stella lightly on the shoulder. 'Thanks for helping,' she said, and departed.

Coffin leaned forward. 'I see your part in this, Stella, you brought her in. Don't tell me you are also a helper at Star Court? No? Well, tell me, who is Josephine?'

Stella's eyes grew round with surprise. 'She's Josephine. You don't know Josephine? You mean you didn't recognize her? She was the great model of the 'fifties and 'sixties, everyone knew her, her face was on everything.'

He thought he did recall the name and now he considered it, he could see it explained the way Josephine held herself and moved. 'So what's she doing at the Star Court?'

'Oh well, she's been down, you know, right down, touched the bottom . . . she had a bad time, drugs, drink, she went through it all, got beaten up herself once or twice.'

Perhaps more often than that, from all Stella had heard. 'And I think she's paying back all the help she got herself.'

'So she doesn't work any more?'

'I don't know what she lives on,' said Stella, answering the unasked question. Not much, she feared.

'She's right, though, we ought to look into the case of the other girl.'

'She's got a conscience, has Josephine.'

'You're not suggesting that she had anything to do with it?'

'Of course not. I mean she cares about people.'

'It's more complicated than she realizes.' He drew a pattern on the cloth with his spoon. 'Do they have lads, male students, working at Star Court?'

'Shouldn't think so, they avoid the male down there and you can understand it. Even the security staff is female.' Ah yes, Our General, Coffin thought, no doubt supplied by her, wonder how they'd perform as Valkyries. Stella went on: 'Why? Is a male student missing too?'

'Could be,' said Coffin. 'It's complicated.' He could tell her that Martin Blackhall was missing, but he decided not to. Stella could be discreet, but not always.

He meditated the problem: a university and a refuge for battered women, two institutions at opposite ends of the social picture, yet reaching out touching hands to each other. Bloody hands.

He sat silently for a moment, his own problem sitting on his shoulders. Who knows how long he'd be able to help anyone? Stella looked at him with big, soft eyes. For once she seemed in a sympathetic mood.

He was badly in need of someone to go to for advice, but unluckily she was the very last person he could ask.

'What's up?' said Stella. 'Feel like more coffee? Or a glass of wine?'

Yes, definitely in a sympathetic mood, but it was no good.

'Sorry,' he said to Stella. 'I've got to get back to work.'

'Me too, I have a board meeting: your sister's trying to cut our money.' Letty Bingham kept the theatre on a rolling budget. Funds were tight at the moment, the theatre was

30

doing well, but this was a recession, and Letty had other interests, other responsibilities. Stella liked and admired Letty Bingham, a beautiful, well-groomed woman whose clothes and way of life she admired and even envied, but Letty was sharp about money. They had battles; sometimes Letty won and sometimes Stella. No bones broken, but you had to struggle. 'I have to fight it.'

'You'll fight.'

They both stood up. Stella reached down for the dog's collar. 'I'll take Bob.'

'He's yours.'

Philippa, hurrying home, after what had been a very satisfactory and heart-warming meeting with Marcus (she called him Marcus and she was Philippa), went into Max's the Deli on Old Church Street, hard by the theatre and St Luke's, where she walked into her Brunnhilde.

Lydia Tullock was buying smoked salmon roulade and a half-bottle of champagne.

'Just bucking myself up. I felt I needed it after what I'd been through.'

Philippa knew what was required of her, there had been a raid on a shop in Spinnergate Tube station and Lydia had been there. 'Is that the Spinnergate thing? I heard you saw something.'

'Saw something! I was there, my dear. I was just walking up to buy some tights in that little boutiquey place as you come up the escalator when I heard the noises and saw the assistant trying to fight off a youth, with another boy just coming up to attack.'

'How awful for you. What did you do?'

'Just stood still. One youth pushed past me, that one got away and the other would have done, but he was absolutely fallen upon by the most splendid girl in a kind of leather tracksuit, she hit the second boy and knocked him right down. Skull-cracking,' said Lydia with some pleasure. 'Ambulances and bodies all round.'

'It must have been exciting.' Lydia had all the luck.

'Of course, I was worried for my voice.' She touched her

31

throat, draped in a silk scarf. A Dufy print in pink and blue, Philippa noted, and therefore probably from Hermès. Lydia always had the best. 'That's where the strain always shows. Otherwise, I should have run after our defender and offered her a lift home. But she cleared off . . . motorbike. Lovely young creature . . . not beautiful, plain of face, but a marvellous flow of muscles.' Lydia gave the beaming smile that suited her plump face. 'I shan't say I saw her hit him, though, she might get into trouble if he dies, and she was such a creature.'

Philippa listened: her friends' sexual inclinations were always a subject of interest to her, but she decided now, possibly with a shade of regret as she herself admitted with shame, that Lydia's emotion was purely æsthetic.

'I wonder if she can sing?' she asked, her chorus line of Valkyries being always on her mind.

'Shouldn't think so, dear,' said Lydia, 'but I saw some marvellous soft leather jeans in Bond Street that would just do for Siegfried.' Except that he was about six feet round the waist. 'I must take my little snack home. What are you getting, dear, something nice?'

'Pretty nice,' said Philippa, not willing to admit to an economical choice.

From the back of the shop, Max called, 'Here is your vegetarian terrine, Mrs Darbyshire.'

'I thought you'd given that up, Phil,' said Lydia, clutching her luxuries to her ample bosom. 'Mustn't stint on food, you need building up.'

Philippa ground her teeth and watched her Brunnhilde depart. Tired, she walked home. On the way she nodded and smiled at a passing young constable on the beat. You never knew, and with searching eyes like that he would make a very visual Hagen, and with such a chest, he must have a voice. She gave herself a shake, she was getting obsessed with Wagner.

That evening, that same young, sharp-eyed constable saw the blue and white sweater as he walked on the river path

32

by the old foundry works. It was a well-known spot for the river to deliver its burdens.

The young man picked the garment up, saw the label and recognized it for an expensive article. Missoni, said the label, and a discerning girlfriend (she was a barrister and they had met in court) had educated him about the value of that name.

He knew at once it was something that could be important. When he saw the initial on the front, he connected it instantly with the missing girl Dean.

CHAPTER 3

Day Three to Day Seven

Time passed, a slow, and painful passage for those closely concerned with the two missing students. Sir Thomas kept his appointments and tried to avoid the sympathetic comments of his colleagues as the story got out. He preferred not to discuss it. His wife, a distinguished physician, flew home from Berlin where she had been giving a series of lectures. He would have preferred not to discuss it with her too, but that was not to be.

She refused to be met at the airport and drove herself home in her own car.

'I hope you had it in the long stay car park,' said Tom Blackhall.

'I won't even answer that one.' Victoria Blackhall travelled light, just one bag suspended from her shoulder.

'Cost a fortune otherwise.' This was about the level of their communication at the moment. If they got in too deep there were things that might be said that were better left unsaid.

'You need therapy, Tom,' she said, going into the hall. It was long and spacious, with an impressive stretch of carpeting and a few good pieces of furniture, all of which belonged to the university, but the pictures on the walls, a

33

Freud and a Sturrage, belonged to Victoria and were probably worth more than all the furnishings put together. She disliked the furniture, calling it fake Georgian, which was unfair as one or two of the pieces had scraps of authentic old woodwork melded into their carcasses. 'Speech therapy.' She dumped the big soft piece of Louis Vuitton on the floor. 'And if it had cost a fortune, it would have been my fortune.' She knew it irked him that her income, all earned, was considerably larger than his. In the Blackhall household, money spoke. It defined status and pecking rights.

'Can we have a truce?'

'Done.' She held out her hand. She was always the less aggressive of the two, though quick to defend her rights.

'How was the conference?'

'What I want to know about,' said Victoria carefully, 'is Martin. But since you're asking, the meeting was great and I was great.'

'Martin . . .' Her husband hesitated. 'No news.'

'Is that good or bad?'

He hesitated again. 'I don't think it's good.'

'I don't either . . . What do the police say?'

'They don't say.'

'I must get unpacked. I need some clean clothes . . . I bought you some German brandy . . . it's probably horrible but you used to like it.'

A long time ago that had been, before the honours and horrors of his position had fallen upon him. Fallen? No, not fallen like the gentle dew from heaven, but bitterly and fiercely struggled for. Part of the trouble, really.

The autumn sun poured into their bedroom. 'Damn those thin curtains, they don't hide a thing.' Victoria yanked down a blind which had been installed at her own expense. Curtains in this house were a sore point with her. A later generation would discover that the handsome pair of red silk damask curtains in the large reception room downstairs were a fake, just for show, they could not be pulled together, money having run out when the decorators got to the curtaining. The light revealed the shadows under her eyes and

34

the lines and hollows a sleepless night had brought her.
Victoria was older by a little than her husband and the
years had treated her less well.

As she unpacked, Victoria said: 'He could be suicidal
. . . I have wondered about it.'

'Martin is quite normal,' said Tom fiercely. 'You're not
a psychiatrist.'

'You learn to observe in my job.'

'I know much more about students than you do, my dear.
You think you do, but you don't.'

'I don't want to believe he's dead, but I just do. I think
Martin is dead.' She put her hands to her face. 'Oh God,
I can't bear this. I do love him.'

'I know you do. So do I.' He put his arm round her
shoulders and drew her head on to his shoulder. The truce
was holding.

Suddenly she raised her head and looked. 'You're keeping something back, I can tell. What is it?'

'Suicide might be the best of it,' he said.

'What do you mean?'

'Martin is suspected of doing away with the girl.'

'She may not be dead . . . Who suspects him?'

'James Dean for one . . . Probably the police too, but
they aren't saying.'

Or if they didn't think it now, then they would as soon
as they remembered about Virginia Scott. They must have
remembered now, the police were good at remembering
that sort of thing, their computers told them—would tell
them—that Martin had been her friend too.

But for the police, it was a matter of reason. Evidence
and reason, these were their tools . . . James Dean now,
that was different. Emotion there.

'I've half a mind to phone Dean, see what he knows.
More than I do, I suspect.' He had that feeling about Dean,
that knowledge of some sort was tucked away inside him.

He reached out for the phone by the bed and dialled.

'No, don't,' said Victoria, her voice sharp. 'Leave it, just
leave it.'

*

Jim Dean also went about his business. He had no wife, so he turned his anxiety upon himself. He could quarrel with himself, hate himself, easily enough, no trouble there.

He could also hate Martin Blackhall, that too presented no difficulty. His suicide, if it had taken place, he would have regarded as a positively good step. He considered the possibility of killing him.

But to do that, it would be necessary to find him. The police would be of no use there, a private detective must be found. No trouble there either, he knew one, if not two. Use of them came his way in business at times. But he also had an underground link to a CID officer in the Second City Force.

But he hesitated.

He toyed with a gold propelling pencil, decorated with his initials by Asprey's, which had been one of his first purchases for himself when he started to make money. He wanted to handle gold, just as he wanted to wear soft leather.

He could pick up the telephone and say, 'Hello, Harry, how are things?' and get a response. But it would mean going behind John Coffin's back and he had a healthy respect for that man's acumen.

The telephone rested on an alabaster stand set with gold. It matched a pen which matched the pencil.

He liked everything about him to be of the highest quality and massive, made of quantities of the best possible materials, whether gold, silver, silk or wood, but actual design he left to the professionals so that his office, as with his home in Chelsea Bank, looked beautiful and expensive but unlived in. There were no looking-glasses in his house except in his bathroom where he shaved, and even that one was small and could be folded up to put away. No photographs around either, but he had a drawerful which he did look at occasionally.

All the same, his office reflected his personality much more clearly than his home: in the window, which was a sheet of shining glass, he sat at a large pale wood desk, gleaming and polished, but with its surface covered by a layer of papers and files, while he faced the green screen of a computer. Attached at right-angles to this desk was a matching work surface with a small filing cabinet on top, and with three telephones hitched on to faxes and answering machines. He worked in a self-created nest of business equipment.

No pictures on the walls of this office, no flowers, but a group of soft leather armchairs stood round a low marble table.

It was late in the afternoon, everyone else—secretaries, assistants and receptionists—had all gone home, but he still sat there. The telephone on his desk rang once, but stopped ringing before he could pick it up.

Not the CID then with news, or they would have gone on ringing. Why hadn't Amy been found?

Then the white telephone on his right hand did ring. He let it ring out for a few minutes, then he answered it. He knew it must be the police. Call it telepathy or precognition or just a good guess, but he knew, and almost knew what it was. They had found something.

'This is Sergeant Donovan here, sir. CI Young wondered if you'd be good enough to come down to Spinnergate . . . Yes, the Lower Dock Road entrance. Yes, something's turned up . . . Been found.' Donovan knew he was doing it badly. 'Yes, an article of clothing . . . No, I don't know more, sir.' He knew more but had been instructed not to say.

Dean took a deep breath. Here we go, this is what you wanted. 'I'll drive over at once.'

He was relieved to be going. Action at last. He couldn't credit this step forward to John Coffin, things turn up as they will, although sometimes human hands can help. As a former policeman he knew that much. But he wanted movement.

He parked his car round the corner from Lower Dock Road in Spinnergate, using Malmaison Street which he thought he remembered of old as a street of low repute. He had been born round here and surely he remembered his mother (who had had social aspirations which, in a way,

37

he had justified for her) saying he must not play with the children of Malmaison Street? But Malmaison Street had had a lift in the world and he had to squeeze his relatively modest Rover between a Jaguar and a Rolls, though there was a battered old lorry three hundred yards down towards the river, which suggested that Malmaison Street was struggling to hang on to its old reputation.

Sergeant Donovan was waiting for him by the door. No need for introductions, Dean thought, he seemed to be known, and he allowed himself to be led straight into the room where two men were waiting for him.

One came forward. 'Chief Inspector Young. I'm in charge of this investigation.'

'I'm glad there is one,' said Dean. 'Thought there never would be . . .'

'No, it's always been a case, sir,' said Young smoothly, 'but things move slowly sometimes.' He gave a nod to the other man in the room, never to be introduced, who led the way to a table in the window.

On it lay the blue and white sweater retrieved from the mud of the Thames.

'We think this might be your daughter's.'

Dean stared down at what he was being offered. 'Where was it found?'

'On the river bank, not far from the Old Leadworks Wharf.'

There was a long pause while Dean looked and considered. He knew what he had to say, but he found the words hard to get out; they stayed in his mouth like pebbles.

'It could be Amy's,' he said at last. 'I don't know all her things. But yes, I think she had something like this. Seem to remember it.'

'I thought you'd say that, sir,' said Archie Young, quickly whisking the cover back over the table. 'I think that settles it. I'm pretty certain in my mind it belongs to your daughter.'

'Have you showed it to Thomas Blackhall?'

'No. Doesn't seem to concern him as yet.'

'Who found it?'

38

'A constable on his beat.'

'I'd like to speak to him.'

'Later, if you don't mind.'

'How did it get where it was found?'

Archie Young shook his head. 'No idea. Could have been dropped in the river elsewhere and been washed up there. It is a place where the river deposits what it's got. One of them. Well known to be.'

Dean nodded.

'Or it could have been dropped there in the first place,' went on Young.

Dean asked the difficult question: 'Do you think it means that Amy is in the river?'

'Not necessarily,' said Young. 'I don't see that at all.'

'Where is she, then? I want her found.' He didn't say alive or dead, but both men understood he meant it.

Young said: 'These were found in a pocket.' He pointed to two objects laid on a small plastic tray on his desk.

One was a small white handkerchief. The other was a sodden piece of paper that had been straightened out and dried.

'I don't know about the handkerchief,' said James Dean. 'One white handkerchief looks like another.'

'No initial on it and no laundry mark.'

'I suppose it is hers, has to be . . . And that's a bus ticket.'

'That's right, sir. You can just make it out. Route 147a, run by an independent operator. This route runs through Spinnergate and out towards Essex.'

Dean frowned. 'But she has a car. I don't see her using a bus. Perhaps it's an old ticket?'

'The stampings on it show it was bought on the day she went off, and from checking the number, it looks as though it was purchased between eight and ten on the evening she was missing.'

'Someone else may have bought it, and she just picked it up.' He didn't believe that, or even sound convincing to himself.

'Could be, but it was in the pocket of her sweater, wedged

underneath the handkerchief.' CI Young went across to the wall opposite the window and drew down a map. 'Come and have a look at this.' He pointed. 'We can tell from the ticket that whoever bought it got on at the stop at Heather Street. Here.' He put his finger on the map. 'That's just beyond the university . . . and the ticket would take that person through to the end of the line. But the route passes Church Street and a few yards up the road takes you to Star Court House where she worked.'

'So she might have been going there? But the ticket would have taken whoever bought it much further?'

'Yes, but there's no conductor on these buses, you put in the right fare yourself.' He shrugged. 'If you haven't the right change, then you overpay and get more of a trip than you use.'

'I never wanted her to work in that place,' said James Dean. 'I hated it and all it stood for.'

Then he said: 'Does the driver remember her? Did any-one see her? One of the passengers?'

'We are inquiring. The driver doesn't remember. It was late in the day. One of the last buses out on his shift and it was crowded.'

'Bunch of drunks,' said Dean viciously. 'What would they see?' He started to walk up and down the room. 'Can I ask you about the Blackhall boy? Any sign of him?'

'Not so far. He might have been on the bus, we asked about him too, but no result.'

'Flush him out. You won't find him lying dead anywhere.'

'We don't know your daughter is dead yet, sir. We mustn't jump to conclusions.'

'She's dead. I'm telling you.'

He had moved on from his first demand that she be found, CI Young observed.

'What about the car? What's that telling you?'

'Forensics are working on it.'

'That was my car. I drove it for a few weeks, then I gave it to her. That was because she didn't like taking valuable presents, I had to persuade her it was a car I didn't want and wouldn't use. She had that sort of conscience.'

'I'll pass on to Forensics that you have used the car,' said Archie Young gravely. 'They'll need to know.'

'Yes. Is that all you want from me?'

'For now, Mr Dean.'

'Have you got a daughter?'

Archie Young shook his head. 'No, no children.'

'You're probably lucky.'

Archie Young said: 'She may not be dead, sir.'

James Dean paused at the door, looked at Archie as he spoke and gave him a bleak half smile. She's dead, the smile said.

Young said: 'If you receive a ransom demand, I hope you will tell us, sir.'

'There has been no demand to me. I'd be surprised and glad if there was one.'

'Amy could walk in the door tonight and wonder what we were making a fuss about.'

When Archie Young reported this afterwards to John Coffin, as requested, he said: 'He looked at me as if he didn't believe a word of it.'

'He probably didn't,' said John Coffin. 'Did you believe it yourself?'

'Half and half. I was just trying to sell him a bit of hope.' He added: 'He's really wild. I don't like the look of him.'

'What do you think he will do?'

Young considered. 'Bash something up, that's what he'd like to do. Either the university or Star Court.'

Yes, the old Jem Dean had been that sort of a man. Too soon to say what the new Jim Dean was like.

'What do you make of the bus ticket?'

'Don't know. Someone bought that ticket, and it was in her pocket. Miracle it was still there after being in the water.'

'It is surprising, but you do get luck occasionally.' If it was luck, so far it didn't seem to have helped. He was keeping an open mind on the bus ticket, it needed thinking about. 'What about the Blackhalls?'

'Sir Thomas telephones regularly to ask for news. Nothing to tell him, no sighting of either the boy or the girl. He doesn't like that. I think he's nervous that somehow Dean will find the boy first.'

'Better keep an eye open,' Coffin advised. 'Watch the university campus and Star Court.'

'I'll be around myself, asking questions,' Young assured him. 'I want to see both of the missing students' rooms.'

But Dean did not go to either of those places. Or not on that day, whatever he was going to do later. After leaving the police headquarters, he got into his car and took a ride. Not unnoticed, as it turned out later. There were one or two people in Coffin's area who also seemed to notice everything and one of them, indeed the best, was Mimsie Marker who sold newspapers from a stall by the Tube station at Spinnergate. If she didn't see events herself, and after all even Mimsie could not be everywhere although it sometimes seemed as though she had been, she had contacts and friends to pass on the news. Mimsie was a kind of sieve, through which all local information could pass.

Coffin had other things on his mind, not only this case and the security for the Queen's visit, but he had a sister, Letty Bingham; he had his late mother's memoirs which he had edited and which Letty wanted published; and he had Darling Stella. And there was always the cat, Tiddles.

Stella also wanted his mother's memoirs published, because she had a TV producer lined up who would turn them into a four-parter with Stella as his mother.

Coffin found the idea gruesome . . . Stella as his mother? Considering all that had passed between them, it was incestuous. Obscene. Stella didn't see it that way, of course. It was work. Acting.

'I don't like to think of you as my mother,' he had said uneasily.

'Oh, don't be silly. I'd be your young mother.'

Exactly, Coffin had thought, but he could not drag his mind away from Amy Dean and Martin Blackhall. Gone,

42

both of them. There was a nasty odour of death and decay in the air.

Stella too took a keen interest in the case: the university, and Sir Tom in particular, were patrons of St Luke's Theatre, and she herself had helped in an appeal for money for Star Court House. Naturally she was on the side of women, she said. She didn't know either of the two missing students.

'Can I do anything to help?'

Coffin didn't think so, police work was police work. But Stella helped them in recreating the scene when the two students were last seen, standing by Amy's car. A WPC was found, sufficiently like Amy to play her part, but they had trouble with a double for Martin, no police officer was a match and none of Martin's fellow students was willing to volunteer. So Stella discovered a young actor who was a match in height and colouring, and after talking with Lady Blackhall and studying photographs, she coached him in the walk and mannerisms of the young Martin. As luck would have it, he was young Darbyshire, Philippa's son, who had just got his Equity Card. He was also, with suitable make-up, going to be one of the non-singing Valkyries. This had infuriated Our General (who had been approached for help), who thought it was all right for women to act like men but wrong for men to invade their territory.

'It's the golden thread,' Stella explained to Coffin. 'Haven't you noticed it in life, there is a golden thread linking event to event . . . that's what Josephine has taught me. Josephine is a bit of the golden thread here, isn't she?'

Josephine, the Valkyries, Our General, some thread, Coffin thought. 'Thanks for helping with the reconstruction scene,' he said.

They were in Stella's living-room in the apartment which had been created out of the ground floor and old vestry of the former St Luke's Church. There was an ecclesiastical touch to her kitchen which had strong oak rafters in the ceiling, but her living-room had been nicely secularized. Not much cooking was done here as Stella had long since mastered the art of proxy cooking, buying in what she wanted from Max at the Delicatessen or Harrods and putting it in the microwave.

Because they shared the ownership of two animals, one cat, one dog, the two of them had regular what they called 'interchange' meetings when Tiddles was forcibly returned to the Tower and John Coffin, and Bob was repatriated to Stella. Both animals would emigrate again as food and prospects looked better in the other place. Tiddles was suspected of having yet a third home, so far unidentified but strongly tipped to be the kitchen of the bar-restaurant in the theatre. He had been seen carrying a chicken leg from somewhere.

Stella's living-room had recently been refurbished on the strength of the contract signed for her TV series. 'Should be good repeats,' she had said as she chose a set of expensive Italian leather furniture, soft and quilted so that you could tell every chair cost as much as a diamond. Of course, she had had new rugs, Spanish these, and thick natural linen curtains with that unironed, crumpled look that was so valuable and sought after at the moment. 'We ought to be sure of a Christmas showing, maybe more.'

The film about the two missing young people went out on all the main TV news programmes. With any luck they would get some hard information; there would certainly be some loony responses from those who had seen the couple on the Shetland Islands, in New Zealand or embarking on a space ship for Mars.

Some other traveller on bus 147a that night might remember the girl or the boy, or both of them together. A slim chance, but possible.

The report of Archie Young's interview with the staff at Star Court House arrived on Coffin's desk the day after the TV filming. Young reported that the trio of women in charge (the place was a kind of cooperative, self-governing as far as possible, with one paid and trained social worker) had been polite but not helpful.

Coffin dropped into Archie Young's office to speak to him. Not a popular habit, he knew, but one he meant to continue. Apart from anything else, he was always interested to see Young's office, a tiny slip of a room, but with a long window-sill which got the sun and on which he was always growing seedlings and small pot plants. Today he had some elderly-looking tomatoes, running up the window on frames, heavily fruited, but unripe.

'Isn't it time you picked those?'

'I'm waiting for them to ripen.'

'They look past it to me,' said Coffin judicially. They were unhealthy, infected with some mould, but he wasn't a plant man himself, and if he had set himself up with plants in pots, then his resident cat Tiddles would have done something unpleasant to them. 'So how did it go at Star Court? You didn't seem to get much.'

'Didn't get anything. They wouldn't open up.'

'Being deliberately obstructive, are they?'

'Not really, just naturally prickly and difficult, I think.' Archie Young sounded as if he was still assessing what they had said. They were a strange bunch, living a kind of communal life while fiercely preserving every inch of privacy that could be managed. He respected them for that, but had found Mrs Rolt, the administrator, polite but distant and the one who wore rags and tatters with such an air a puzzle.

'Are they protecting someone, then?'

'I don't think so. They just don't believe in men. And particularly the police. They've got their own protection down there.' He looked at his Chief. 'You know about that? I sort of probed around there but they wouldn't talk.'

'Our General? Oh, certainly. I can see she might be a conversation stopper from all I've heard.'

'I didn't meet her, I gather she keeps her distance, but I think she might have been in the house. Just the way they acted.'

'I think I will go down there myself. Find an excuse. After all, that bus route does pass very close. Amy Dean could have been there.'

*

45

He called early that evening, after a committee on Policing in the Community had ended a perplexed and anxious session. This particular committee which, mercifully, he was not required to chair, never got anywhere and never would in his opinion in spite of high motives and good will all around. There must be something like dyslexia of the soul, he thought, that impeded people of different groups when they talked of certain matters: you just couldn't read each other right. He thought that contact with an outfit of women trying to get on with their lives in their own way might be just what his spirit needed.

And he wanted to ask questions about Amy and Virginia.

Star Court House could have been a slum. As it was, it came very close to being one, a battered old house that seemed to match its function, but it was saved by the fresh paint on the front door, a strong defiant red, and the row of fierce orange geraniums that lined the windows. No pot plants could be put outside or stood by the door, they would be stolen or vandalized. Unluckily, it was that sort of neighbourhood, a kind of no man's land between three tall housing blocks and a sad, undernourished-looking park made up of a circle of grass and a children's paddling pool which was empty.

But it was on a good bus route and near a busy main road. So it was accessible, a place you knew how to get to, although not the sort of place a taxi-driver would happily take you to. But then few of the women who arrived could afford a taxi, most of them walked from the bus, even if at home they had a choice of cars, or had been prosperous, coming here they seemed to prefer the anonymity of the bus.

There was no obvious sign of the protection of Our General and her gang, but he was reliably informed that if you made a nuisance of yourself not many minutes passed before you regretted it.

Watch your back, his informant had advised him, but he didn't expect to be attacked: his help had been sought. Star Court might not like him or his sex but they trusted him as a person.

He rang the bell. After a wait, he was inspected through a hole in the door, and then the door was opened.

It was Josephine.

'I thought it was your eye,' he said.

'We knew you'd come.' A large white overall covered her fine-coloured flutter, and she had toned down her make-up a little, this was her working garb. 'You're the second. We had an inspector down here.'

Chief Inspector Young would not like being downgraded. 'All right if I come in?'

She opened the door wider. 'Enter.'

The house was not quiet, he could hear women's voices down the hall, laughter, a child calling out, music, but it sounded friendly.

'Come into our interview room.'

'Oh, do you have one?' He was interested in knowing how they worked.

'Have to have, can't bounce people straight into the kind of madhouse that we sometimes have here.'

They went into a small room, with several armchairs and a dilapidated sofa. Someone had been smoking in here not so long ago, leaving a strong smell of cigarettes and a deposit of ash on the floor.

'I'll call Maisie, Mrs Rolt, she wanted to talk to you.'

He knew the name: Maisie Rolt had got the centre running single-handed in the face of a lot of opposition. 'Is she all right?' He had heard that she had been attacked by an unpleasant form of cancer.

'Fighting back,' said Josephine with a smile. 'That's our Maisie.'

Left alone for a moment, Coffin occupied himself with opening a window to empty the laden ashtray. The grass underneath the window was thick and uncut, more than a match for any nicotine.

Maisie Rolt came into the room quietly, but without Josephine. She was wearing blue jeans, a dark blue sweater and bright red beret drawn down low on her forehead. She looked cheeky and alert and she smelt strongly of onions.

'Sorry about the smell, onions do whiff, don't they? But

47

we're having sausages and mash for supper tonight and a fried onion does liven it up.'

'Sorry if I have interrupted the cooking.'

'Jo's carrying on. Sit yourself down.'

Curiosity impelled the next question. 'Does Josephine live here?'

'Of course not. She's got a flat in one of the tower blocks on Planters.'

'Is she all right there? Any trouble?'

'She did have a bit at first, got mugged, and her TV stolen, but she made powerful friends and they look after her now.'

Ah yes, Our General again. 'Protection?'

'You could call it that, but not for payment. But you didn't come to talk about Jo.'

'I wouldn't mind.'

Mrs Rolt smiled. 'There's a story there, and one day I might tell you, or she might.'

'Or it might come out.'

'Things do come out in the end,' agreed Maisie Rolt.

'I thought you would be glad to know that a solid investigation into Amy's disappearance is under way.'

'I am. She hasn't just gone off, she wouldn't do that. She was very regular in coming here. We didn't count on her; help is always useful but we can manage; but it was just not in her character for her to drop out. She'd arranged to take a party to the swimming pool, the kids were all ready, she would never have let them down.'

'Yes, I see that.' He hadn't known about the swimming pool trip, and it did carry some weight with him, although with students, he thought, you can never be sure. 'So you had no warning she might not turn up?'

She shook her head. 'No message, nothing, just silence. I found that disturbing. It upset the whole household. And I take that seriously. If some of the women here think it's bad, then it is bad.' She took a deep breath. 'They learn to smell trouble.'

'You don't ask me if I have any news.'

'Because I know you haven't, you would have said

48

straight off, you're that sort. Besides—' she smiled—'I have my own sources, I know there's nothing.'

Ah yes, Our General, he thought, and possibly Mimsie Marker down at the Tube Station, she was the great communicator.

The door swung open and a small child appeared, a boy probably, although it was hard to be sure, his or her outfit was unisex: longish hair and a kind of kilt with pants.

'Hop it, Darren,' said Maisie. 'Nothing to do with you.'

'The soup's boiling over.'

'Tell Jo, or your mother, or anyone you can find. On no account touch it yourself.'

'If it is boiling over,' she said as the door closed. 'Just wanted a look at you, I expect. His mother probably sent him in, she has fantasies about what goes in this room.' Maisie gave a hoot of ironic but friendly laughter. 'And so would I if I'd had her life. Ask no questions because I'm not telling you.'

'What can you tell?' He was beginning to see what Archie Young had meant. Not so much difficult as baffling.

'I never tell much about anyone really, that's what I'm good at, keeping quiet. It helps here. Essential. If I was a gossip I'd have been killed by now and this place would have gone up in flames . . . But it was the two of them, Virginia and now Amy. I talked it over with Josephine and she felt the same.'

Coffin kept quiet.

'I didn't want to think it was our fault.'

'How could it be?'

'You don't know, do you? You never know when one thing leads to another until it's too late. But the girl came to us here, said it was part of her course. I checked, and it was, so all right, but she did more than she need have done, and so did Virginia.'

'Just kindness of heart?'

'Could be, but it worried me then and it does now. They didn't come together, but they knew each other. I don't like coincidences that end in disappearance and death. Was it something they got into because of coming here? I don't

49

know. We're clean here, no drugs, nothing of that sort. I watch for it. I didn't ask them why they came, beyond the first query, which is standard. I mean, I have to look out, we do have some dubious characters whose motives are not very nice. I can suss them out. These girls were not like that. I'm glad of help and I don't dig into people. I'd go mad if I did. We have enough trouble here as it is.'

It was quite a speech and he wondered what emotions lay behind it.

'We had a man round here asking questions. No, not one of your lot, I can always tell them.'

'A nuisance, was he?'

Mrs Rolt smiled. 'He was seen off. We had a couple of guardian angels who dealt with him . . . Debagged, I think it was called once. Anyway, he left without his trousers and he hasn't been back.'

Powerful ladies, Coffin thought.

'How often did Amy come here?'

'Once a week regularly, and other times as we needed more help. She did office work, typed letters, filed them, kept an eye on the accounts. Talked to anyone who wanted to be talked to, some don't. She seemed to know by instinct. She was good. Good at what she did and a good girl.'

'Did the boy, Martin, come down here?'

'Once or twice but we didn't encourage it. He was awkward.'

'We are still trying to form a picture of what might have happened. You know Martin is missing too? His wallet was found in Amy's car.'

'She loved that car.' It was not an answer but he concluded she had known about Martin, and possibly that was part of her alarm. Did she think he was guilty of violence?

'In confidence—' he almost stopped there, no question of confidence, soon it would be known everywhere—'I can tell you that a sweater that has been identified as Amy's has been found. There was a handkerchief inside it, and with it a bus ticket. A ticket on the route that runs at the bottom of this road.'

'I don't think she ever used a bus,' said Maisie. 'Always came in the car.'

'Someone bought that ticket. And on the day she disappeared. It was wedged beneath a handkerchief.'

'She never used a handkerchief, always bits of tissue crammed into her pocket.'

'It was clean. Might have been just decoration.'

'I don't think so. I'd say it wasn't hers.'

'Her pocket in her sweater,' he persisted.

Mrs Rolt shrugged. 'You asked me.'

Darren put his head round the door. 'There's ever such a smell of burning in the kitchen.'

'I'd better get back,' said Maisie Rolt. 'I'm afraid I haven't helped. Just pushed your questions back at you.'

'At the beginning of an investigation like this, questions are as valuable as answers.'

'Thank you for saying that . . . Would you like to stay for supper? I dare say it won't all be burnt.'

To his surprise, he heard himself say yes, he would, thank you, but not tonight, some other time?

Suddenly she said: 'I'll tell you what I feel: we weren't using her, she was using us. She was getting something, we were giving her something, and I don't know what it was.'

Darren burst in again, and said: 'Our General says she won't bloody be a Valkyrie and nor will any of her girls. The lads can please themselves if they want to act bloody women.'

At the same time the telephone rang, and as Coffin left, he heard her dealing with a call from someone called Angela, temporizing on whether Angela could help at Star Court.

As he walked down the garden path a figure dressed in black leather swept along, nearly knocking him over. He saw the gleam in her eye as she flew past.

Second time of asking, he thought. She meant to get me if she could.

Our General. Rosa Maundy, a rose with many a thorn, he thought. Maundy was an old Spinnergate name, you got them on the records way back to the first Elizabeth when they had been Thames watermen. Our Rose. He knew a

51

bit about her now, she worked for her father who ran a small haulage company, it was her power base. A story there too, and he would find out when it suited him, which might be quite soon if she kept trying to kill him.

He walked to where he had parked his car and drove westward. Sometimes you can walk just so far and no farther.

At the Tube station in Spinnergate, where he stopped to buy an evening paper, Mimsie Marker was packing up to go home.

'Saved you a paper.'

'You always do.'

She folded it up in the professional way, as taught her long ago, pocketed the money in the leather bag that hung in front of her like a kangaroo's pouch and became confidential.

'About those kids that have gone missing, pair of students.'

Coffin waited.

'Saw Jim Dean today.'

'Oh, you know him, do you?'

Mimsie didn't answer that as not being worth comment, she knew everyone. 'He bought a paper, just like you, then he waited for the bus, but he didn't get on it. Had his car parked and he got in and followed the bus.'

'What number bus was it?'

'147a. But you know that, or you wouldn't have asked.'

A good example of Mimsie's maddening hit-the-nail-on-the-head way of thinking.

'I thought you ought to know. Wonder what he was up to?'

'Did you see him come back?'

'No, I reckon he went all the way to the end.'

'And what's at the end, Mimsie?'

'Nothing much. Depends what you want. Woods and marsh mostly.' Her eyes were bright and alert. 'Used to test the big guns there once when Woolwich Arsenal was alive.'

'Thanks, Mimsie, that's interesting.'

52

'Thought you'd say so.'

He hadn't disappointed her. She watched him sit in his car till the right bus came along, and then drive slowly behind.

He followed it out, past the road which led to Star Court House, out through the dingy inner suburbs to where they lightened, grew more pleasant with pretty gardens, then beyond that to where the houses were scattered, past a cemetery and a crematorium and finally to a cluster of houses round a bus stop. At this point, the bus turned round and came back. End of the road.

Coffin stopped his car and got out. Across the road from a parade of houses, newly built, isolated and windswept, was a stretch of scrubby, empty land with a belt of trees.

He paced it slowly, looking at the ground. There were signs of the passing of a car along a muddy track at the side. On the grass itself were tyre marks.

Hard to say how recent these were. It was probably an area where lovers came. It had that look about it, not to mention the odd spoiled condom lying about.

Under the trees several years of leaf fall lay thick and mushy. He thought he could detect signs that the layers had been disturbed so that here and there the darker, decayed deposit had come to the top. He moved the leaves with his foot.

The earth underneath had been opened, then pressed back. Something or someone had been buried here.

Coffin went back to his car where he made a telephone call, then sat waiting.

When the police van arrived, he took the team of diggers to the spot he had found. He watched while a canvas barrier was set up to protect the area, then he stood back. Very soon he was joined by Chief Superintendent Paul Lane, not pleased to be taken away from his evening at home. Coffin could imagine the grumble going on inside: One more of the Boss's flights of fancy.

'Nice evening, isn't it, sir,' said Paul Lane. It was, in fact, beginning to rain. 'For digging, that is,' he added morosely. For standing about it was damp and cold.

The two men watched in the rain which began to grow heavier. A small crowd of spectators had appeared, as they always did on these occasions, alerted by some underground set of signals.

'Have to get lights up if we don't finish before dark,' said Lane. It was dusk already. 'No problem, of course,' he added without conviction. Then he said: 'They've got something.'

A muddy figure was heading towards them from out of the enclosure. 'A buried dog, sir. Sorry.'

'That's it, then,' said Paul Lane, putting up his collar against the rain. 'Might as well be off.'

Coffin stood where he was. 'No. Go on looking. There will be an indication of a disturbance somewhere. Find it, then dig again.'

He took pity on the Chief Superintendent. 'Come and sit in the car and tell me what's been going on.' He himself had had to cancel a dinner engagement with Stella Pinero, who had not been pleased. 'I hope something has.'

Earlier that day, Chief Inspector Young had received the first forensic reports on the girl's car. Nothing very helpful, he had thought: traces of the clothes of the girl herself, fingerprints, possibly hers, her father's (he had acknowledged using the car), and possibly prints of the boy, Martin Blackhall. It would all need to be worked on and checked.

But later, during that afternoon, Chief Inspector Archie Young in company with a woman detective had entered and searched the student room lived in by Amy Dean. This room had been locked for days now, so that when they went in it smelt stuffy. Even sour. Young wondered if there was the smell of drugs; there was certainly stale cigarette smoke.

On the outside it seemed the room was orderly and tidy, but when the drawers and cupboards were opened, there was a different story.

Sordid, dirty, beneath apparent order.

The drawers and cupboards were full of soiled, crumpled clothes. Underclothes, tights, sweaters and jeans, all pushed in the drawers and shoved into the cupboards, not hung up, all disorder and dirt which spilled out in front of them.

Young looked at the woman detective with him who raised her eyebrows and shrugged. 'Bit of a slut.'

Or mute signs of a confused, unhappy girl, who wanted to be dirty?

The diggers ceased their work and came across to the car.

'Found something, sir. I think you'd like to look.'

The two men got out of the car to hurry across the grass. The diggers had gone down several feet into the Essex clay.

Under the soil was a roughly made coffin.

'Better get it opened.' Lane spoke gruffly, more moved than he had expected.

'No.' Coffin was abrupt. 'No, let's wait until Dean and Blackhall get here.'

'It'll mean waiting some time.'

'No, they should be here any minute. I telephoned earlier.'

'My God, you were sure,' said Lane.

'Yes, I was sure.'

They watched as first one car and then another drew up, from which Sir Thomas and then Jim Dean got out. They watched in silence as the two men approached. Coffin walked over to them and murmured something. Lane saw them nod, then the whole party moved to the edge of the pit to look down at the coffin.

Ropes were fitted and slowly the coffin was drawn up.

'Open it,' said the Chief Commander.

Behind them a girl got out of one of the cars and came running towards them.

Tall, slender, in jeans, fair hair floating over her shoulders. Sir Thomas muttered under his breath that she shouldn't be here, not his idea. 'Get back, Angela,' said James Dean.

'You promised, you promised! I want to know.'

Jim put his arm protectively around the girl. 'Go back.

55

I promised you could come. I promised I would tell you. But you can't look.'

A chisel levered at the wood, the coffin opened with a crack.

CHAPTER 4

Day Seven. A long day

Things had changed. In the old days a killer usually left the body lying around. In special cases he might chop it up, put it in a trunk or deposit it around the countryside. The body might be shrouded, the murderer did not always want to see the victim's face. But a wooden box, that was something different.

Coffin felt that once they knew how that had happened, they would know the killer.

Of course, he could be wrong. He had been in the past.

He was hungry, he was tired. His day had started early and was still going on. He had the beginnings of a headache, and something inside that might be indigestion but felt more like tension. He had lost a button from his jacket, and as he drove home he saw that his hands were dirty with one nail broken, so he must have been down in the hole, moving the earth away with his own hand, and drawing back the wood from the dead face. Had Dean got his hands dirty?

He needed a bath, a change of clothing, and a drink. But more than this, he needed to talk to someone. Someone who could understand his own particular problem.

There was only one such person. And to see him seemed more important than the bath and the drink. Besides, Mat was usually good for a drink, provided you settled for his own special brand. Last time he had visited him the brew had been camomile tea.

He sat for a moment, looking up at the tower of the former St Luke's Church where he lived. The Post Office had recently informed him that his address was now No.1, The Mansions, St Luke's Old Church. He could see his cat Tiddles outlined at one window, so that meant he ought to go in and feed Tiddles.

Which would mean reading any post that might have arrived since he had left and listening to any messages on his answering machine. Suddenly he knew he wasn't going to do any of that. He waved to Tiddles, turned the car and drove off.

As he waited at a traffic light on red, he meditated on his position. He liked his work and thought he did it well, but he had his critics. He had not set up the organization of the Second City Police Force. This had been the creation of a Home Office Panel specially set up for the occasion. He had just walked into it, but he managed it his way. His way.

He drove south to the old docklands, taking the Blackwall Tunnel under the river, mercifully free of traffic at that time of day, and followed the road into Greenwich, once the home of English kings. After a long period of decline, it had become fashionable again with many of the fine houses enjoying the elegance they deserved. He parked the car in a side street near the theatre where Stella had once worked and then walked towards a street running south.

There it was, a quiet shop, not brightly painted, making no pretences: Matthew Parker, Bookseller. His old friend Mat had retired from the Force and started a secondhand bookshop. Not what you expect from a CID sergeant who never seemed to open a book, but Mat was making a go of it. Although it was late by now, the shop had light in it and was still open. It was always open, especially to Mat's friends. He treated it as a kind of club.

He pushed at the door, setting the bell ringing. 'Hello?' he called out. Mat appeared from an inner room. He was a tall, burly man who was older than he looked. A widower of many years, he dressed for comfort in soft old trousers of no special shade, a thick sweater in a tone of grey (although Coffin sometimes wondered if it hadn't perhaps once been white) and tan leather slippers.

57

He seemed unsurprised to see John. 'Wondered if you'd be in.'

'How's business?'

'Mine's all right. How's yours?'

'So-so.'

Mat went over to the door, locked it and drew down the blind. 'Think we'll shut up for the night. Not been a bad day. Five customers, two bought something and one tried to nick a book.' A rumbling laugh provided a comment on this. 'Come out the back. I've got a fire there.'

Coffin took a careful path through the bookcases and the piles of books spread around the floor. He was always amazed that Mat knew what he had in stock, but he seemed to.

'Not bad for an old copper, is it?' said Mat, looking at his domain in pride. 'Want a drink?'

'What is it?'

'Well, you can have cocoa, but it's made with water. Or join me in a cup of green tea, first picking, best quality. It's the finest tea you can buy. The Japs love it, buy it all the time. Go in to Fortnum and Mason and you'll see them queuing up to buy.'

'Tea, then. Do you shop in Fortnum's then these days, Mat?'

'No, but my daughter does, and she buys it to keep her old dad happy.'

He might have said, 'And off the drink,' because his departure from the Force had had something to do with his heavy drinking. He was off it, now, though, and as far as Coffin knew had not touched a drop for five years. He always said so, anyway.

'I'll take the tea.' Coffin wondered what the green tea would be like, emerald maybe, but the cupful looked just like tea, weak pale tea. Not much flavour either, he thought. He was a strong dark Ceylon tea man himself. But Mat was sipping away with pleasure. But he had ladled in three spoons of sugar.

'I thought you'd be along,' said Mat.

'Oh, why?'

'I hear things . . . Smoke?'

'No, thanks.'

'I shouldn't,' said Mat, comfortably lighting a long dark object that he called a cigar.

'You hear things before I do, then.'

'You've never been a great listener, Jack.' Mat was the only person in the world who called him Jack. 'Watcher, yes, but listener, no. Too busy with your own ideas.'

'I hope that's not true.' Coffin drew the letter he had received out of his pocket. He had read it twice, with mounting anger. 'I've had this.'

Mat put down his cup of tea (he never used mugs and that same loving daughter who bought the tea also provided bone china to drink from; she was rich, ran a successful hairdressing establishment in Jermyn Street) and took up the letter. He read it through slowly once and then again.

'Short and to the point. Signed Frank Darely. Who's he?'

'A kind of local czar,' said Coffin. Frank Darely was a councillor and had always seemed friendly. No doubt this letter was meant in a friendly way, but it was cheek and angered Coffin. 'He carries a lot of clout, and of course he's on the Police Committee.'

'Big in local government, isn't he?'

'Got friends everywhere.'

'Yes, he sounds that sort,' said Mat judicially, studying the letter again. 'Quite friendly put. A kind of advance warning.'

'He is friendly, damn him.'

Frank Darely had written briefly to say that he had reason to believe that Coffin would shortly be asked to appear before a special sub-committee on the matter of certain relationships of his that the Police Committee felt were not what was expected of the Chief Commander who must be whiter than snow.

'Reason to believe,' said Coffin. 'He bloody knows.'

Mat clicked his teeth. 'Manners, manners, the dog doesn't like bad language.' Mat, who had been among the most profane of heavy drinkers in his day, had cleaned up his act so successfully that even damn was rarely heard on his lips. There was no dog.

'There's always been a division on the Committee between those who wanted me and those who thought I was a big risk. I've always known that, knew when I was asked to let my name go forward . . . You know what my career has been like. Patchy. I've had my downs.'

Mat was silent; he had shared in one of those downs himself.

'I take risks, I know I do, I'm not conventional in the way I handle things. I know that too. I've got my enemies.'

'Anyone special?'

'How special do you want? One of our MPs has his knife in, he'd like to get me out. The other one, Mary Backham, she's not too bad but she might be gunning for me on the feminist issue. Although I've always been in favour of women.'

'You certainly have, Jack,' said Mat thoughtfully. He might have added: 'And not always wise,' but he chewed on his cigar while he considered and Coffin waited. Oddly enough, the tea seemed to be a powerful stimulant, so that he felt less tired and more cheerful.

Mat folded up the letter and handed it back. 'I'd keep a copy of that, if I was you . . . And what's upsetting them?'

'Oh, Stella, I suppose, and perhaps some of my sister's goings-on in the property market, but mostly Stella.'

'I remember Stella. Nice lady.'

'Everyone's allowed their bit on the side, several sides,' said Coffin fiercely. 'Adultery and marital rape, we can take all that, but not for me. I ought to have a nice, neat respectable married life and be an example to everyone.'

'Have you thought of getting married?'

'I was once.' And a disaster that had been.

'To Stella, I mean?'

Coffin got up and started to walk about the room. Pacing up and down.

'The dog doesn't like that,' said Mat placidly.

'You haven't got a bloody dog.'

'How do you know?'

60

'One day you'll say that, and a dog will walk through the door,' said Coffin in a fury.

Mat began to laugh. 'We'd get on fine, my daughter says I'm a fantasy myself.'

'I don't know if I want to marry. Anyway, Stella has a husband. They never meet but he's still extant. An ex-actor, he has some sort of agency.'

'It adds to the picture a bit, though, doesn't it? Especially if he is making trouble.'

Coffin stared at his friend. 'He isn't.'

'Perhaps Fred Darely knows better.'

'You mean he's been put up to it?'

'It could be. You'd better have a word with Stella, see what she knows.'

'We're barely talking,' said Coffin unhappily. His good mood had been very temporary.

Mat poured them both some more tea. Then he got up and put a log on the embers, giving them a stir as he did so. He relit his cigar with a stick from the fire. A scatter of sparks fell on his shoulders, which he ignored.

Coffin patted them out. 'You'll go up in smoke one of these days.'

Mat ignored him. 'Drink up the tea while it's hot.'

'The thing is, should I take this letter, this whole business, seriously?'

'They are taking it seriously,' said Mat.

'I thought you'd say that. Damn.'

Mat drained his cup, put it down. 'Want me to tell you what you should do and how you should do it?'

Coffin made his way home to St Luke's feeling clearer in his mind after his talk with Mat. He trusted Mat, one of the few old friends who had seen him at his worst. Mind you, Mat's worst had been something sensational too.

He drove home in a leisurely fashion, not as tired as he had been, and more cheerful. All seemed quiet in Spinnergate as he drove through. A patrol car passed him, recognized him and flashed its lights.

61

He knew the message would go back to base: WALKER is driving home.

He let himself in and walked up his staircase, where he met Tiddles who seemed pleased to see him. 'Thanks, old boy.' He patted Tiddles's head. 'In my present mood, any support is welcome.'

There were two messages for him on his machine. One, which had been there for some hours, was from Stella. She wanted to know where he was, asked him to get in touch, and sent her love.

Some faint trace of strain there, he thought.

The second message was from Chief Superintendent Paul Lane asking for a meeting, tomorrow if possible. About the box in which the girl was buried.

CHAPTER 5

The next day. Day Eight

The box was an amateur production, roughly hammered together out of pale new planks of wood. By the look of it, it had not taken long to make.

'Bit of a cheap job,' said Paul Lane to the Chief Commander. It was the next day and they had met in the car park as Coffin arrived, both in a hurry, both glad to talk. 'Just thrown together. I thought you'd want what we got as soon as maybe. Just whacked together.'

'But interesting it should be made at all,' said Coffin. He hadn't slept well and had eaten no breakfast.

'You think so? . . . I tell you it made my flesh creep a bit.' He screwed his face up in a frown. 'Nasty.'

'It could have been made in love.'

Paul Lane looked alert and sceptical. Let's keep our feet on the ground, his face said. 'I'll let you know if the lab boys pick up anything from the coffin.' He had come to have a reluctant respect for his scientific colleagues and their technical expertise. Many a good case had been got

62

into the courts with their help. And the odd one lost, of course, but don't dwell on that. They had set up an Incident Room on the spot in a pod, a mobile van with appendages, and all the technicians were at work, overtime no worry, which pleased some and not others. 'Going over the ground down there, inch by inch. There'll be something.'

'Keep looking for another coffin.'

'You think he made himself a coffin and then dropped himself into it?' Silly joke and no one laughed. Least of all Paul Lane when he realized the Chief was serious.

'We'll keep looking,' he said.

'I'm glad I caught you.'

'Yes, I've left some papers at home.'

He watched his boss drive off to collect some papers he had left behind. Not like the Chief Commander, he thought, to be forgetful.

'It was the girl in it, of course,' said Stella. They were walking side by side, round and round the small courtyard that the architect had contrived between St Luke's Mansions, where they lived, and St Luke's Theatre now up and running in the old church itself. The architect called it a cloister and was proud of the small arcaded walk. Stella was walking round and round it, accompanied by Bob, as she thought about her next part. She had the script with her. She learnt her words better if she walked them into her brain. But she was also thinking about the future of the main theatre ... the workshop theatre was safe, she thought, since its demands were modest. The big theatre was dark at the moment, it had a production they had brought in from Windsor coming in next week for a month, but after that ... 'So it was the girl,' she said again. She said it sadly. Sometimes she felt that death came close to her too often through her relationship with John Coffin.

They had met in the cloister, Stella on her third circuit, Bob on his fourth or fifth because he moved faster, and John Coffin coming back home to grab some papers. Or so he had claimed, but it was really an excuse to get back into his own home for a bit. He had sat there, slumped in a chair and thought about Jim Dean and his own troubled past. Things were getting dug up and not only bodies.

They were all pleased to see each other, Bob most of all, because he felt he had a hope of a meal: Stella had overlooked his last feeding time, she grew forgetful when she was in rehearsal, and he was hungry. He associated John Coffin with food, so that was good. He sat down and looked up hopefully.

'Poor kid,' said Stella.

'It was her.'

'You knew it would be.'

'Yes, I think I did,' said Coffin, considering. 'It seemed likely.'

'And no signs of the boy?'

'No, we still have no idea where he is.'

'How did Jim Dean take it?'

Coffin considered again. How had Dean taken it? 'He took it very well. He was expecting it, I think.'

He was not surprised that the news of the discovery in the woods had reached Stella before he told her, Spinnergate was a village in many ways. A brief mention in some of the London papers had not included the identity of the body.

'He won't leave it there, though. He's very angry.'

'With whom?'

Again Coffin considered. 'Everyone, I think, including himself.' Most of all himself, he had thought, as he had watched Jim Dean's face. 'But with the boy. He blames the boy. And certainly he is angry with the police.'

'Why?'

'For being too slow.'

'You were as quick as you could have been.'

'But not quick enough, apparently . . . And slow about finding Martin Blackhall. He talked about getting a private detective to look for the boy but I intend to talk him out of that.'

Stella was thoughtful. 'I don't think I remember Jim Dean.'

'He was after your time. And before it.' He gave her a

64

loving smile. There had been a hiatus in their relationship during which they had not met, although he had always been aware of where she was. During this time they had lived different lives. He had buried his years in the wilderness; Stella had triumphantly risen above hers. She always had a quality of the phoenix.

But it was in this buried decade, right at the beginning of it, that Coffin had known James Dean. They had been paired for a while, then Dean had left. He suspected that Dean had links still in the Force, possibly among his own men. No harm in that, there were always networks, he used them himself.

'How did the girl die?'

'She was strangled. Manually.'

'So it was murder?'

'Oh yes, no doubt about that.'

'But of course,' said Stella thoughtfully, 'it always looked as if it would be. I never thought anything else. Not that I knew the girl, but when a girl like that is missing, you always think: Ah yes, well, she's dead, poor kid. Someone's got her . . . I suppose the boy is likely to have done it?'

Coffin shrugged. 'It's hard to like the human race sometimes.'

'But you go on trying . . . That's what I love about you.'

'I don't keep trying all the time.'

'Well, I don't love you all the time.'

Coffin laughed. 'I'd noticed that. Now I know why.'

'There are other reasons . . . You can be maddening.' She bent down to stroke Tiddles who appeared from behind a pillar. 'I wish I'd been around when you knew Dean.'

'It didn't last long. It wasn't the best time in my life. And I wasn't a very nice person to know.'

Stella picked up Tiddles and looked into the distance. 'You realize you make me feel sad when you talk like that.'

'I wasn't very nice to you, Stella.' He saw himself: young, brash, self-centred.

'That was earlier. And I wasn't very nice to you.' Far from it. She had treated him badly. Walked away, left him, with barely a goodbye. She couldn't do it now. Life had softened her, made her more tender.

'Ah well, I don't dig it up very often.' Keep things buried, he thought, but they get dug up like bodies, all the same.

'Well, I suppose you wouldn't.' She put Tiddles down, but he hung around, he had something on his mind. Food, probably. Bob too acted hungry.

'But I learnt something in those years and it's stayed with me. Done good service. I learnt when to get worried.'

'And now?'

'Yes, I'm worried now. Something bad is going to happen.' He didn't use the word evil, it was not professional, but he smelt it.

'What?'

'I wish I knew.' In his career, he had met most varieties of evil, but life had taught him that there was always scope for more.

'I'll tell you all about those years one day, Stella.' Or as much as was suitable, she wasn't as tough and cynical as she pretended. 'There were some good patches and some bad patches, some mad weeks and some weeks I was too sane, and I think I've ended up sane streaked with madness and that seems the right mixture for a policeman.'

They parted in the cloister, Coffin going back to his office and several boring committees and his own thoughts on the death of Amy Dean.

Coming home late that evening, he met Tiddles at his front door. It was a night for hunting. Tiddles debated and then shot up the staircase ahead of John Coffin.

James Dean was waiting for him at the head of his stairs.

'How did you get in?'

Dean did not answer directly. 'I wanted to see you. Privately. On our own.'

He was holding a bottle of champagne. On the table was a tray with smoked salmon sandwiches. Tiddles advanced hopefully.

Dean waved a hand. 'I went to Max's Deli, ordered a light meal for us both and told him you wanted me to await you here. He gave me his key.'

66

'I'd forgotten he had one.' Dean had always known how to get in where he wanted; he remembered that and one or two other things as well. Money no doubt had passed hands; he must remember that too.

'To do Max justice, it was not Max himself, a girl, one of his daughters.'

'Oh yes.' Dean knew how to handle women, always had, the younger the easier. Look how he had managed the girl, Angela. She had been soothed, quietened and sent back to Armitage Hall in Dean's own car with a policewoman. Dean himself had taken a taxi.

'Nice-looking kid.'

The Beauty daughter, then. Stupid that one, and not as pretty now as she had been three years ago. Some bloomed at fifteen and went off. She might end up a plain forty-year-old. Then he checked this bitchy thought: it was just redirected anger at James Dean.

'You haven't got your pretty lady with you.'

Coffin prickled at this description of Stella Pinero who was so much more than that.

'So what is it?' He observed with pleasure that the cat had already got his paw round a sandwich and was removing it to the floor. 'Why champagne?'

'Not a celebration of a death,' Dean said savagely. 'I want to talk. I'm going to give you a week to find the boy and then I am going to send in my own detective.'

'I strongly advise you not to do that.'

'But I don't take your advice, do I?' He was pouring the champagne. 'Or I didn't in the past. It was one of the reasons we parted company. Here, take your drink.'

Coffin accepted the drink reluctantly, he was still angry with this invasion of his privacy. 'Not the only reason. And we didn't part, as you put it. You left the Force.'

Dean said: 'I don't trust that bastard Tom Blackhall and that wife of his. She's too clever. I don't like clever women.'

'Is that the real reason?' Or did she turn you down once? He knew Dean's reputation. 'Do you trust any of us?'

'You found my daughter. You got her dug up. I give you that.'

Coffin said thoughtfully: 'The bus ticket led us there.'
Then he added: 'You led us there.'

'No, I was just driving around. I'd given up. I still don't
know what she was doing on the bus or who was with her.
The boy, I suppose, but you were the one that persevered.
You always were. Remember the time we were looking for
the Hadden rapist? You stuck at it.' He poured some more
champagne.

'But you don't trust me to find the boy?'

'You're only human.' He shook his head. 'And I want to
make very sure that he gets what's coming to him.'

'He may be dead.'

'I don't think so. His wallet was in the car. That says he
was there.'

'It also says he may not have left the car willingly. People
don't leave their money and bank cards behind if they can
take them with them.'

'He may not have noticed. Depends on his state, doesn't
it? You and I know that murderers don't behave rationally.'

'Yes, I do know that.'

'And always leave something behind. Some trace. He'll
have left his spoor. Find him.'

'CI Young will be checking passengers on the bus. Something might come from that.'

'Well, see he gets on with it. People forget things. How
many people were on that bus? He'll never track them all
down. What about the driver? Is he the sort to remember?'

'Young's a first-class officer with a good team.'

Dean gave a grunt and sank back into the chair. Coffin
acknowledged the raw pain inside the man. Both of them
knew too much about what was going on, what was happening to his daughter's body, the people involved, the police
surgeon, the pathologist, the technicians. He was not surprised at what Dean said next.

'Remember viewing your first post-mortem, John? Not
nice, eh? How did you feel? I was sick, you weren't.'

'Everyone felt the same.'

'The inside organs don't look too bad, once they've been
cleaned up. In fact, they're kind of interesting. I remember

thinking that. But it's not what you'd want for your nearest and dearest.'

Coffin saw he was shaking. He touched Dean's arm gently. 'I'm sorry, Jim,' he said.

'Yes, I wish I hadn't remembered. He was an old man, that one . . . She was all I had left.'

'I know.'

'No, you don't. For you it's just business. D'you think I don't remember how coppers look? I've seen that look before in other eyes, and was surprised to see it now.'

'You're doing me an injustice.'

Dean let a long pause go by. He can talk before I do, Coffin decided. Damn. And I'm not sure about this wash of emotion. I never have been sure about him.

Dean said suddenly: 'I didn't want her to go to the university, I didn't want her to take that sociology course.'

'What did you want?'

'She had a place at a finishing school in Paris. I wanted her to go there. But no, she had to choose this place on your patch.'

'Not my fault.'

'I think she already knew the boy Martin. Seem to remember him around the place.'

'At school together?'

'No, he was at one of those schools for smart, difficult boys, the schools where clever academics send their sons when they can't manage them. They met at a party somewhere . . . on the river.'

He knew a lot about it, Coffin reflected, he must have watched the girl. Perhaps he had used one of the detectives he spoke about.

'And that place she worked at. Star Court. I was dead against that. Why did she have to go there?'

'Part of her course, I believe.'

'That's what she said. Perhaps. I don't like that place. Take it apart if you have to.'

Was that really why you came here, thought Coffin.

Dean went to the window, glass in hand. 'Nice view you've got here. I like to see the river.'

69

Coffin joined him at the window. He drew it down a fraction so that the night smell, still damp and full of autumn, floated in. 'Just a glimpse. You don't hear much these days. Never the big ships talking to each other like you used to. I miss that sound.'

'No, those days are over . . . Remember that night on Phoenix Wharf?'

There was a long pause while Coffin picked up noise and smell from the past: a foggy November night, fog sirens wailing sadly from the river, the peremptory hoot of a tug in the distance. The remoter sound of traffic. The smell of dampness and dustiness and oil, all mixed up. London as it was all those years ago.

'Never forgotten.' Buried the memory, of course, but he was digging it up now.

'Dark night, wasn't it?' said Dean. 'That was why we got lost.'

Coffin dragged another memory out. 'Didn't get lost, we were misled by that man who was supposed to be pointing out the way.'

'Yes, you always said that, I was never so sure.'

Misled or just lost, Coffin could see it now: the darkness, the river on his left, the tall black buildings of Phoenix Wharf on his right. What had been stored in there, that it all smelt so oily? Dean had been behind him. In front . . . the figure that was meant to be leading them to the rendezvous suddenly disappeared.

He thought now, as he had thought then: We were fools to have believed him, we have been led into a trap. He could smell his own fear.

Ahead, a shape loomed up through the fog, another behind.

These days, he thought, we wouldn't have gone in without proper back-up. Asking for trouble. Young fools.

He had hesitated, then shouted. Probably the worst thing he could have done. In the darkness came the flash of a gun, he had half turned, then Dean had pushed him down, and in the same second fallen on top of him. The bullet had gone into Dean's chest.

70

He could remember the weight of Dean on top of him, the rush of blood, instantaneous it had seemed, spouting out. He could remember the smell. Him or me, he had thought, and it was Dean that had got hit.

Then he had dragged himself from under Dean's body and got on with the job.

Well, the men had been caught, although not by him, and he had got Dean to hospital.

'You saved my life,' he said to Dean. 'I knew that then, although I was too bloody-minded to say so.' But that had not been the true reason, there was another, blacker reason, a feeling of treachery, that perhaps Dean had known more than he should about what was going to happen, and had not been the one meant to be shot.

I was always jealous of him, Coffin admitted silently, it distorted everything so that I never knew what was truth and what just suspicion. He pushed the idea down to the past where it belonged and turned back to the safety of the present.

'Although I can't remember much about it, I understand you got me to hospital in time and offered your blood.'

'But it was the wrong sort. Our bloods don't match.' Just as well, he had thought at the time, my blood would have clotted in his veins. He had kept his bloodstained clothes bundled up in the back of a cupboard till they began to stink, then had put them in a small case. He had carried the case round with him for days before eventually dropping it in the river. Dean's blood, shed for him, and he had very mixed feelings about it.

Gratitude did curdle inside you sometimes.

'You get a buzz out of action like that,' said Dean reflectively. 'Or I did. I suppose I recognized the danger signals, you get hooked on that sort of thing . . .'

'Was that why you resigned?'

'No, not really.' Dean was thoughtful. 'Just seemed like the end of one life and the beginning of another . . . I'd met a girl . . . Her dad offered to put me in his business . . . I didn't marry that girl.'

'So I'd heard.' There had been the usual gossip.

71

'It wasn't me that jilted her, she threw me over, but it gave me a start. Her father felt guilty. I always got on better with him than her, sex apart . . . When I did marry, that was a bit of a disaster. Suppose I hadn't got the trick of being married, it's not a skill you pick up in the Force. But I did better second time round. She died, though. I expect you heard that too. You had a bit of a bad time yourself, from all I've heard.'

'Sort of,' said Coffin. The doctors had kindly said that he had reacted badly to some drugs.

'You married, didn't you? Not too good from the word I got.'

'You hear a lot.'

'Things get passed round. There's a network, you know that . . . You didn't trust me, did you?'

Coffin looked at him silently.

'And you don't trust me now.'

'Is that what you think?' True and yet not true.

From below Coffin heard Stella's voice floating up from the garden where she was calling for Tiddles who was up with him, and the past receded and the present came back into full view. Darling Stella, always real.

'That's your woman, isn't it?' Dean stood up. 'Seen her act. Brilliant. I must be off. I've said what I wanted to say. We've finished the champagne and the cat's had the smoked salmon.' He put on his coat which was of cashmere, soft black, with a dark velvet collar. Inside it, he looked tougher than ever, like a successful boxer out for the day.

Coffin said: 'Hold out your hands, will you?'

Dean hesitated, then did so, stretching out both hands in front of him.

Coffin examined them, turning them over. Clean, white, the nails carefully trimmed. No sign of recent manual labour.

'So?'

'Someone made that coffin.'

'You can't suspect me.'

'Murder is very often a family crime, Jim. You and I know that much.'

72

Dean buttoned his coat with careful hands and put on his gloves. For a moment he said nothing. Then: 'I wasn't her family any more. Have you found that out? Her family was the university and Star Court.'

He turned towards the door. 'I'll see myself out.'

Coffin followed him down the twisting staircase. At the bottom, he said: 'Jim?'

Dean turned. 'Yes?'

'I'll remember what you said.'

Coffin held the door open. 'One more thing.'

He held out his hand. 'My key, please?'

News of the discovery of Amy's body, and of the circumstances of her burial, lapped in wood, soon spread throughout the campus. The news travelled fast from Armitage, where it had been heard first from Angela, to Barclay and Gladstone. The further it got from Armitage, where Amy had lived, the more the story got distorted (she had been raped, tied in bonds, buried alive, and cut in bits), the more the guilt of Martin Blackhall was held to be obvious.

The fact that he was the son of their Rector made the gossip hotter and sent more of it underground. But Sir Thomas was liked. Not much known by the student body, but liked. He meant well by them, they thought.

Some decades earlier when, on what in retrospect seemed like the whim of the then government, many new universities had been conceived and brought to difficult birth, it had been suggested that one such university could be sited in that very area of dockland (already running down into decay and needing something to give it life) which was to be the heart of the Second City. It hadn't happened then, but twenty years later and another government, another desperate need to upgrade an area that had outlived its original reason for being, and there it was.

At the time of the first suggestion, Thomas Blackhall had been an ambitious young academic in Oxford, his eyes set on achieving a chair somewhere. Professor Blackhall, he thought, had a good ring to it. He was not married then and living in college. Tom was the son of a butcher, not a

73

rich man but a good one, who had handed on to his son a fine physique and a beautiful voice. From his mother he had inherited brains. It was a winning combination. A professor in Cambridge at 32, which he had achieved by a judicious move, married to a prizewinning medic, with a child, he had begun to look around for the right university to head. One or two near misses had discouraged him. His timing was wrong, he thought. But he sat industriously and intelligently on several important committees and chaired at least one with distinction. Things were looking up.

One evening at a college Gaudy night he sat next to a cabinet minister. The minister knew that the University of the Second City was about to be put together (cobbled, was the word he had used in Cabinet), and he thought Tom was the man for it. Especially as the Minister for Education had another candidate for the post and it would be a pleasure to defeat his fellow minister. He had met Tom Blackhall before, they had sat on a committee and crossed swords but the minister liked a fighter.

Blackhall's name was put forward and he was asked to apply. He talked it over with his wife.

'Never going to be in the first rank, not in this century, that has to be faced, but I might make something of it.'

'And then move on?'

'I like London,' he said evasively. 'It might suit me.'

So he had come, just a little later than John Coffin. He had welded together the disparate and sometimes warring elements of his new institution into a whole.

It had not been easy. Student trouble, drugs, drink, rent strikes, he had survived all those, only to run into trouble with an indigenous population which eyed with some envy those it thought were having it easy. Town and Gown do not make good neighbours. But in the end the Second City was coming to be proud of its university. One Nobel Prize, several illustrious Gold Medals in the arts and sciences, made everyone happy.

The university was helping to create the very city it was planted in, giving it a character, a status, a sense of corporate identity.

I keep the peace here as much as you do, he had wanted
to say to John Coffin, and you'd better know it. I am part
of the balancing act.

Not unnaturally, when they met there was a slight sense
of rivalry between the two men. They were polite, even
friendly, as men can be when they are eyeing each other
with care.

The relationship between Tom Blackhall and his wife
had undergone strain now that they were thrown together
more than they had been for years.

'Coffee?' Lady Blackhall looked as though she had slept
badly, but she was dressed and made up expertly as usual.

'Thank you.'

They were always polite to each other, never more so
than now. Old friends used to wonder how they talked to
each other when they were alone, but no one ever heard
shouting matches or even anger.

But there was one subject that was never raised between
them, although it was the cause of constant silent combat.
He wasn't, you see, her first husband. She was always conscious that she was older than he was in a quiet, unobtrusive
way that might show up more as the years went on.

He couldn't quite avoid that topic now, though. It had
to come up.

'Things like that don't happen, do they? I know guilt
seeds itself but not to the children. We're not living in a
Greek drama, are we?'

'I don't know, you're the historian. I'm just a scientist.'

'Blood.' He had taken a sleeping tablet the night before
and it had loosened the tongue as it was apt to do lately.
'Blood guilt. That because I behaved badly, I will be punished through Martin.'

She got up, put her hands on his shoulders, hard. 'There
was no blood, shut up about blood, the man who was my
husband drowned.'

'Sorry.' He tried to take her hand, but she moved away.
'I didn't mean it literally, it was that sleeping pill last night.
Gives me bad dreams.'

She went back to her coffee. 'I'll prescribe something

75

better for you,' she said briefly. 'And don't think like that. Don't touch the idea. Martin is not dead.'

'I don't want him to have killed the girl.'

'Not that either.'

'She was trouble. I always saw that.'

Victoria Blackhall was surprised. 'I didn't know you knew her.'

'Of course I knew her. I'm the Rector here. I try to know them all.'

'I've heard you say so.' Her tone was neutral.

'Over three thousand here. About three hundred of them, I do know. Faces, anyway, damn it. I try . . .' It was a lot of faces. They were all photographed on arrival, and these pictures he studied carefully before meeting a group. 'Once I knew Martin was interested, then I took a good look. And I didn't like what I saw.'

'Oh, with a rich father like that she would be spoiled.'

'No, not spoiled, not indulged in the way you mean, but something wrong with her.'

His wife said: 'I thought she sounded a nice child.'

He ignored that. 'And you know what Martin's like.'

'I do know,' said his mother, who loved him. Tall, blond, handsome, and not stupid. Physically, the image of his paternal grandfather, the handsome butcher. 'And don't go on about blood. It's just an organ of the body. It's the genes that carry inheritance, not blood. I know about blood. My job.'

'I know about blood too. I'm the butcher's boy, remember?'

He went back to that bit of their past before they had married. He couldn't leave it alone.

'I wonder if the police will dig it up.'

'Why should they?' She wanted to say: 'And nothing happened,' but that would not have been quite true. They had committed adultery but not murder.

'Plenty of talk at the time.'

'All forgotten. No one remembers now.'

He laughed without amusement. 'If you think that, you don't know the academic world . . . It will all be neatly

76

tucked away in someone's letter, some diary somewhere, ready to be brought out at the right time. We shall be publishable.'

'Stop going on about it, and let's concentrate on Martin.' She began to move about the room in a restless way, unlike her usual careful poise. 'I'm sure he'd telephone if he could. I wonder if he's gone away . . . Scotland, he loves Scotland. Or Italy.'

'He didn't have any money, no wallet, no credit cards. All left behind. He can't have gone far.'

'Do you think . . . a friend could be hiding him? Perhaps on the campus? No one checks on the student rooms, do they?'

Tom Blackhall shrugged. 'The student feeling is that he killed Amy. He wouldn't get help here.'

The telephone interrupted them. Tom Blackhall picked it up. 'Dean?'

'No news of your son, I suppose?'

'No, none.'

'You'd tell me, I hope, and not cover up?'

'I would not cover up,' said Sir Thomas with cold anger.

'I've given the police a week in which to find Martin, then I'm going to bring in my own detectives. Will you join me?'

'No.' Tom Blackhall was brief. 'I'm leaving it to the police.' He put the telephone down. 'Dean,' he said to his wife. 'He wants to hire a detective.'

'And?'

'You heard. I won't.' He put his head in his hands. 'Oh God.'

'Stop worrying about the past.'

The Rector picked a Meissen dish from the table by the telephone, aimed deliberately at the window and threw it. 'You fool,' he said. 'I'm not worrying about the past. I'm worrying about the future.'

It was a long time since his wife had seen him indulge in such violence, and she knew that it was usually she who brought it out in him.

77

A student, passing below, heard the crash of glass and looked up in surprise.

No explanation about the broken glass and china was made by the Rector nor by his wife and the mess was cleared up by the usual cleaner. The glass was restored by a member of the Works Department, a quiet man who never speculated about anything, having found that in his job a lack of imagination was an asset.

The only comment was made from wife to husband. Tight-lipped, Lady Blackhall said she would be claiming on the insurance for the piece of porcelain and that now she was going out.

'Where?'

'Work. You'll be better without me for a bit.'

'Leave your telephone number so that I can get in touch with you if I have to.'

'I shall be at St Luke's Hospital all the morning. I have a clinic there.'

'I have the feeling that something, anything, might happen.'

His wife went away, having assessed her husband's mood with some anxiety: he might be on the edge of a breakdown. She would watch him, she loved him, as she loved their son, but they were not easy men. As she drove herself to work, she wondered if the old man, the butcher, was to blame, handing down to them a complexity of spirit they would not own up to. There was an edge, a boundary, in life, and both of them would, on occasion, leap over it. Tom had done so once. A tough man, Sir Tom was called, but his wife knew better.

He thinks of what is happening as a kind of punishment, she told herself, but it is not. There is no connection between what is happening now and our past, unless we choose to make it so.

She slowed down as she approached the hospital, and felt better. The sight of the old grey brick building was familiar and friendly.

St Luke's Hospital, as with so many institutions in the

78

Second City, was made up of a clutch of new buildings tacked on to an aged centre which had been a Poor Law Infirmary and was thus a monument to solid, sensible, uncomfortable Victorian building. Several wars and many bombs had not dented it. During the war against Hitler, the basement had housed the Auxiliary Fire Service, while those patients not evacuated had nested above.

Dr Blackhall's clinic was held in the older part of the building about which the smells of generations of patients and disinfectants still seemed to hang. In spite of this, she enjoyed her work there. She came only once a week but they counted as good days. St Luke's was an excellent teaching hospital, attached to the university and with a growing reputation. Dr Blackhall's clinic attracted interesting cases, referred there from other hospitals for her speciality which was disorders of the blood. A first-class team of registrars and housemen was attached to her.

She worked on that morning, her ear always on the alert for the phone call that might come. One of the good results of having committed several sins yourself, she thought, was that it made you sympathetic to the oddities of life (and she got plenty of those in her clinic in that district), you were tolerant of those of your patients whose ways were not as yours.

It was a big clinic that day, so she was able to avoid lunch in the canteen without comment, only stopping later that afternoon for a cup of tea. She was sipping it, and signing some letters at the same time when she was interrupted.

'Dr Blackhall?' She looked up, it was Agnes Fisher, the Ward Sister from another department. They were old friends, she had trained with Agnes's mother, now retired into a happy marriage. 'May I have a word?'

Victoria Blackhall swung round in her chair. 'Of course, Agnes. What is it?'

'I've had a few days' leave,' began Agnes nervously, wondering if Dr Blackhall knew that she had put on one brown shoe and one black, but deciding not to mention it. 'Just before I went off, we had an emergency admission: a

79

girl had been attacked in a robbery in a shop in Spinnergate. She was brought in here, together with one of her attackers. He had no ID on him. Badly hurt and unconscious, both of them.'

She hesitated. 'I didn't see either of them then, and now I have done . . . His face is very swollen and bruised still, but I think the young man may be Martin.'

Victoria Blackhall stood up quickly, knocking over her chair. Agnes put her hand on Victoria's arm, checking her. 'Of course, there is a police constable sitting by his bed . . . I suppose he is under some kind of arrest.'

CHAPTER 6

The day continues

As she hurried through the corridors of the hospital, Victoria Blackhall summoned up in her mind the names of all those who might be useful to her and her problem son.

This was a crisis to be tackled as well as she could and she must rely on herself, she had the feeling that Tom was going to be of no use. It was woman's work here.

I don't know Commander Coffin, she told herself, but I have met his sister Letty Bingham, and I know Stella Pinero pretty well. And then there was Philippa Darbyshire, we've sung in the Bach Choir together.

People who sing together, hang together, the chant went through her mind as she turned the corner.

No one hangs these days.

Her destination was a small side ward off the Albemarle Ward in which the Intensive Care Centre was placed. This was part of the new building. A policeman was sitting outside the door. Along the hall was another constable, a woman, and she rightly concluded that here was the attacked girl, the victim.

The room was small, painted white with green curtains. There was a nurse by the bed, who looked up from her task of adjusting a drip. Seeing a white-coated figure with a familiar face, she smiled and got on with what she was doing.

Another police constable sat by the door; he stood up as Victoria passed him. 'Sorry, doctor, you can't come in.'

She ignored him and went to straight to the bed.

'Doctor, please . . .'

A bruised face, hair which had been cut back from the forehead, a helmet of white bandages. It must have been a bad injury. He had fallen backwards, it seemed, hitting his head. Eyes closed.

She took his hands, they were pitted with little flaky wounds as if something had been chipped out of them. She looked at the nurse.

'We had to pick the bits of wood out of them.'

The policeman started to say something, but she ignored him.

'There's something wrong with him beside the head injuries.'

The nurse had now got Victoria's face in focus and knew her. Dr Blackhall was a respected and admired figure in St Luke's. Slightly feared as formidable, but trusted.

'Yes, a virus. He was soaking wet, we think he may have been in the river.'

The policeman managed to get his word in: 'If it's a medical matter, of course . . . but otherwise . . .'

'I only wanted to see if this is my son.'

The police constable was flustered. In his youthful experience, admittedly limited, doctors, and especially such commanding ones as this lady, did not have sons who might go down for a stretch for attempted robbery with violence. 'And is it?'

Victoria Blackhall looked down at the bruised and battered face. His eyes opened, he stared up at her.

'Mum.'

She took one of those battered hands. 'I'm here, darling.'

A whisper. 'Mum. I didn't mean to hurt her.'

Sharply, she said: 'Stop it. Don't say another word.'

*

81

Outside, on her way to telephone her husband, she leaned against a door, took a deep breath and thought about her son's condition, about his immersion in water, about his hands which had handled wood and about the two girls, one dead, one gravely injured. What had been going on?

Wood and water, she said to herself. Wood and water. Rationality made a play to be heard, she must listen to reason. It can't mean anything . . . And yet I have said it . . . Perhaps that is what retribution is: you make it yourself.

I shall not say this to Tom. He has the night horrors in the daytime already.

The news spread around at once, evoking different reactions in different places.

The hospital was the first to know, beating the police by a short head. John Coffin was alerted by a telephone call from Chief Superintendent Paul Lane. Then the news was transported to the theatre, where a rehearsal of 'The Ride of the Valkyries' was taking place. Star Court heard nothing that day, it was not quick at noticing the outside world, but Josephine was told the next day on picking up her morning paper from Mimsie, who had heard the story and slept on it. Jo looked so ill these days she was sorry she had told her.

The hospital, on the whole, held its breath and kept quiet. Dr Blackhall was a well-known and respected figure there, no one wanted to cause her more pain than they had to. She had cancelled her clinic appointments for the coming week, leaving her Senior Registrar to stand in for her. No one expected her to be away longer than that: she was a professional, after all. Nor did they pain her by looks of sympathy as she walked through the corridors, although one very senior colleague did give her a hearty slap on the back, but he was known for doing that sort of thing.

For the police it was another matter and Chief Inspector Young was round to the hospital at once, where he was soon joined by the team that had been investigating the

82

robbery in the shop. Sergeant Hill got there first, having been alerted by the constable in the room.

Two men, both concerned with questioning one young man about two different cases. The two of them met in the hall outside Martin Blackhall's room. Martin had been conscious and they wanted to get at him.

'Inspector Vernon is on his way over,' said Hill, anxious to be polite to Young who was known to be in with the Big Man himself. Or so the story went. He himself had spoken but once to the Chief Commander and had found him courteous yet alarming. Like everyone else he knew the tale of the Chief Commander's life; how he had come up through the ranks, how he had a mad mother and a rich half-sister, how he had spent a period out of favour because of some special circumstances (not known about but thought to be secret and dangerous work which sent him mad too) and how he had come back. Stella Pinero had her place in the saga too but they admired him for that. She was a woman of importance.

'I want to speak to this young man,' said Archie crisply. 'He must have had quite a busy few days if he strangled and buried one girl and then went in for robbery with violence.'

Hill remained silent, life with his superiors having taught him the virtues of a quiet tongue.

Archie Young continued his monologue: 'What was he up to? Wanted the money to escape, I suppose . . . Could be on drugs. That might explain a lot.'

Archie opened the door and looked into the cubicle where Martin lay, but his way was blocked by the nurse.

'Dr Chain says no visitors.'

'Oh, come on, nurse. We're police officers. This is important.'

She was nervous, but held her ground. 'Doctor says not . . . And in any case, the patient is not fully conscious.'

'Let me have a look.'

She moved a pace back. 'Just look and no more.'

Archie Young pushed ahead of Hill. He saw what Victoria had seen: a bruised and swollen face, with bandages covering the head. He observed a scratched hand resting on the bedcover.

His spirits took an unexpected dip, he was touched by cold. He had the sense of something very wrong. He did not use the word Evil, it was not a word in his vocabulary, but he was puzzled. He felt something more than he could express.

A feeling like that was not to be endured, and he rallied.

'His mother knew him. That's good enough for me.' He stepped back. 'Let's go.'

Hill remained circumspect. 'I'll hang on till Vernon gets here.'

'Right. Then come on over, both of you, to my office. We need to talk.'

Not two cases but one, with two investigating teams involved. Three, if you considered those handling the matter of the car found in the territory of the Met.

One thing, Archie Young decided as he drove back to Spinnergate, we can give up looking for a dead body in Essex. Work had gone on there since the discovery of the coffin with Amy Dean's body in it, but nothing had turned up and now he thought he knew why.

The hospital, having triumphed as an institution over the police by imposing a delay for medical reasons, resumed its own busy life.

One more thought came to CI Young as he waited in the heavy traffic, banging an impatient hand on the steering-wheel: Have to get round to the university on the quick or the Blackhalls would have that sewn up too. He had no illusions about whose influence had operated back in the hospital. No word might have come from Sir Thomas or his lawyers as yet, but his shadow had gone before him.

In the main refectory of the university there was a quiet buzz of gossip as various medical students got back from the hospital and spread the news that Lady Blackhall had identified her son.

Angela, Beenie and Mick were about to eat a late lunch. Mick deposited a large tray on the table. 'Three cheese salads. It was about all they had left. Oh, and coffee for us, Beenie, and fruit juice for Angela.'

'I'd have liked coffee,' said Angela.

'Get it yourself, then.' Mick sat down and picked up a fork. 'I thought you weren't drinking coffee because you thought you had caffeine poisoning.'

'I'm over that now and back on the caffeine.' She moved the cheese around on the plate. 'This salad is disgusting.'

'Looks all right to me.' Beenie dug into her salad. 'I'm hungry.'

But although all three had healthy appetites, today the food was chewed without interest. Angela anyway had been causing her friends worry since the discovery of Amy's body.

'Don't let's talk about Martin and Amy,' said Beenie. 'Not till we've eaten.'

'Thrashed it out already, haven't we?' Mick muttered.

'No, there's more to say.'

Angela kept quiet. Her friends noticed and exchanged glances. She had been so much closer to Amy and Martin than either of the others. Knew more about Amy and her problems. There had been problems. Who said sex was easy, thought Beenie. She gave a small shrug which Mick interpreted as: Keep off anything dangerous for the time being.

He might or might not take notice of that warning; he was the man in this group and would make his own decisions. But he did notice a new bruise on Angela's arm.

He poured sugar into his coffee with youthful abandon: he had no weight worries, he was never going to get fat. Hunger worried him much more, he was nearly always hungry. Even now, he looked round wondering whether to go back for that extra roll and cheese. The canteen girl knew him and liked him and might therefore hand it over without charging. The university awarded them so many points a term for food in the canteen. Beyond that allowance (and Mick usually ate his way fast through it) you had to pay in hard cash which no student ever admitted to having

85

much of, and certainly not Mick who operated on an over-draft at the bank and loans from his family.

He stirred his coffee and decided against the roll. 'How was Star Court?' Angela could not refuse to answer a direct question.

'They've accepted me to go once a week. I was there today.'

'Good, was it?'

'I think I was helpful. I did jobs that weren't getting done. They watched me a bit, but I understood that.'

'Anyone been rough with you down there?'

'No.' Angela flushed and drew her sleeve down over her forearm. 'Just banged myself.' Lies and more lies, Beenie thought. What is with this Star Court?

'Wish you wouldn't go down there. I know you said you were kind of doing it for Amy but you give too much.'

'It helps me. I like doing it.'

'You mean you get something from them?'

'Give, get.' Angela shrugged. 'Sometimes it's the same thing.'

He wondered more than ever what had drawn Angela and Amy to Star Court. For Amy it had been part of her degree course, she was doing a paper on it for her tutor, but he sensed something more. Something personal. Started by Amy, he thought, but now carried on by Angela. And before that there had been Virginia. 'Shall I come down and give a hand?' he tried experimentally.

'No.' Angela was quick to say no.

Strangers keep out, Mick thought, men not wanted. But he put his considerable brain power to work.

Across the room a cluster of medical students, white coats flung over chairbacks, notebooks and files stacked on the tables, were bursting into laughter. One male student had a skeleton on the table.

'Showing off,' said Beenie. She leaned forward. 'We ought to talk about Amy and Martin now he's turned up.'

'Don't want to,' said Angela. 'Nor do you, do you, Mick?'

'Thought we'd hashed it all over.'

'No,' said Beenie. 'Besides—' she lowered her voice still

86

more—'see those two men sitting over there, having coffee, and pretending to be one of us?'

'Police,' said Mick, glancing over his shoulder. 'They've been all over the place for days, we all know them. And it isn't their feet, it's the way they look at you.'

'Right. Well, rumour has it they've found something in Amy's room.'

'Such as what?'

Beenie shook her head. Her information, reliable because she had heard one of the detectives say so himself, went no further. Angela got to her feet. 'I'm going.'

Mick watched her walk from the refectory. 'We said something wrong there.'

'I'm keeping an eye on her, don't you worry.'

'Have you thought there's something that Angie and Amy have in common.'

'Someone,' said Beenie promptly. 'Martin.'

'Well, that, yes.'

'What, then?'

'A look,' Mick said thoughtfully. 'Let's recapitulate.' This was a favoured expression of his, much used in his essays when he wanted to think things out on paper and didn't know the way forward. 'Our friend Amy has been killed, strangled. Martin is suspected because he seems to have been the last person known to be with her. Mark you, I say known.' Beenie nodded. 'Martin is in hospital, suspected of having tried to rob a shop in order to get money. To escape with, we presume. He muffed it and got knocked out himself. Badly. The girl shop assistant is not too good either. Then there is Virginia, who died last year. Also murdered. Possibly by Martin? Both girls worked at Star Court, home for battered ladies. And finally, there is our Angie, about whom we are worried because, inexplicably, she seems to be going the way of Virginia and Amy.'

'You're soft on her yourself, I think,' said Beenie. 'I could eat another roll.'

They got up and strolled over to begin negotiations with the girl at the counter.

One of the visiting detectives said to the other one: 'I

wish I could lip read. I'd like to know what they were talking about.'

'I can't lip read but I know what they were saying: that we've found something.'

'And have we found something?'

'Haven't we just.' They indulged in this sort of repartee occasionally. After a particular triumph.

Under the floorboards of Martin's student room which he did not share with anyone, they had found a tin box in which was the torn-up, cut-up or, as forensics were to show later, the sliced-up-with-a-knife photographs of Virginia, the very first girl killed.

'He's lying there in his bed, not speaking, not saying a word, all tucked up and comfortable, and all the time he had that picture under the floorboards in his room.'

The two of them left the university precincts soon after this, having warned the university security staff against people trying to get in.

'No one inside, right?'

They drove off, they were in a hurry to report and get home. One had a girlfriend he was keen to meet and the other was singing in a choir that was joining in an amateur production of Wagner. He thought he was meant to be a dwarf.

Philippa knew that one of the chorus singers was a policeman, because the beloved Marcus had told her. All in all, she thought him one of the most unlikely Nibelungs she had ever seen, but he had the voice, Adrian said. She also knew, due to the excellent intelligence service that Spinnergate operated (it was, after all, a village), that he was working on the case of Amy Dean. The woman who cleaned her house was a friend of the woman who helped behind the bar where several police officers gathered, that was how it worked. Hardly anyone thought about the woman quietly polishing the glasses with a soft cloth. Quite a few police officers drank in that pub which was across the road from their HQ, so that some information often seeped out that way. Even the Chief Commander had been seen there on occasion, although not saying much. Perhaps he was conscious of Daisy and her sharp ears.

Circles do interlink, Philippa thought with unease. Must be careful what I say. She gave the policeman-Nibelung, whom she was introducing to his costume, a sweet smile.

He looked baffled, both at what he was required to wear and her smile. 'I don't think I can get my legs into this.'

'Oh, I think you can. Try.'

He took the garments and retired behind a screen. They're not decent, he thought. Or won't be when I'm in them. A sort of leather jerkin and tight leggings. A kind of little cap for the top of the head. He felt like a mixture of something out of *Snow White* and a garden gnome. He supposed he could sing in such clothes.

As he emerged he could hear one of the Valkyries complaining about her breastplate, and when he saw it he didn't blame her. Even Madonna couldn't wear that, he thought.

'No, it's not really steel,' Philippa was saying. 'Of course it's not steel, it just looks like it. Painted. Anyway, the Gods wouldn't have had steel. Not period. Iron or bronze.'

The Valkyrie started to say something about the boy Martin being found and then stopped when she saw him. Must know he was a policeman. Now he got a look at her, he saw that she was the chief Valkyrie, Brunnhilde, a kind of super Girl Scout.

He put his head down and moved into the rest of the Nieblung chorus, most of whom were complaining about their costumes too. He knew the face of one of the Nibelungs: a student. His eyes and Mick's met and admitted a relationship.

While they awaited the arrival of the conductor and the musical director, he sat down and thought about what he had discovered under the floorboards in Armitage Hall that afternoon. It had been his hands that had lifted it out.

'Saw a mark on the floorboards,' his report had said. 'Lifted the board, and this tin box was underneath.'

Inside was the coarsely shredded photograph, in colour, of a girl. On the back, when pieced together was the word Virgin.

Short for Virginia, he supposed. Virginia Scott. Dead a year ago. Made you think.

Lydia Tulloch was also thinking. The boy Martin had obviously been badly hurt by the black-leather-dressed girl and she had witnessed his beating. And it had to be said it looked as though the leather girl had enjoyed what she was doing.

It was justified, of course, she told herself, if he had just attacked the shop assistant, but I suppose I ought to say. There had been that milkman, he saw something, maybe leave it to him. Could I recognize the girl again? Hard to say.

She wondered how the police worked. Reports in duplicate, memoranda and meetings probably, much like the university where she had been a unit in the administration before coming into her inheritance from Aunt Dolly.

She felt so sorry for the Blackhalls.

She took herself off to stand with the rest of the Valkyries. Centre stage of course, that was where Brunnhilde stood.

The meeting in John Coffin's room had been going on for some time. Superintendent Lane, and Chief Inspector Young were present and talking. Inspector Vernon was looking on.

'Do we know who knocked Blackhall out?'

'Yes, we have a good idea. One person saw from a distance and gave a description. Milkman on his round. He described a figure that makes us think it was the girl they call Our General. But it's a guess, we can't prove it. We need a good witness.'

'Have you questioned her?'

The Chief Superintendent looked at Archie Young, who admitted with reluctance that they had not. Our General could not be reached.

'Of course, we'll get to her,' he said, with more confidence than he felt, having had dealings with Our General before. 'And if it's not her, then it's one of her lot. A girl wearing dark clothes belted off on a motorbike before the police got there. It has to be her. Exactly what she was up to isn't clear. Whether she was part of the break-in gang or whether she stepped in to protect the girl.'

90

'You'll question the gang?'

'Sure. But it's hard to lay hands on them.'

'How is Blackhall?'

'Recovering. The doctor says we will be able to question him soon.' Whatever soon meant, he thought cynically. 'The Blackhalls will have their lawyers all round him by then, though.'

Coffin nodded. He accepted that would happen.

'And the girl shop assistant? What's her name?'

'Helen Foster. They say she can't be questioned yet either. But naturally we're anxious to get what she knows. If anything. The medicos say her memory of what went just before her injury will have gone.'

'Met that before,' said Coffin. Two girls in the case now. Amy Dean, already dead, and the other, Helen Foster, in a state of shock.

And now there was this suggestion that the case really began with the girl Virginia Scott, who had been dead for over a year.

The first report on the finding of the tin was already available to the men in the room.

'Now there is this photograph . . . torn up,' said John Coffin.

Or, as the forensic scientists were about to tell him, sliced up with a knife.

Down at Star Court House, there was no conversation on Martin Blackhall or what he might have been up to, they had other troubles there. A quarrel had broken out among two residents, so that Maisie had had to intervene; the supper had been burnt and was almost uneatable, and money was short. Also, they were threatened with a visit from the local councillor they liked least. Tempers had been strained and Josephine had gone home, glad of the relative peace of George Eliot House. Perhaps she had had enough of other people's troubles, they no longer took her mind off her own position but made them worse.

*

91

Josephine at home was different from the Josephine to be met with outside. At home, she took off her fluttering finery, removed her turban to reveal grey braids of hair, and put on a loose white shift of the sort that models wear between fittings in a couture salon. She had several of these, one of which was always fresh. This was in summer and autumn; in the real, cold winter, she wore a sort of black robe, belted at the waist.

Her flat, on the third floor of a tall block, was austere and clean, no clutter and no litter. It smelt empty. The furniture, such as it was, had been bought in Greenwich market or off a barrow in Peckham, she knew where to find the cheap old furniture that was also good. A sofa, two armchairs and a little bureau, made up her home, and she had stripped them down herself and repainted them white or ash grey. No colour here. Josephine was good with her hands, so the work was well done. She used to say she could have built a house if she had to.

She had never had to. In her time she had lived in a smart flat in Mayfair, a country house in Perthshire (only not for long, dogs and country were not for Josephine), and dwelt in an apartment overlooking Central Park, New York. She had also dossed down in a slum in Bermondsey, spent several nights in a cell in Holloway, and lived out of a box under Waterloo Bridge.

Good times, bad times, but helped by Maisie Rolt and Stella Pinero, she had struggled up again.

The doorbell rang. She was expecting a visitor.

She let Our General in. They were friends, not ordinary friends, they were not ordinary women, and they had nothing in common except their sex and a certain view of life. And some similar experiences.

The General liked fighting: it was a pleasure to her to find a side and battle for it. Josephine did not like fighting, but for women in trouble, because she had been one, she would always fight. She had almost, but not quite, learnt to fight for herself too.

'Thanks for coming.'

'A pleasure.' Rosa Maundy was a sturdy young woman

92

with mighty muscles which she worked on, and a badly blotched face which she blamed on her father. No love lost there.

Josephine had the kettle on already. 'Coffee or tea?'

'Caff, please.'

They sat opposite each other, Josephine drinking herbal tea while Rosa Maundy stirred the sugar into her coffee. For a time they did not speak.

Then Rosa said: 'I'd like to kill that policeman.'

'Which one?' It was a fair question, Rosa having had many a brush with the law one way and another, usually getting the better of them, but going to prison once. It was where she had met Josephine. Then sought her out under Waterloo Bridge and directing Maisie Rolt to her. Maisie had then told Stella. It was a chain.

Rosa didn't answer. But she gave Josephine a look which said: You know whom I mean.

'I don't think of him as a policeman,' said Josephine.

'That's the way to think of him. It's what he is. He ought to have it marked on his collar like a dog.'

Josephine gave a hoot of laughter. She could still laugh at some things. Just. No longer at herself. 'He'd love that.'

'I'd have a shot at doing him, if I thought I'd get away with it.'

'Don't talk like that, Rosa. I don't like it.'

Rosa leaned forward. 'For you, I won't.'

Josephine put her hand on Rosa's wrist and held it for a moment in her cold, dry fingers. 'You've done your bit, Rosa. You helped me.'

'It was a two-way thing. You pushed, I pulled.' Rosa finished her coffee, swirled round the few dregs. 'You didn't get me round here just for a cup of coffee.'

For answer Josephine got up and went to the bureau where she opened a drawer to take out a wrapped package. 'I want you to take this away and keep it safe for me.'

'Isn't it safe here?'

'You know what it's like in this block. I could be broken into any day. Only luck this wasn't taken before . . . I'm

93

protected by you, I know that, but it may not work for ever.'

Rosa raised her eyebrows. I'd like to know why not, she was saying. 'So I just keep it? That's all?'

'Open the box when you think fit. Use your judgement.'

'What will tell me?'

'Circumstances,' said Josephine, 'circumstances. You never know.'

'What's in it? Don't say if you don't want.'

'Just personal things. Keep them for me. You've got somewhere in your father's office.' Rosa managed the office in her father's haulage firm when he was away. He was away a lot, encouraged so by his daughter.

Rosa considered. She didn't trust her father not to poke around, so Star Court House might be safer. Maisie Rolt could be trusted.

'Right. I'll do it for you. Do more than that.'

'Well, haven't you?'

Rosa punched her friend jovially on the shoulder. 'Gotta go, that crazy woman wants me to sing in opera!' and went away. Josephine washed the mugs they had used and put them away. Next to a half-bottle of whisky, which was there just in case.

CHAPTER 7

The next day

All the reports came flooding on to John Coffin's desk, together with reports from committees, memoranda for future committees, petitions, pleas, and protests. All the materials which made up his working day.

He took up the forensic report on the car: of little value. Plenty of traces of the girl and the father but nothing of Martin Blackhall except a handprint on the door and the wallet that had been found in the car.

Some blood traces, but her blood and not his.

There was an additional report on the wood used for the coffin: the wood was elm, machine cut into planks. These planks had then been cut, by hand with a small-toothed saw, then nailed together roughly.

Not the job of an expert carpenter but done neatly enough to suggest someone good with their hands. Probably a man, the nails had been driven in hard.

Coffin was thoughtful as he put this sheaf of papers down: he knew that the experts could identify by the cut of the saw and the grain of the wood the source of the planks.

If they could find the source.

Two officers had interviewed the driver of the 147a bus on which the ticket found in the blue and white jersey had been issued. He remembered nothing and no one. Pressed, he said Yes, there were a few regulars.

Names: Mrs Howard
   Jack Edwards
   Someone called Coney ... might be a nickname.

Mrs Howard and Jack Edwards had been tracked down and remembered nothing of the other passengers on that night.

This left Coney who had yet to be found.

Coffin put down this report and went on to the next one. Two female officers had gone to Star Court House to interview Mrs Rolt.

He read what they had to offer: nothing much there.

A male officer had gone to the haulage firm where Rosa Maundy worked. Rosa was 'away on business'. He noted that they had been dealing with a consignment of wood, a few planks of which remained. He made a note of this in case, the source of the wood for the girl's coffin not having yet been traced.

In the university a team of officers was interviewing all students and teaching staff, while another team was talking to all those workers in the kitchens, cleaning and security departments. There were also typists and secretaries to be seen. It was a big task and not yet complete.

Here too was a source of wood. A pile of planks rested

outside the Works Department. This was noted, and specimens taken. There might be a match.

In the hospital Martin Blackhall was recovering, but had not yet been subjected to more than a token questioning. Paul Lane had attached his own comment here:

I think we will have enough to hold him for questioning. We have the attack on the girl in the shop. He was certainly involved but we need the girl's evidence here, which we will get. (Lane had underlined this bit.) *And we have his own words to his mother: 'I didn't mean to hurt her.' Which girl, I ask myself? And where did he go in the river, and why?*

There was yet another paper for him to study. An additional forensic report on the photograph found under the floorboards in Armitage told him that the picture had been sliced up with a sharp knife.

He was conscious of having to absorb too much detail. He needed time for the important things to become apparent.

Coffin put down the papers on his desk. He set in motion all the answering machines and faxes which operated all night, repressing the desire to silence them for ever, and went home. He was early for once.

But there was one positive action he advised: Question Amy Dean's friends about the slashed photograph

St Luke's Mansions, where he lived in the tower, had changed a little in the years he had lived there. White paintwork had dulled down to London grey, plants and bushes newly planted four-odd years ago, had grown. Everything had a settled look, the years had been kind.

He and Stella Pinero were the oldest inhabitants. Dwellers in the middle apartment seemed to come and go. Some places are like that: tipping out their residents every so often.

He let himself in his front door and went up the winding staircase, meeting Tiddles coming down. He turned back to let the cat out.

'Got shut in, old chap? Mrs Fergus forget to let you out?' Mrs Fergus cleaned his house once a week, leaving some of his possessions gleaming while others collected dust, and everything that would move just a little out of place.

He went into his sitting-room, adjusting one picture as he passed, and moving a bit of Venetian glass back to where it should have been. It was amazing how she did it, the woman had no sense of balance at all.

But she had a strong sense of what mattered, and had left a note on the kitchen table.

Sir,
    You are out of all cleaning materials, soap and lavatory paper. These I will shop for. There is no milk in the fridge and no cat food, and these you must buy.
F. Fergus.

She writes a good note, Coffin thought, well put together and to the point.

He turned dutifully to the door to start on the shopping. He had found it paid to heed Mrs F. Fergus's little notes. Max in his delicatessen would welcome a customer, even providing food for Tiddles, and he could take the chance to mention the matter of the key, which had been handed out to facilitate the delivery of wine and groceries, not to let in stray visitors.

He rounded the corner to where Max's store had spread now into two shops, beating the recession and proving without doubt that people round here in Upper Spinnergate loved to eat.

The left-hand shop, or the north-west shop if you had a sense of direction, was now a neat little eating place which you reached through an inner door in the shop proper. Several tables were taken, including the big round one in the window usually reserved for St Luke's Theatre staff and performers, most of whom he knew by sight. But he didn't recognize this tableful of weary-looking faces, except for Philippa Darbyshire's. He decided what she had there were a clutch of Valkyries and a few Nibelungs. A post-rehearsal discussion group, he decided, and not looking too happy about it either. Did one of the men recognize him? The tall one in the middle, he had an aware look.

To his surprise, Stella Pinero was hunched over a cup of coffee at a table in the corner, with Bob crouched at her feet. Bob was allowed in on sufferance (*Only Guide Dogs for the Blind and Hearing Dogs for the Deaf*, said a notice on the front door) because he was a local hero for services rendered.

Stella looked as if she had been crying. No tears or anything like that, but a redness round the eyes and a kind of pinched look to her mouth. She raised her head, smiled sadly and drank a sip of coffee. Bob gave a little moaning whine, he was a sympathetic dog.

'Hello, Stella, didn't expect to see you. I'm just doing some shopping.'

'Come and join me.'

'Let me do the shopping first.' When he returned with his big recycled paper sack full of food that he could eat and so could Tiddles, he sat down with his back to the room so that he could get a good look at Stella who might be in trouble. He nodded to the group in the window. 'What's going on over there?'

Stella managed a smile. 'Bad rehearsal, I think, and Marcus threatened not to work with them any more.'

Coffin raised an eyebrow.

'Professionals don't really like working with amateurs.' Stella herself, tolerant as she was, would be wary of such an arrangement. It might be wrong but there it was. So easy to lose status in the performing arts. 'And of course, Lydia can be a handful.'

Coffin turned round to study the table behind and met the interested gaze of the man who seemed to know him. The chap smiled, Coffin smiled back. 'I don't see their Brunnhilde.'

'Lydia was here, but she stormed out . . . I think that's the way to describe it, she looked thunderous enough. Some trouble with her breastplate, she said she wouldn't be able to Hail the Sun adequately if she was wearing it.'

Coffin nodded. He knew the scene from *The Ring*, one of the most moving and beautiful, yet also the most richly comic unless well done.

He finished coffee. 'What's up, Stella? Because something is, I can tell. Is it me?'

A quarrel did rumble between them occasionally, but he had thought that at the moment they were all clear.

'No, it's the new TV series. I think I've just lost the part . . . Jack Tickell is producing and he's never liked my work. He savaged me at rehearsal today.'

'I've heard he always does that.'

'No, he wants me out. He'll manage it, Equity rules or not.' Her voice dropped. 'It's an age thing.' She turned her face towards Coffin, she looked piteous. 'It's bloody when it happens.'

For a moment words of comfort froze on his lips, he was stopped by the genuine pain of the moment. It is hard on actresses. After a certain age, parts dry up. Not many around for those in the middle. Once you get into the nineties, there are plenty, but the bit in between can be difficult.

And then he thought: But this is Stella! She is marvellous, it can't happen to her. He reached out to take her hand.

'Let's go outside,' she said. 'Walk home with me.'

They went out into the dark street, accompanied by Bob who frisked ahead, intent on getting what pleasure he could out of the night.

'You could be wrong, Stella. Tickell would be silly to lose you.' She did panic over things, but she was a shrewd professional judge.

'I hope he thinks so . . . he's got a girl he wants to put in,' she said savagely. 'I don't think they're living together and from all I heard of her, they never will be, she likes to keep her options open.'

She must be hurt. Stella often made jokes about her colleagues and rivals but she was rarely catty and never about a younger actress.

She sighed. 'Oh dear, I can remember being the rising young star . . . Remember! And it doesn't seem so long ago.'

'I never look back,' said Coffin. 'Not if I can help it.'

Bob, trotting along, had seen a Dalmatian across the street. He hated Dalmatians with the passionate dislike of a mongrel for a dog of breeding. He hurled himself forward.

A car approaching swerved and braked and skidded towards Bob. Stella gave a cry and leapt forward to grab Bob by the collar. The car struck her a glancing sideways blow before she could reach him. She fell backwards on to the road.

Coffin rushed forward to pick her up, her eyes were closed. He held her for a moment, trying to control his own breathing. The driver, white-faced, helped him carry Stella to the pavement. 'I couldn't help it, I couldn't help it,' he was muttering. Coffin ignored him.

Then Stella opened her eyes. 'If I've broken my leg, I'm going to kill that damned dog.'

Across the road, Bob, unscathed by traffic, had just been dismissed with contempt by the Dalmatian and was about to limp back.

'All I've got is a badly bruised leg.' Stella lay back on her sofa and held out her hand for the brandy that Coffin was offering her. She would have preferred gin but brandy seemed more suitable for an injured lady.

'You could have been killed.'

'You look worse than I do.' This was true, Coffin was white. 'Where's Bob?'

'Eating,' said Coffin. 'You ought to go to hospital.'

'What, and miss a performance. I go on, broken leg or not.'

'Good joke,' said Coffin sourly. 'Just as well you haven't really got a performance tonight.' He was still shaken.

'I would have gone on. Sarah Bernhardt went on with one leg, didn't she? I could go on with two legs and a limp.'

He knew she would have done. Any actress would. You faint with pain after the curtain goes down.

Stella closed her eyes. 'Wouldn't it have been awful if I had died? Killed saving Bob.'

'Yes, it would,' said Coffin. He was realizing how terrible it would have been.

'Was the car driver upset?'

'Very.'

'It wasn't his fault.'

'So you both said.'

'And was Bob upset?'

'He was when I dragged him home,' said Coffin grimly.

Stella leaned back on her cushions. The accident seemed to have cheered her up. 'You know, I think I'll get the better of Jack Tickell after all. I won't lose that part. Want to bet?'

'No.'

'Do you know, I think I'm hungry. Could you manage a sandwich for me?'

In her kitchen, with its unused look, Coffin dug into the bag of groceries he had bought at Max's. Parma ham, French bread, Brie cheese, tiny little tomatoes. They would do. Two tins of salmon meant for a cat.

Somewhere out there Tiddles must be raging with hunger.

He made some coffee, in the making of which he now had considerable skill, knowing not to boil the water and exactly how much powdered coffee to dump in a cup. His sister Letty was continually giving him expensive and gleaming glass and silver coffee-making machines, one of which even ground the beans; these he ignored. He found some plates and carried in the tray.

They sat, eating and talking in a companionable way. It felt cosy, as near to domesticity as they had ever come. Stella had a child and had once run a household, but one would never know it, she had sloughed off anything of the housekeeper she had ever had. But her child was reported happy and successful and deep in her own career.

'Are you worried about this case?' asked Stella.

'No,' and to his surprise he was telling the truth. He felt a cold remoteness from Jim Dean and his daughter. Not nice, he thought, but true.

'You usually are.'

'Not this time.' Must be a reason for it.

'Of course, I know you've got the boy Martin. Do you think he is guilty?'

'Probably. But it might be tough to prove. Gradually the

forensic evidence will mount up. If there are traces of his clothes or skin on the girl, that would be a help. But sometimes all these magic tricks fail to come up with anything we can use.' They could point the way and sometimes offer the sort of proof that judges and juries loved, but not always.

Stella said: 'Go on, this is interesting. You've never talked to me like this before.'

'She was strangled, and buried in a coffin. How did the body get where it was buried? Did it go in the coffin? Or was she killed and the coffin made and brought to her? Or made on the spot . . . lots of possibilities.'

'How could a boy like Martin do all that?'

'There were wood splinters in his hands. He could have got them making the coffin.'

'I suppose you could look at the wood.'

'All flushed away down a hospital sink . . . there may be some still in his hands waiting to be dug out, but I doubt it.' His mother would have checked on that, or even the boy himself.

'And we would have to find out how he got the wood and where from and how it was transported to Essex.' He added: 'He might have been able to lay his hands on wood.'

'I suppose I can imagine a sensitive boy who hadn't meant to kill her but to whom it had somehow happened, a quarrel, a sexual frenzy, wanting to bury her.'

'Could be,' said Coffin, reflecting with sad irony that life with him had certainly opened Stella's mind to the various ways of violent dying.

'What do you think?'

'Timing matters,' he said cautiously. 'The boy turned up, having apparently been in the water somewhere and been caught trying to rob a shop. It's a complicated situation with him. But it's the way a guilty and frightened boy might behave. We don't have to look for reason and balanced judgement here, just panic and disorder.'

'It's how I would be, if I'd killed a person,' said Stella, her eyes dark. 'Poor lad.'

'The girl herself is a puzzle.' Not Jim Dean's daughter

for nothing. 'What was she up to? Victims sometimes seem to go looking for death.'

'What a terrible thing to say.'

'They were worried about her at Star Court House. Josephine must have told you that. Not the first death either. There was the other girl, Virginia . . . She was a helper at Star Court too.'

'You can't suspect them of anything.'

Coffin did not answer directly. 'Josephine came to me, remember. Whatever happens, she came to me . . . If Martin Blackhall did kill Amy Dean, then he may not have been in it alone.'

Stella was troubled. 'Tell me what you really think.'

'I think she was killed elsewhere, possibly in her own car, and then transported to Essex. Or in the car in Pickerskill Wood. I don't know at what point she was put in the coffin. Or why. And that's about all I do think at the moment.'

Or by whom, but he knew that Paul Lane and Archie Young thought they had the killer. No proof but the right man: Martin Blackhall.

'Time matters,' he said again. 'Who had time to do all that was done?'

Stella said: 'I have never heard your voice so cold.'

She got up. 'I think I want to get to bed. Help me, please.'

Hobbling and leaning on his arm, she reached her bedroom. 'I'll take a shower.'

'Want help?'

'No, I can manage. Wait for me, though. Don't go away. Wait till I'm in bed, then say good night. And there's something I want to say first.'

While she was fidgeting around, creaming her face, combing her hair, seated with her back to him at her looking-glass, she said: 'I wouldn't tell you this if we hadn't been talking freely, and you may know and it probably has nothing whatever to do with the case . . .'

He sat waiting, wishing these were days when one could smoke, and conscious of the dark cold hole inside him that you might call hate.

103

'Victoria Blackhall has been married twice. Her first husband was found head down in a small lake in Oxford. He'd been drinking, but there was a lot of talk. Everyone knew about Tom and Victoria, they'd been very public. I was playing at the New Theatre in Oxford at the time, and I knew them all.'

'Accident or suicide?'

Stella shrugged. 'I suppose it was an accident. Who knows?'

'The Oxford police must have investigated it as a mysterious death.'

'Yes, and I think that was exactly where they left it: a verdict of accidental death. But a lot of people blamed Tom, there was gossip.'

'I bet there was,' said Coffin. 'Doesn't seem to have touched his career.' Academics were broad-minded chaps these days, what was the odd divorce or suicide? What was it Tom Blackhall had said himself? One of my professors is up for dangerous driving and another has seduced three pupils.

Did this story make any difference? What did it amount to? Two young people (Tom Blackhall had been very young) and behaved wildly. They had been the subject of gossip and had no doubt felt guilty. But it had no connection with what was happening now. The two of them had survived and prospered. Victoria Blackhall was a powerful lady, and one not liked by James Dean. Might be something personal there . . .

But James Dean just didn't like successful women.

When Stella was in bed, leaning against her pillows, she said: 'I think the way you feel about this case has to do with James Dean himself. I don't know what he did to you, but it must have been bad.'

'He saved my life,' said Coffin in a hard voice.

'You are detaching yourself from this murder in a way you never do. It has been your strength and your virtue. Because he saved your life, however much you resent that, and you appear to do so, I think you owe it to him to find out who killed his child.'

'You hit hard, Stella.'

For answer, she took his hand. Her own hand was soft and cool, smelling of rose geranium.

As he sat there, holding her hand and telling her how it had been, Bob came in and stretched out on his feet. He went on talking. Stella smiled and murmured back at him in a friendly way. Then she was quiet.

Presently, he saw that Stella was asleep. He tucked her in, patted Bob's head and let himself out of her apartment. Stella would bounce back. She always did. She might lose a part and break a leg, but she would be there again, at the top of the tree, waving.

As he walked the few paces home, he recognized that Stella had got through to him. She had cracked something open.

She was right. He had not been straight with himself about this murder. Too many old emotions had entered in. Now he must make it his honest business to find out how and why Amy Dean had died.

CHAPTER 8

The night of that long day and into the next week

His thoughts kept time with his feet on the stairs of his tall abode. One thought a tread.

You have to know these people.

And their backgrounds.

Do I know them?

The answer was: Some, but not others.

It was a long staircase and he was only half way up.

Tom Blackhall he knew. Probably in more detail than Sir Thomas guessed. He had information. It was part of his job. He hadn't really needed Stella to tell him what she did. It was on record.

Victoria Blackhall? He knew her too slightly and not

much about her career. But he could find out, her academic and medical career would be on record, and he could talk to people she worked with. He had heard she was held in high esteem.

Josephine? He knew her not at all, but there was a feeling that he could know her if he chose. Dig into her corners, seek out the depths.

Jim Dean, his old partner. Oh yes, he knew Jim.

He was almost at the top of the stairs, he paused to look out of the window. That was London there below in the moonlight. Not the smartest or the richest or the most beautiful of Londons, but his, with its cruelties and its criminals and its poverty. Also what it had of richness and goodness and human companionship.

Not to mention its busy, cheerful eccentrics like Philippa Darbyshire, so happily engaged with the choir and the Wagner production. She was a bit Wagnerian herself in size.

Martin Blackhall, another one to know, and possibly a very important one, but he might be just a boy dragged into the picture by bad luck.

And two whom he would never know now: Amy Dean and Virginia Scott.

He would tour around, ask questions, go to this place and that. Watching, and listening.

And all the time, a ghost would walk beside him.

It was a question where to start, but the answer soon came. To the place where the girl was last seen alive. To the university.

He drove round, not an occasion for walking, found a place to park his car, and asked the man in the porter's lodge where he could find Mick Frost and Rebecca North.

'Beenie and Mick, sir,' said the man cheerfully. 'Oh, they'll be in a class now, but hang about and you might see them coming across the quad to the library.'

'You seem to know them well.'

'Oh, I know all the students, by sight anyway. Some better than others. It's my job. I know that pair.'

'So you knew Amy Dean?'

'Yes, and I know you too, sir. That's why I'm talking. Don't do it to everyone.' Across the room the telephone rang. 'Oh, excuse me, sir, I'll have to attend to that.'

Coffin went out into the sunshine, and strolled around until he saw students pouring out of a door in a corner of the large white building. He collared one and asked to be shown Mick Frost.

'Mick? Oh, he's not been at this lecture. I'm a medical and he hates us.' The lad, tall and carrot-haired, looked around. He pointed. 'You could try his room in Armitage. If they let you in, a snooty lot there ... Oh, wait a min ... That's him, though, coming out of that door.'

Coffin made his way across the grass, students on all sides of him, some running, some walking head down in deep abstracted thought, others in friendly groups, but all apparently going somewhere important and at once, and none of them interested in him.

'Are you Michael Frost?'

'Yes, that's me.' Mick looked at him alertly. He knew Coffin, having attended a lecture the man had given the year before on Crime and Punishment. Mick was more or less in favour of punishment, of the right sort, and he had thought that the speaker had felt the same. A good bloke, he had judged.

Coffin introduced himself, noting no surprise on Mick's face. 'Anywhere we can talk?'

Mick nodded. 'Over here.' He led the way towards the library and Coffin followed. All the students seemed to have disappeared, the quadrangle was empty.

Mick sat down on the steps outside the library portico, and Coffin lowered himself. He recognized it as the site where Amy Dean had been photographed. He was probably sitting on the very spot.

'I hope I'm not keeping you from something?'

'No, I had a class, that's just finished. I've got a tutorial in an hour's time. I was just on my way to the library.'

The porter was an accurate observer of Mick's ways, Coffin reflected.

'Tutorial,' he said absently. 'That's an interview with your tutor, is it?'

'To read an essay, discuss it. Of course it's not one to one, or even two; usually three or four of us. We take turns to read. We're supposed to be imitating Oxford, only economy style.'

'You and Rebecca North were Amy's closest friends?'

Mick was willing to concede this. 'Yes, I think so. Except for Martin, of course. And Angie.'

'Oh yes, Angela.' The girl who had come rushing forward to look at Amy's burial place, and been restrained by James Dean himself. 'Where can I find her and Rebecca?'

'Beenie's in Bloomsbury for a lecture. Angie's working in her room, as far as I know.'

Was he nervous? Alert and a bit jumpy. 'I want to talk to you about Amy and Martin.'

'I don't think there's much more I can tell you . . . I've answered a lot of questions already. People keep asking the same questions . . . I feel like a plucked chicken.'

'You know that Martin has been found?' Mick gave a short nod. He knew; they all knew. 'What sort of a relationship did those two have?'

Mick frowned. 'Fairly close,' he said in a neutral, give-away-nothing tone.

'Lovers?'

Mick remained silent.

'Come on, we already know Amy was not a virgin.'

'Ask him.'

'I will when I can. Now I'm asking you.'

There was a long silence, during which Coffin watched a solitary girl student make her way from the gatehouse to a side door of the library.

Mick relaxed, took a deep breath and managed a smile. 'All right. Fine. But in spite of what you seemed to think I don't know every detail of my friends' lives. I don't know if they went to bed with each other. They didn't tell me and I didn't ask.'

'But you think?'

'I think not . . . He was in love with her, but Amy wasn't in love back.'

'Thanks.'

Then Mick relented. 'Amy might have told Angie what was what, and Angie might have told Beenie . . . but as it happened, no one told me.'

'And Martin didn't say anything?'

Mick shook his head. 'I don't really know him that well.'

'Who does?'

'Not sure if anyone does. It is difficult for him, being the Rector's son. He ought to have gone to another university, not this one. Don't know why he didn't. He's bright enough.'

'You don't think it was Amy . . . she was here?'

'Could have been,' conceded Mick. He was pretty sure it was, but didn't want to say so. 'Can I ask you a question?'

'Go on.' But I may not answer.

'You're the boss figure, like our Rector only more so. Why are you going round doing the questioning?'

Polite but bold and self-assured, Coffin thought. Wouldn't mind having him work for me.

'I know Mr Dean,' he said formally. 'What is it you are studying?'

'History. But I'm going to be a lawyer. Or I might sing.' But that was a fantasy and he knew it.

'You'll be a good lawyer,' said Coffin. 'What about considering the police force?'

'Money,' said Mick, still polite. 'I don't think there's enough.'

'You were one of the last people to see Amy alive.' He didn't make it a question.

'On the campus, yes.'

'Did you notice what she was wearing?'

'The Sergeant and the Chief Inspector both asked me that. The answer is no, I can't remember.'

'Did she own a blue and white sweater with pockets?'

'You'll have to ask Beenie or Angela about clothes.'

'Did you ever ride with Amy in her car?'

'Yes, several times, she was generous with lifts. She liked using the car.'

'Do you know if she used the buses much?'

Mick said: 'I've been asked that before and the answer is no. As far as I know she never used a bus. She had the car, after all.'

'Did you ever go to Star Court House with her?'

'No, never. I didn't encourage that business. Not that she took any notice.'

'Why didn't you like her working there?'

Mick shrugged. 'Hard to say. Seemed to alter her . . . Well, perhaps not alter, just seemed a character change of some sort. Perhaps I imagined it . . . I don't like talking about this. Seems disloyal.'

'You may be helping to find out who killed Amy.'

Mick looked sceptical. 'OK, if you say so.'

'I believe Angela Kirk works there too?'

Mick shook his head. 'You'll have to ask her.'

'Would you say Martin Blackhall was capable of violence?'

'No,' said Mick shortly.

'Did you know Virginia Scott?'

'No.'

'But I understand she was studying history, as you are?'

'It's a big school and she was one year ahead of me. We didn't know each other.'

'But Martin Blackhall knew her.'

'He may have done. He gets around more than I do. I'm a worker.'

'And he isn't?'

Mick did not answer.

Coffin got up from his seat on the stone steps. 'Thank you for answering all those questions.'

'No trouble.'

'I'm sorry that I wasn't much help.'

'Oh you were. You have told me, whether you meant to or not, that you were anxious about Amy. Your anxiety seems to centre about Star Court House. You have told me that she was emotionally stirred by her contact with that

110

place, and emotion can be an important pointer when a girl is murdered.'

Mick opened his mouth as if about to speak and then shut it again.

'And you have been very careful to distance yourself from Martin Blackhall.'

Mick went white.

'And to know nothing about Virginia Scott who was also killed and who also went to work in Star Court . . . What is it you have on your mind, Mr Frost?'

When Mick said nothing, Coffin went on: 'I can probably get it out of Miss Rebecca.'

Mick considered. Yes, Beenie might blurt it out. 'All right,' he said, his voice unsteady. 'Someone was beating Amy up. At least we thought so. At intervals. Beenie and I saw the bruises. Star Court House is a place for people like that, isn't it? What's the connection? I don't know. You work it out.'

'And that's why you don't want Angela to go there?'

'What do you think? And the sick thing was, the thing that really bugged me was, we didn't understand Amy's attitude. She couldn't push off the bruiser, whoever, not me, not Martin, we're not into that.'

'Do you know anything about a slashed photograph, one of Virginia Scott?'

'Oh, that.' There was a long pause. Coffin waited. 'Amy did that herself . . . we saw her. Martin tried to stop her, took it away. I don't know what he did with it. Burnt it if he had any sense. I told you she was sick.'

'She needed help.' It was a mark of a disturbed and unhappy girl.

'We told her to go to the Student Counsellor but she didn't. Just tootled off to Star Court House.'

'Who took the photograph?'

Mick shrugged. 'I don't know. Not Martin.'

Coffin looked at Mick with a mixture of irritation and sympathy. Still something there he wasn't getting. He took a card from his pocket. 'This is where I live. If you think of anything you want to tell me, you can find me there.'

111

Mick stood up, a shade of relief on his face. He'd not said too much. There might be more to say, but he would consult with Beenie first. 'Oh, I know where you live, sir. I'm singing in a production of extracts from *The Ring*. I pass where you live every time we rehearse.'

Coffin took his card back. So be it. 'And there's always Chief Inspector Young,' he said, not without a touch of malice. 'You've met him?'

'Oh, sure.' Mick was beginning to edge away. And hoped not to meet again.

'One last thing.'

Mick looked nervous. 'Yes?'

'Can you tell me where I can find Angela?'

'She might be in her room. Armitage 23. And Armitage is the block on the north-west side of the campus.'

As he walked away, Coffin glanced back to see Mick, not walking sedately towards his tutorial as might have been expected, but running like a hare into the university library.

Inside the library, Mick slowed down to avoid being noticed but made haste towards the main reading-room. He walked through it, to the stacks behind.

'Beenie! Thank goodness, I've got to you. I told that policeman Coffin that you were in London at a lecture or he'd have been after you. He asked far too many questions and he's a friend of Dean.'

'That's lethal,' said Beenie.

'It's Angela we have to think about now.'

Beenie sighed. 'We love her, don't we?'

'Oh, everyone loves Angie. Just like they did Amy. Got that way with her. The kitchen love her, the security staff love her, her tutor loves her, the Rector in his ivory tower loves her.'

'If he knows her,' said Beenie.

'Oh, he knows her all right,' said Mick.

Beenie gave him a long, thoughtful look, and Mick got back to what was worrying him. 'We have to decide what we are going to say.'

'What did you say to him?'

112

'I think I said too much . . . The trouble is I half wanted to say it all. Confess. He's got that way with him.'

Beenie meditated. 'We don't actually know anything. You said that yourself.'

'He's suspicious. He was asking questions about Virginia Scott.'

Beenie said: 'I heard that the police found a box in Martin's room with her photograph in it, all cut up.'

'Yeah, well, we know about that, don't we?' said Mick. 'I told the copper Amy did the slashing, he was asking. A sharp bloke. I had to do it, but I wish I hadn't now. Nasty.'

'The whole thing is nasty. Maybe we should let it all out.'

'If it wasn't for Angie we could. We've got to protect her. And the best way is to keep quiet and try and get her out of it.'

'Like we protected Amy?'

There was a pause while one of the librarians came from behind the stacks with a trolley of books.

Then Mick said: 'I don't think anything could have saved Amy.'

'Do you think she heard anything?' asked Mick, watching the back of the librarian.

'No, they never hear anything,' said Beenie with confidence. 'They don't think of us as people, just students, not quite human.' In her way Beenie returned this attitude, regarding the librarian as a kind of book transport with arms.

'She gave us a look.'

'Just doesn't like us being in the stacks. Thinks it's her territory.' It was in fact a forbidden area for students but Beenie always got away with her invasion. Sometimes she thought she must be truly invisible without knowing it. 'Didn't hear a word.'

But she had heard, and was wondering what it was all about and what she ought to do about it. She knew who they were, and of course everyone was talking about the murder. Not much else was being talked about, except the

113

deficiencies of the new Head Librarian and the general shortage of money in the library world. They were all under suspicion here, that was the feeling. Each and every one of them. She favoured Martin Blackhall herself. You could never trust those good-looking ones.

She found herself humming as she moved. Annoying, not what she should be doing at all, but one of the young lads who worked in the library was singing in some choir and was forever trying out bits of it when he thought no one could hear. Now she was doing it, she who despised Wagner.

Wouldn't it be something if she could contribute to the police case? Go to that nice-looking policeman and say what she knew?

No, she would telephone, she knew her voice was her best feature.

John Coffin, on his way to the Armitage Building, passed the Maintenance Department and was thus able to get a sighting of the neat pile of wooden planks, some of which might have provided Amy's burial chest. He looked but passed on; not for him, specimens had already been taken and were being inspected in the Police Forensic Laboratory.

He walked into a narrow hall lined with notice-boards which were themselves covered with posters, lists of names, and notices of meetings, lectures and admonitions about fire risks and cigarettes, and almost slipped on a highly polished stone floor. At the end of the hallway was a tea and coffee dispenser, with a notice saying it was out of order, and next to that a machine selling condoms, in two shades and two weights. This appeared to be in good selling order.

There was a lift, but he chose to walk up the stairs, reasoning, from the number he had, that Angela's room was on the floor above. He passed the white doors numbered in brass, before coming to a stop outside a door that had, in addition to its number, the picture of a rabbit and the name ANGELA.

Did she think of herself as a rabbit? He rapped on the

114

door. No answer came, but he heard movement behind the door. He knocked again. 'Angela?'

Silence, but he would swear she was pressed against the door, listening.

'I am John Coffin, I am a policeman, Chief Commander of the Second City Police. I would like to talk to you.'

A pause, then the door opened a crack. A pretty, distracted face looked out at him.

'Angela?'

'Of course I am.' She swallowed, and took a deep breath. 'What do you want?'

'To talk to you. Can I come in.'

She leaned against the door, long pale hair falling across her face. Perhaps just a bit like a rabbit, but an appealing one, with big blue eyes. Yes, they were lovely eyes, he thought, now they were focused on him. What people used to call speaking eyes, although he was not sure now what they were saying. 'I suppose you are a policeman?'

'I can prove it.' He put his hand into his pocket.

'No, it's all right. I recognize you; I saw you when . . .' She hesitated.

'When Amy was found? I remember you, too. May I come in, then?'

She thought about it, giving a quick look at the room behind. 'If it's important.'

When he got inside, he understood her hesitation. Chaos reigned. Clothes, books, papers, all lay scattered around. He wondered if she always lived like this. Some of the clothes looked none too clean, either. Amy too had favoured squalor, he remembered. Perhaps a disease they caught.

'I'm packing.'

'You're going away?'

'I'm going to take a term off. Perhaps the rest of the year. I've spoken to my tutor. She thinks it's a good idea.'

'You were pretty close to Amy?' She nodded dumbly. 'Is that why?'

'Sort of.' Not much of an answer, but all he was going to get.

Not really an articulate girl, our Angela, he thought, but

115

with eyes like that who needs a tongue. Or is it that she just doesn't want to talk to me?

'So what will you do?'

He saw the faint look on her face that suggested it was none of his business, but she answered politely enough. 'I shall take a temporary job. I might be working at Star Court House.'

'It's about Star Court House that I wanted to talk . . . You and Amy put a lot of your energy into your work there.'

She cleared the one armchair of its burden of clothes and books, nicely mixed. 'Do sit down.' She herself sat on the bed on a pile of papers. 'I'm doing the sociology special like Amy, she put me on to Star Court. It's interesting. I don't mind doing it. I've got a case history to complete.'

'Don't you feel like a case yourself sometimes?'

She looked at him bleakly and knowingly. Not a look he liked to see on someone like Angela. 'No.'

No change there, he thought, watching her. She moved restlessly, and several folders fell off the bed and exploded on the floor, where they joined a tweed coat and a pair of jeans.

'Taking all your possessions with you, are you?'

Possessions, property, he realized what a policeman he sounded.

She looked at it as if didn't matter to her, was of no interest, as if she was only packing it for something to do. Burning energy that she was lumbered with.

'I suppose I could shove it all in a drawer. But some other student will have the room. Be glad to come into residence, a lot of us have to live out in rooms.'

There was a large trunk in the middle of the room, already half filled. Packed you could hardly call it, thrown in looked more like it.

She moved forward gracefully, brushing against him as she threw some books off the bed on to the floor, thus clearing a place for herself to sit down. Through her fringe of hair, she gave him a half smile, then lowered her lids over those amazing blue eyes.

The eyes said she didn't dislike him.

116

He had met that look before in other eyes, and was surprised to see it now.

'You're very distressed about Amy, I can see that. I'm sorry I have to talk to you now.'

She bent her head in that manner at once submissive and inviting. He could see that if you were given that way it could be exciting.

'She was my best friend. We shared a lot.' Her voice dropped on the last sentence. 'I feel guilty, as if I could have saved her.'

'How could you have done that?'

There was a pause. 'No way.'

'I was surprised to see you running out of Mr Dean's car that evening.'

'I made him take me. He didn't want to . . . but I guessed you'd found Amy's body and I wanted to see. But he wouldn't let me.'

'If he had been willing, I would have stopped you.'

'I don't understand that . . . I suppose you think, both of you, that you were protecting me.'

'I don't know what Mr Dean thought but for me it was a professional matter. You had no place there.'

'It would have been better if I had seen Amy, I needed to see her . . . When my father died, they wouldn't let me see him, and so I never believed he was really dead.'

'You can believe your friend is dead,' said Coffin soberly, wondering how much truth there was in what she said. He believed in the dead father. He could almost have predicted that. 'Did Amy have a blue and white sweater?'

'Yes, I've already said that. And no, I don't know if I've seen it recently. Maybe yes, maybe no. And if you're going to ask about the bus ticket, no, she never used that bus. Never got on a bus. Said they made her sick. And that route is always late and crowded.'

'So you did talk about it?'

Angela flushed. 'I used the bus to go to Star Court House.'

'Ah.' Yes, of course she must have done. Too far to walk and no car.

117

The bus and the ticket came in somewhere, he was sure of that. The way it was tucked into the pocket suggested care, forethought.

He had the sudden conviction, what was known among his subordinates as one of the Guvnor's flashes of light, that the sweater had not been washed up by the river, but deposited on the bank to be found.

'You know Martin Blackhall has been found?'

'Yes, he didn't kill Amy,' said Angela swiftly. How they all protected each other, Mick and Rebecca and now Angela.

'I didn't say he did.'

'But people think so.'

Angela stood up. 'I think I'd better get on with my packing.' She pushed her hair away from her face and her shirt, loosely buttoned, fell away from her neck. She put one hand delicately on her neck, in that same manner at once submissive and inviting.

As if she could not help herself, she smiled. She held her hands up, palms facing him, fingers curled back, and moved the hands slightly towards him. An invitation, if he had ever had one, by God.

Just for one second, his own hands moved forward, he almost touched her. Then he drew back sharply.

'No more questions,' he said. 'Thank you.'

'Yes, sure. Sorry if I wasn't much help.' She held the door open for him and closed it behind with a small but decided bang.

Outside he paused. You learn something about yourself all the time, no matter how old you are.

He was thoughtful about Angela's behaviour. She puzzled him. Might ask Stella about it, he thought, get the woman's point of view. That is, if Stella was giving him the time of day.

As he walked down the stairs, he thought: No, there had been no deliberate display. It was unconscious. She had been created by nature to appeal, to attract, to be a perpetual invitation. It was built into her.

And when the shirt had fallen away from her arm, he

118

had seen a trio of small bruises, spread out like fingers.

The porter on duty at the main entrance saluted him as he went past. Coffin stopped. 'I know you . . . Robinson, Fred Robinson.'

'That's right, sir, I thought you'd remember. I worked with you on the Greenwich Tally-Ho murders. Never forgot that case, brilliant work you did there.'

'So you got out?' He was surprised now he thought about it. Sergeant Robinson had looked like a man powering himself to go right to the top. He'd put on weight, but he looked content. 'Weren't you just moving over to the Major Crime Unit?'

'Took early retirement . . . The wife was very ill, didn't look as though she was going to make it, and I wanted to be with her for as much as I could for what we'd got left.'

'I don't blame you.' He probably wouldn't have done it himself, not at that age, and that was a mark against him. 'How is she?'

Robinson smiled. 'Doing very nicely. I'm not as worried as I was.'

'So you came here?'

'Not straight away . . . I worked for Mr Dean, on his security staff. Daughter still does, on the switchboard. But there wasn't a lot of free time there either, not what I wanted for me and Alma, so when this job came up, I applied and got it. Mr Dean gave me a very good reference . . . There's more responsibility here than you might think.'

'Can't be easy at the moment.'

Robinson puckered up his lips in a way that Coffin suddenly recalled. 'No, it's a bad time. Second time round too . . . Never cleared up that first poor girl.'

'Were you here then?'

'Last year? Just joined.'

'So you didn't know her?'

Robinson shook his head. Behind him a telephone began to ring. 'Saw her. Nice-mannered girl, always polite, more than you can say for some of them . . . Perhaps she was too polite.'

119

'What does that mean?'

'I don't know why I said that, sir,' said Robinson, as if he had surprised himself. 'Perhaps polite wasn't the word, more docile . . . I'm not saying she was a natural victim, but going that way. You get dogs like that sometimes, you can just look at them and say that one will get his throat bitten open.' The phone continued to ring. 'I'd better answer that, sir. I'm the only one on duty at the moment. Bit of sickness around.'

'I'll remember what you said about Virginia Scott.'

'I hope you get the chap who did it.' He looked directly into Coffin's face. 'Perhaps you've got him already.'

'The file isn't closed,' Coffin said.

As he drove away, he asked himself what he thought he had been doing here in the university?

What was I really up to? I am looking for a guilty man. Well, certainly that. But as well? Deeper down?

I am worried, I am miserable, because I think this whole investigation is going all wrong and I can't think of what to do about it. Because at the same time, I have the feeling my career, my whole life is going down the drain. I am thrashing around because I have a big problem inside me.

The traffic streamed past him on the main road, he had to wait at the traffic lights for a moment to cross. He took the opportunity to draw in a breath and try to get a grip on things, tell himself to go back being a reasoning man.

To be honest I was trying for questions, any questions, to see what I turned up . . . And I did get something. I got to know one aspect of Angela. And I saw that bruise on her arm.

And as an extra, a straight tip from an inside voice that Martin Blackhall did for both of them.

He thought he would give Star Court a miss, he had been down there recently and he didn't think they would welcome him again. They were not that keen on men and policemen. But then he saw Angela drive past him in a taxi, presumably on the way to Star Court but with no luggage that he could see; he was surprised that she had moved so

120

soon, and curiosity about her reception from Mrs Rolt and Josephine, not to mention that passionately interested small boy, led him to drive briskly in that direction. He liked inquisitive small boys, he had been one himself, but he hoped not to meet that one on this visit.

He drove up the slight hill, so that it was some time before he came in sight of Star Court House. When he saw it, he stopped dead.

Parked at the kerb was a line of six motorbikes, each with a black-leather-jacketed rider astride. It was still daylight, but each bike had the headlights shining. A wasteful, defiant, but somehow telling gesture. Ready for anything, it said.

The riders, goggled and helmeted, let him pass, but as he walked in the gate he saw an inner cordon of black-jacketed figures lounging about the grass. A couple straddled the path, obstructing his way.

Our General had called out her troops.

He halted at the gate. 'Can I come through?'

'Who are you?'

He identified himself. 'I want to see Mrs Rolt.'

He got a suspicious look. 'Wait where you are.'

He decided to be patient, half amused by the parade. He could pull rank on them, demand to be let in, but to do so would reinforce all the suspicions they had already about men and policemen. In any case, they would probably have ignored his demand, he doubted his ability to fight all of them, and he would have lost face. In playing this game with Our General, you had to play by her rules.

While he was waiting he was making an observation of the assembled blackjackets. Not all girls, he noticed, at least a couple of older women, and one or two lads. He wondered if they were armed, and decided that he wouldn't be surprised. They'd have something to fight with apart from bare fists. What had the Valkyries used? Swords, if he remembered rightly, and a bit of magic. But they had to be careful about whom they loved or powers could be lost. He wondered where this outfit's sexual inclinations lay?

Our General came out of the front door and advanced down the path towards him. They met half way.

'What's all this parade in aid of?' he said.

'Protection.' Rosa Maundy put her arms across her chest and stared at him. Seen close to, she had a bold, strong face, with narrow eyes under dark brows. She was not beautiful, and wore no make-up, but there was something attractive about her very strength. She was a leader, he granted that much.

'But why?'

'A woman is hiding here from her husband. She came in today. We've heard he is on his way round.' There was movement, people gathering in the hall behind her, but she ignored this.

'You could have called the police.'

Rosa grinned, showing strong white teeth in a smile without amusement. 'What do you think we are? Think we do this for fun?' She spaced her words, dropping them like hard stones into a pool. 'He—is—a—policeman.'

No, not hard stones, he thought. More like a bucket of cold water right in the face. Coffin was halted. For a moment, he could find no words. 'Who is he?' he demanded.

The flurry in the doorway behind her resolved itself into three figures. Mrs Rolt and another woman on either side of a third whom they were supporting.

'We don't regard our friends as exhibits,' said Rosa. 'I wouldn't let you see her in the ordinary way . . . But this time you can. Maisie and Dr Gray are taking her to the hospital. Stand aside.'

To encourage him, she gave him a hefty shove to the right.

'You may know her . . . if you can recognize her face.'

They were supporting her because one leg seemed damaged so that she was limping; they were guiding her because her eyes were hidden by a great swelling. Her face was distorted, tilted to one side. She looked like the victim of a bad road accident. Coffin recognized the result of a thorough beating-up. She was not to be recognized.

122

What he could see, though, was that this was a middle-aged lady wearing good shoes and well-made skirt and jacket. No throwout from society, but a middle-class woman from the professional classes.

'Know this lady, do you?' asked Our General. 'Know her face?'

Coffin shook his head, trying to draw away as they passed, although he saw that the woman was past noticing him. Then he saw the crisp red hair, just beginning to go grey. Dyed? It didn't look dyed, he had never thought it was.

'Betsy Coleridge,' he said under his breath.

Mrs Harry Coleridge, wife of Chief Inspector Coleridge, soon due to retire from the Force with honour.

'And don't think this is the first time,' said Rosa. 'He's been at it for ever.' She turned aside. 'Come away. That's enough. Don't stare.'

Coffin drew back into the garden while Mrs Coleridge was helped into the doctor's car and Maisie Rolt came back into the garden.

She didn't seem pleased to see him. 'What do you want?' Her voice was gruff. Her face looked more pinched and tired than he remembered, but she was dressed in cheerful yellow and blue. 'Hurry up, please.'

He was surprised into stiffness and formality, 'On the matter of Angela.'

'Which Angela?'

'Angela Kirk. She's helped here.'

'Oh, that Angela. Can't help you there, don't know anything about her.'

'I thought she was here.'

'Well, she's not.'

'On her way, then.'

'Not as far as I know.' She frowned. 'Oh yes, she did ring up with some offer of help. I turned her down. Silly girl. Now is that all?'

For the moment it was, he thought, not dismissing his interest in Angela but moving aside. 'About Mrs Coleridge . . . I had no idea.'

123

'You weren't meant to have.'

'You can dismiss the guard. I'll have a word with Coleridge.'

'I wouldn't advise it. I've met him, you know.' She turned back into the house. 'But the girls won't go. I don't give them orders.'

'Come from the All Highest, do they?' said Coffin, looking at Our General.

'Just about.' Maisie allowed herself a smile. 'I'm off to the hospital to bring Betsy back—if she's not kept in. Suit yourself what you do.'

There was a movement among the gang. They were lining into a battle order near the gate. Two of them in front, then three, four behind that. Quite effective as a fighting formation, he thought, and turned round.

A car was coming up the road, slowing as it approached the gate of Star Court House.

Coffin walked towards it. Harry Coleridge turned his face towards him as he came up. He stared at Coffin, first without expression and then with surprise. Continued to stare for a long, silent moment. Surprise melted away from his eyes, the pupils contracted, the eyes narrowed, and dislike, even hate, took the place of surprise. His face went white. Then he started the car and drove off.

That's one of my enemies, Coffin thought. Or if he wasn't, then he is now.

Maisie Rolt drove them both to the hospital. 'If you want to come, leave your car and come with me. Someone will pick it up for you, I expect.'

'Why do you want me with you?'

'I want to talk.' Her irritation had disappeared. 'Sorry if I was short with you about Angela, but that girl gets on my nerves. She's taken to hanging around Star Court. Says she's trying to help, like Amy. She claims she's doing it for Amy, that it's what Amy would have wanted. I don't like the attitude, it's patronizing. It's not what we want. It worries me.'

'But you were worried about Amy,' he reminded her.

'Not like that,' she said illogically.

'She's said that she's taking a term off and coming to work with you. I thought she'd be there now.'

'She isn't,' said Mrs Rolt in a decided voice. 'And I can't be bothered. You've seen the sort of problems we have. And we're still upset about Amy. I suppose the boy did it?'

'No opinion on that yet,' said Coffin cautiously.

'Looks obvious,' said Maisie, driving the car forward at speed and turning a corner. 'Whoops, hang on.'

As they drove, Coffin found himself thinking about Harry Coleridge. He was badly shaken. All those years he had worked with Harry and thought of him as nothing but a pedestrian, dull, quiet man, who was an efficient administrator and not much else, while all the time this had been going on behind the façade.

He had never known him well. As young men they had worked in different districts and their careers had moved them apart, but he had always known his face and his name. When he had taken his new position as Chief Commander, he had been glad that Harry Coleridge had stayed on in the area to join his headquarters team. Harry had had the choice, he could have left and taken promotion elsewhere, but he had chosen to stay and had been seen as the quiet face at committee meetings while his signature at the bottom of a report was guarantee of a job well done. They had never met socially, and he had never thought of Harry as a friend, but he had felt comfortable with him.

No more. There had been that in Coleridge's look that suggested a long-held dislike now unveiled. Coffin was shaken.

Could Coleridge's have been the voice of the anonymous telephone caller?

No, that voice might have been uttering a threat, but it had also been sending a warning. From what he had seen of Coleridge today, that man would rejoice in Coffin's downfall.

He might even have been one of the people trying to organize it; Coffin was beginning to get the strong feeling that it was being organized.

He was thrashing around trying to sort out things. He took a deep breath, so deep that Maisie Rolt looked at him. 'Don't get too worked up. I'm not that bad a driver. Nearly there now.'

'I hope Mrs Coleridge will be all right,' he said, as he got out of the car.

'She won't be going home.' Maisie made it a brief statement.

'No. Can't blame her. I would never have thought it of Harry Coleridge . . .' A man with two faces. But perhaps he was like that with Stella. Not always open and honest.

He felt he had met an enemy and at the same time got a look at his own secret face. The one he would not want Stella to see.

He hesitated about going with Maisie Rolt to see Mrs Coleridge, but found himself dismissed.

'You can leave me here.'

'Betsy Coleridge,' he began, 'shouldn't I . . . ?'

'She won't want to see you,' said Maisie bluntly. 'You get on with what brought you here in the first place. The boy, I suppose? You go ahead. If he killed Amy, go and get him.' That was the tough ruthless side of Maisie Rolt showing from under the tender concern. She probably believed in the death penalty for men.

Outside the room of Martin Blackhall, he saw one of the CID sergeants, known to him by name only. By the unsurprised look on Sergeant Duke's face, he knew that the word had gone around that WALKER was out and on the prowl.

Duke turned away from his conversation with the uniformed constable who now had a chair to sit on in the corridor. He got up hastily as he too recognized Coffin and saluted.

Duke seemed genuinely pleased to see his Chief Commander, as if he had a problem he was glad to offload. An unsmiling man, he smiled.

'You've heard, then, sir?'

'So the boy's conscious?'

A faint look of surprise appeared on the Sergeant's face,

though his tanned, battered face never showed much expression. 'Well, yes, he is. Has been for a few hours, but that's not all. The girl has come round, the shop assistant, and wants to talk.'

'You've spoken to her?'

'No, sir, I haven't. The CI said to lay off, he's coming down himself.' But his eyes, those pebble-grey, hard eyes said that he had listened and heard something.

'I'll go in and see her myself. Third door down, is it?' There was another uniformed constable outside this door.

'I'll come with you.'

'No, stay where you are.'

He nodded at the police constable on guard outside the girl's cubicle, entering to the sound of voices. The nurse by the bed seemed to be trying to calm the patient.

'Lie back, dear.'

'No, I want to talk, to tell.'

Coffin stood at the door. The girl in the bed was propped on pillows, her head swathed in a turban of white. A tube was attached to her arm and another further down, but her eyes were wide open, staring at the nurse. Neither of them took any notice of John Coffin.

'May I talk to your patient?' He introduced himself, his voice more hesitant than he had meant it to sound. Truly, he shouldn't be here, he thought, but he meant to stay.

The nurse turned round, taken off guard, slightly flustered. 'No, not without Dr Mallet's permission, I don't care who you are.'

The girl began to pipe out that she would, she would, she would talk. Her voice was frail and thin. But determined.

She began to flail at the nurse with her hands.

'Can I help?'

'No, go away. I've just turned out one of you.'

'Something's wrong,' said Coffin. It was a tiny room, and he was almost on top of them.

'I think it's an abnormal reaction to one of the drugs, it can happen, she'll calm down in a minute, then go to sleep.'

Right, he thought, I'm hanging on.

'Please leave this minute.' The nurse turned back to her

127

patient, but the girl reached out and grabbed Coffin's sleeve, pulling him towards the bed.

'He was so brave . . . He tried to fight off that man . . . that one had a gun . . . he was so brave, he helped me.'

Coffin leaned forward, ignoring a protest from the nurse. 'Who? Who helped you?'

Our General? One of Our General's cohorts? She had few males. But he knew what the answer would be even before the girl spoke.

'Martin, where is Martin? He helped me.'

Coffin knew he was hearing something important; he looked at the nurse and her eyes flickered as if she too knew she was receiving something vital. He wondered how the sick girl would stand up to questioning when she was out of the shadow of the drugs. Was it fantasy?

But she had the boy's name off pat: Martin.

Archie Young and Paul Lane were not going to be very pleased with him.

The girl's eyes closed as she dropped back on to the pillow.

'She's off,' said her nurse with relief. 'Now clear out, whoever you are.' Relief had sharpened her tongue.

No, CI Young and Chief Superintendent Paul Lane would not be pleased and would not be able to show it, although they might find ways, not being his puppets but men able to discharge their anger.

He wondered what they would make of it. They would probably not believe it and if they did, then would secretly resent the clearing of Martin. But they lived in a shell of normality and his shell was cracking.

I'm like the Queen in *Alice*, he thought, I can believe anything.

And she did have the name off pat.

He walked out of the room into the corridor where he saw that Archie Young, with Sergeant Duke behind, was just swinging round the corner with that rolling walk of his which suggested he might be about to burst into a run. He saw the Chief Commander and hurried his step.

'Didn't expect to see you, sir.' Which was not quite true

as word had gone around that WALKER was out on the loose, and liable to cause trouble. He was on good terms with the Big Man and meant to keep that way. 'Chief Superintendent Lane is out of reach . . .' he said breathlessly. 'What have we got here?' He was cheerful and yet cautious. 'So the girl is conscious. I've been looking forward to that. Now we'll get something to work on.' His eyes were wary, belying his tone. Somehow the message had got through to him that he might not be getting all he expected.

'She clears the boy.' Coffin made the statement blunt.

'We'll see about that,' said the Chief Inspector, moving forward like a terrier approaching a bone. 'And that doesn't touch the Dean case. You coming in, sir?'

'No, I'll leave you to it.' The girl was asleep anyway, but let Young find that out for himself. 'I have someone else to see.'

After all, he would go and check on Betsy Coleridge. A matter of conscience.

He spoke over his shoulder as he walked away: 'Let me know how things go.'

Two days later he found out.

He had managed to avoid seeing Stella (not easy since she had left a telephone message several times and rung his doorbell once), still seeing the bruised, swollen face of Betsy Coleridge.

He had sat by her in the side ward where she had been admitted for observation. He had said very little, nothing about her husband, and she had said less. 'We'll see you through this,' he said, not really knowing who 'we' was, but somehow meaning Maisie Rolt and Josephine and Rosa Maundy, and possibly even Angela. 'I'll be down at Star Court,' he had said. 'You'll see me. But don't worry, this is just between you and me.' He wondered for a moment if she even knew who he was, but then, as he was leaving, she said: 'It's the job.'

A hammer blow, for it was his job too and even more than Harry Coleridge's, for he bore the ultimate responsibility inside the Force. What had the job done to him, himself? And what had he done, was doing even now, to Stella?

Two days passed, two committees and the usual run of meetings and letters to answer, and wondering all the time who among them all knew of his own particular problem but well aware how excellently informed most of the men he met were. They knew. As yet, he had not answered Frank's vital letter, because there was no answer he wanted to make. Answer politely, Mat had said, tighten up your behaviour, find out if Stella's husband is behind this somewhere, because someone is, and get ready to defend yourself. None of which he wanted to do.

So he sat on all these problems while the routine of two days rolled over him. He passed Harry Coleridge in the lift going to his office and he knew from his face that his enemies were assembling.

Then on the third day Paul Lane asked to see him.

'Come in, have a drink?' Friend or enemy, he thought to himself. Lane had been his own recruit to the Force and was as loyal as any, but he probably knew more about Coffin's past and his relationship with Stella than any of them. Mustn't be paranoid.

It was late afternoon. His office was full of sun, smelling of autumn bulbs. His secretary had placed a bowl of them on his desk. She too, no doubt, knew everything.

'Won't, thank you, although I'd like to. I'm on a diet. Wife's orders.'

A happy marriage there, then, thought the observer inside Coffin, now checking everyone with an emotional Geiger counter.

'I'll smoke if I may, though, sir? If I'm on a diet and not drinking, I have to have something.'

'Go ahead.'

'I thought I'd come and have a word with you, sir, because the Dean case is getting tricky and Dean is making a nuisance of himself.'

He'd know how to do so, thought Coffin.

'As things stand at the moment, yes, it looks as though Martin Blackhall is in the clear for the attack on the girl in

the shop . . . She made a statement. It checks out. She says
he came into the shop when the two louts were having a go
at her and tried to stop them. She knows him, says he buys
his socks there . . . She could be lying, of course.'

'But you don't think so?'

'I am keeping an open mind.' Then he said carefully:
'Meanwhile, the Met have arrested two men who match
the description of the attackers, they were trying to rob a
similar shop in Piccadilly . . . We're going to let the Met
see our forensics to see if it matches up with what they've
got.'

'Does she know why Martin was soaking wet?'

'No, she doesn't know anything about that, can't remember, and the doctors say it's pretty remarkable she recalls
what she does, short memory being the thing to go as a rule
. . . Still, there it is.' He sounded regretful, it would have
been a nice tidy solution if they could have got one assailant
for two crimes. 'But it doesn't clear Blackhall from the Amy
Dean case.'

'You think he's guilty?'

'I think he's guilty. Even if he was a hero to the girl in
the shop, I think he killed Amy Dean.'

'Have you questioned him?'

'His mother has him wrapped up in cotton wool. But of
course we shall get to him . . . I have to say that so far the
forensics have been no help. Nothing on the girl or in her
car that ties in with him.'

'What about the bus out to Essex? Anyone who remembers anything?'

'As yet, no.'

Coffin played with a pencil on his desk. It was silver,
with his initials on it, and Stella had given it to him
for Christmas. 'Is that the lot? You can't blame Jim
Dean.'

'I don't, but he knows how to play the tune.'

'Always has.'

Lane said carefully: 'Apart from anything else, it seems
there's this girl, Angela Kirk, a friend of his daughter's,

that he takes an interest in, and we've upset her. Asking her questions. He doesn't like that.'

'It was me,' said Coffin.

'No doubt you had your reasons, sir,' said Lane smoothly.

'One more thing: let me see all you have on that earlier killing, Virginia Scott, wasn't it? It was never cleared up, and must now be considered in this context.'

'Of course we're considering it.' Lane nodded. 'It's all on the computer. You shall have it all.'

Coffin said nothing more. Lane let himself be persuaded to have a drink and they talked for a while, before Paul Lane said he had to go. His wife was singing in the chorus of an amateur production in aid of charity, and he had promised to be home early. She was a Valkyrie.

As he left, he said, fumbling for his driving keys and not looking at John Coffin: 'By the way, Betsy Coleridge is out of hospital. She's going off for a short holiday.'

'Ah.' Nothing was secret.

'I think Harry's planning on taking a bit of sick leave himself.'

No expression in Lane's eyes or face, he might have been talking of a horse.

'A good idea.'

'I thought so.'

At the end of the day, at home at last, Coffin felt a replay of all the events going on inside him. Amy, Angie, Josephine, Mrs Coleridge, Our General. His own problems.

The Blackhalls? An interesting couple. He sat for a moment considering the story as retold by Stella. The death of a husband? A past scandal with surely no relevance to a crime a quarter of a century later? They must get Martin's own account of events.

But something had been nagging at him all the time, one of those subliminal sensations that might not mean anything at all. He went to his answerphone and ran back the tape to that last anonymous call.

132

Yes, there in the background, he could just hear a woman's voice.

CHAPTER 9

The day rolls on

Not a female voice he knew, he thought, playing the tape again, the intonation was not familiar, nor could he hear what it was saying. Just a flash of background noise. Nor could he identify the man sending the message, but the chap was deliberately distorting his voice. Which must mean, Coffin thought, that he knew the speaker.

Well, of course. He knew that what was going on was treachery among friends. The very people you could not trust were the same ones you had trusted most.

Soon now he could expect the call to an informal meeting with the Chairman of the Police Committee. What would be dragged up? His sister Letty and her activities as a property developer?

He poured a drink and pondered whether it had been a mistake to buy this flat from her in St Luke's? But it hadn't come cheap, Letty had done him no favours. Letty would make a statement clearing him, if anyone believed it. A check at Companies House would clear him, but by the time they got to doing that, it would be too late, the mud would be stuck all over.

He took the drink to the window to stare out at the view over the rooftops to the river which he loved.

Or would they attack him on his relationship with Stella?

That looked likely, and he was more vulnerable there. He was ashamed of himself for minding. He ought to stand and shout to celebrate knowing Stella, for being able to love Stella and claim her love back. Unluckily life wasn't always like that.

It was raining and the slates were shiny. The sky was darkening. He turned back into the room to switch on a lamp. This room, with the carefully chosen small carpet with its touches of deep coral, the two pictures which had been bought first and which had, in a sense, dictated the carpet, and the big brown leather sofa which was there for comfort, here was his hideaway. A shell into which he retired from the world outside. He had put it together consciously. One or two books he could crawl into, one or two pieces of music, but mainly it was this room in which he hid for comfort.

Not Stella?

The answer was no. The years, the pattern of life, had forced him to be solitary and now it was too late to change.

He sat down on the leather sofa to finish his drink. Whisky. He had hidden that way once, but mercifully not for long, and seen it in time as no true saviour.

But tonight his sanctuary seemed empty. Even Tiddles, that occasionally baleful companion, was not home. Poor Tiddles, neglected like Stella.

There still was no food in the place. He had a picture of the inside of his refrigerator as containing a heel of cheese which might once have been Brie and a bottle of mineral water.

Suddenly he was hungry. A hunger that could only be satisfied by fish and chips. The nearest eating place was Max's establishment round the corner where fish and chips, as a dish, was not to be had.

He dragged himself upright. He might persuade Max to grill a sole.

Outside, he met Stella, Tiddles and Bob; the trio looked jaunty and cheerful, even aggressive, not like waifs and strays, objects of sympathy at all.

Suddenly, Coffin realized that guilty feelings were just as much a self-indulgence as drink. Stella didn't need his sympathy, she had been fighting her own battles and celebrating her own victories for a long time now, nor Tiddles (God, certainly not Tiddles who was sound in tooth and claw), nor Bob who knew where to put his feet with the best.

Equally suddenly, he realized that the boot was on the

other foot and that Stella was studying him with sympathy.

'You look dead beat.' She patted the bag she was carrying. 'Come on in and have some supper. I've got fish and chips in here, that's why this pair are with me, they can smell it.'

'Just what I was fancying,' he said.

'Got enough for two.' She looked down at the cat and dog. 'For four, if you and I aren't greedy.'

He unlocked her door for her in the small flat which was her share of the old church. Across the cloister St Luke's Theatre had at last been created out of the main body of the kirk. The entrance to this was on the other side, opposite the Theatre Workshop from which strains of Wagner could be heard.

'How are the Valkyries doing?'

'All tickets sold out.' The performance of the Choral Society and the Friends of St Luke's Dramatic Group were always a sell-out, since the relations and friends of the performers formed a conscript audience. 'Mind you, it won't win any prizes, but they enjoy it. I look in at the odd rehearsal to see how they're doing and they've a whale of a time. Amateurs always do, bless 'em.'

Stella went into her kitchen, followed by the other three. She produced paper plates and plastic knives and forks, then distributed carefully adjusted shares of fish and chips to the eaters. More fish for Tiddles than for Bob, but no chips; lots of chips for Bob but not too much fish. What was left, she divided equally between Coffin and herself.

'I got cod because Tiddles prefers it.'

She was wearing jeans and a checked shirt, but the jeans were suede and the shirt of the finest cotton. Her eyes were bright and she was humming as she put glasses on the table.

To Coffin's experienced eye, this meant a man. He was shocked at the sharp arrow of jealousy that went through him. There always would be someone in Stella's life, that was how it went.

'How are things, Stella?' The fish was good, the batter crisp and hot.

'You might well ask.' She poured some wine, still hum-

135

ming. 'But fine, fine. The TV part is still dicey, and I'm up for a part at the National, but I don't think I'll get it, they don't like me there, I'm too commercial.'

Definitely a man, Coffin thought sourly.

'What's the part?'

'A Pinter. You wouldn't think I was a Pinter woman, would you, but it turns out I am. A non-heroine, of course, but I have some lovely lines, and some beautiful pauses.'

They went into a beautiful pause themselves then, which silence Stella broke.

'I shouldn't ask, but I'm going to . . .'

'Don't bother to finish: No, we haven't got anyone for Amy Dean's death.'

'The clever money round here is on Martin Blackhall.'

Coffin was silent.

'You might talk about it.'

He had on his desk at the moment an account written by Chief Inspector Young of his interview with Martin Blackhall. Archie Young was not as a rule much of a writer but he had got across the feeling of this meeting. Perhaps because he had been an irritated man.

This is a short memo which was asked for, it began.

Coffin hadn't remembered that he had asked, but he took this as a measure of Archie Young's repressed irritation at the way the interview had gone.

I asked the questions. I had with me Sergeant Mary Dover, who has had nursing training. Martin Blackhall was sitting up in bed. Present also were Sir Thomas Blackhall and Bryan Pettifer, Blackhall's solicitor. No medical staff were present but were outside the door. A nurse came in twice.

We requested and were refused permission to tape the interview. Sergeant Dover took notes.

There had followed a summary of the question and answer session, spiced by Young's own comments.

I must begin by saying that Blackhall did not look as ill as I had expected him to do; Sergeant Dover agreed, and I came to the conclusion he was being protected by his parents. His mother was not present but she's a well-known and much loved figure in this hospital. I think they would do a lot for her.

Blackhall said he'd like to make a statement: he said he had nothing to do with the attack on the girl in the Stocking Shop in Spinnergate, but that he had come back to Spinnergate on the subway, on his way home after what he called a 'time out', had passed the shop and seen what was going on and waded in. He knew the girl. He says he had hauled off the raiders, one of whom had fled when he was attacked himself. He remembers being hit on the chin, and falling. Thinks he hit his head when he went down.

Coffin could understand Lane's sourness at this point since it would go some way to letting Rosa Maundy off the hook. An accident, I didn't mean to damage him, would be her plea.

He did not know who hit him, but thinks it was one of the female gang that hang out on the Planter Estate. He seems to know about them.

Part of the mythology of the area, thought Coffin.

Wouldn't know her face, wore goggles, but might know her smell. Petrol and sweat. (This sounds like Rosa Maundy to me; she's got an HGV licence and drives for her father. We questioned her once about an assault on her father. He hit her once too often and she broke his jaw.) I don't think Martin Blackhall will identify his attacker, seems to like the gang.

I questioned him about the death of Amy Dean. He denied all knowledge. In answer to my questions he said he knew nothing of her death and disappearance until told by his mother in hospital when he came round. The words he used to his mother about 'not meaning to hurt her' referred to the Stocking Shop incident. He was confused and had meant to say: I was protecting her.

On my further questioning him, he answered that he had quarrelled with Amy Dean and left her sitting in her car in a car park near the Dockland Light Railway. He thinks he must have left his wallet in the car then.

He said the quarrel was 'about nothing special'. Pressed, he said he became aware that there was an affair going on with another man. He didn't approve, this was the cause of the argument.

He did not harm her and did not see her again. He got drunk and went for a walk by the river, he fell into the river while taking this walk, and that was how he got wet and damaged his hands climbing out. It sobered him up and he decided to go back to the university.

Unspoken but there between the lines, was Young's bitter comment: *Believe that if you can.*

He concluded by saying: *I was not allowed any more questions. But to my mind he's the one.*

Chief Superintendent Lane had added a note: *I concur. Think we should press Martin Blackhall. P.L.*

The impression this report had made on Coffin was still strong as he faced Stella, and a flicker of irritation stirred inside him. He turned the fish over with his fork.

Stella eyed him accusingly. 'You don't like it, you don't like cod.'

'It's fine, fine . . . You know I can't say much. I can tell you he is not under suspicion for attacking the girl in the shop at Spinnergate, and it looks as though he was the innocent victim there. One of Rosa Maundy's girls beat him up. We don't know which one, but it was probably Rosa herself.'

Stella raised an eyebrow. 'Oh, you lot. You ought to be looking for the robbers.'

His irritation increased. 'As a matter of fact, that's been done. But I want this other attack cleared up. I won't have it. We'll get someone for it. Tomfool behaviour. Totally unnecessary, caused a lot of confusion, apart from nearly killing Blackhall. I want the gang broken up. They're dangerous.'

'That's not how they see it down at Star Court.'

'I keep the peace here.' He could feel himself getting more and more assertive.

'I've got a lot of time for Rosa.'

'I didn't know you knew her.'

Stella shrugged. 'Friend of Josephine's. Know Josephine, you know Rosa. She's certainly helped there.'

'She's a bloody nuisance. I don't like her and she doesn't like me.'

Stella laughed. Another coal fell on the fire of his anger which was hotting up nicely.

He was getting more and more angry with Stella, and the underlying cause was that new radiance that could have only one reason.

'Oh, by the way, Josephine wants to talk to you.' She added thoughtfully: 'Was it about Angela or with Angela?'

'There's quite a difference.' He was still responding with irritation. 'How do you know this?'

'She said something to Rosa and Rosa told one of her girls, and one of the girls who's performing as a Valkyrie (she isn't singing, just moving round, Philippa likes the look) told Philippa, and Philippa told me.'

As well to know the chain of communication, Coffin thought. Why can't she just pick up the telephone? 'What about just telephoning? My secretaries are there to take messages.'

'I expect it's more personal,' said Stella stiffly.

'I'm home sometimes, and there's always my answering machine.' Could it have been Josephine's voice on that tape? No, surely not. What interest or knowledge could she have of his professional problems?

'I expect she will do something. Take it as an advance warning. If you are interested. Or shall I tell her not to bother?'

'How's your leg?' he asked, trying to switch his mood.

'Not even badly bruised. Thanks for helping me. You were good that night.'

He thought the implication of that was worrying, but he bit back an answer.

'You know when you were talking to me, telling me about

139

Jim Dean and how you knew him years ago. You thought
I was asleep. I was and I wasn't. I was drowsy, but I
was taking it in and I thought about it afterwards. You're
obsessive about him, you bear a grudge, you think he
betrayed you, let you down, and it's not doing you any
good. It was a long while ago, forget it. Throw it off, John.'
So she had been listening and now was drawing conclusions. He had valued that moment as something private
between them. Now he felt a sense of outrage, a judgement
had been passed upon him in his absence. He said so.
'That's the trouble,' said Stella crisply. 'You are absent.
Elsewhere. You are now. Not really here at all.' Then she
pushed the hair back from her forehead. 'Oh damn, I didn't
want to quarrel. Let's call a truce?' She reached out for the
wine and poured some in his glass. 'The wine is good, isn't
it?' she said in a placatory voice.
'It's excellent.' Surprisingly so, since Stella was not
famous for choosing good wine. 'Where did you get it?'
'A present.' She giggled. 'From a fan.'
No doubt about it, he was angry now. Stella was aware
of it too, without knowing why; he could see it in her eyes.
Tiddles leapt up and knocked over his glass. 'Damn.' He
leaned forward, dabbing at his sleeve. 'Let's stop playing
about. Let's talk. What is our status?'
Stella moved her chair backwards an inch, as if he was
coming too close and she did not want this.
'Status, status, what is this status? You can't use words
like that to me. We've known each other too long.'
'Perhaps that's the trouble.' He wanted to say: You're
seeing someone else, who are you seeing?
Stella drew in a breath as if it hurt. 'I know we always
seem to be quarrelling lately, but I didn't know it was my
fault, or if time had anything to do with it.'
Yes, he had hurt her.
Stella believed in hitting back when attacked. 'You've
been in a lousy mood for weeks and I refuse to accept
responsibility for your bad temper tonight. I simply offered
you some food when you were hungry. Which you haven't
eaten, by the way. If you don't want the fish, give it to

140

Tiddles.' She bent down to stroke the sycophant who was weaving himself round her ankles and purring. He was slightly damp from the Sancerre which had dripped over him.

Coffin was conscious of a mixture of emotions inside. He wanted to set things right with Stella, it was his fault but he didn't want to admit it, he couldn't bring himself to say he was sorry.

He stood up. 'I'd better go.'

Stella stood too. 'Yes, you had.'

Stella was tall. Standing up, she nearly matched him for height; he had always liked that, it made so many things easier. A breath of her new scent drifted towards him, sweet, rich, sensuous.

'Nice scent,' he said huskily. He bent towards her. 'Sorry, Stella.'

'Don't. Not good enough.'

He put his arms round her, but Stella pushed him away. 'I said Don't.'

'Stella . . .'

She had pushed hard and he fell back against the table, a glass fell over. He ignored it. A strong, hot anger swept over him. Without conscious thought, his right arm raised itself. He saw Stella's eyes widen, the pupils black. He knew fear when he saw it.

He took a deep breath and dropped his arm. Behind him his hand found the glass, he gripped it, hard, harder. It broke, splintering his palm. His anger was gone, but he felt cold.

They stared at each other. Both seeing what they had come close to.

'I'll leave.'

'But your hand . . .'

He wrapped a handkerchief round it. 'It's nothing.' It was his own blood, thank God.

He stumbled towards the door, a set of conflicting emotions assembling itself inside.

As he walked to his own front door, a voice inside him said: I only wanted to make love to her.

141

But isn't sex itself somehow an invasion? And in my present mood, isn't that exactly what it would have been? Wasn't that just what I wanted to do to Stella? Show her who was master? Stamp her with my mark, like a bloody tomcat?

At this kindred with himself and Harry Coleridge, and whoever had killed Amy Dean, all rapists and men of violence, he went miserably to bed.

In the morning he felt quite different. He awoke, hungry and in a cheerful mood. He was purged of anger.

His feeling for Stella was good, real.

He knew what he must do: what Mat had urged him to do, and what his own heart now instructed him to do: talk to Stella. Tell her the whole problem, let her decide.

It was all coming together, his own particular problem, his feeling for Stella and even his understanding of this terrible murder case.

He had an insight now into the angry, anxious violence of the killer.

And one more factor: there was sex in it.

CHAPTER 10

The morning after. Josephine, Angela, Amy Dean. A double circle like a noose round them.

Coffin found these names written on the pad of paper he kept by his bed. He must have written them and drawn the circle round them in his sleep. As he stared at his drawing sleepily, it did look uncomfortably like a hangman's rope, he wondered what he had meant by it.

Even after a strong cup of coffee he was not sure what he had been up to, but it was his pencil, his paper and his writing.

So what was it Stella had said? Josephine would like to

see you. That must be it. The circle was the mystery, and there was no accounting for the unconscious mind.

Usually a man who threw his clothes on while thinking of other matters, he dressed carefully. Occasionally he had to wear uniform but this badge of office was not required today.

After the explosion of the day before, the weather suited the Chief Commander's mood: it was a cool, sunny, autumn day, the best sort of weather for working and for being happy. Not just content or peaceful, but positively, actively happy.

He might even take a holiday. Go to Venice, and look at pictures. Paris, and drink and eat too much, and buy scent for Stella. Would she come? Damn all expense and all gossiping tongues.

Before he left, he listened once more to the message of warning. An incoming message trying to sell him double glazing had overprinted all but the end of it, but yes, there again was that woman's voice in the background. He heard the tone again, certainly not Josephine's, a higher, younger voice. There was something tantalizingly familiar about the man, though. Someone I know and have spoken to recently, he thought.

He drove towards Spinnergate where Mimsie Marker had his paper ready rolled for him, then walked the few yards to the florist's called Flora's Flowers where he ordered a large bunch of roses to be sent to Stella. No name attached and no message, since none was needed. She would know who had sent them and why. He hoped for a response.

He felt absurdly optimistic, even romantic, everything was going to be all right. He would fight off all attacks, remain in command of the Second Force, and he and Stella would sort themselves out. How and in what manner, he did not know, but it hardly seemed to matter. It would happen. He had married once and it had been a disaster, Stella was still married, but things would be worked out. Even the custody of Tiddles and Bob the mongrel would be settled. They divided their time between their co-owners

143

as it suited them now and would go on doing the same.

'Red roses, sir?'

'No, those pink and white ones, please.' They were the most expensive flowers he had ever bought, but they had a lovely, fragile elegance that seemed to suit how he felt about Stella this morning.

'How many would you like?'

'How many have you got?'

'Just those two dozen, sir.'

'The lot.'

Knowing his sometimes frugal ways (born of long years of never having any money), Stella would read the message he was sending. He might even get a response from her that morning.

What would she say: 'Roses, thank you. You've never sent me flowers before.' Not quite true, but very nearly.

Or would she say: 'Let's drive to Greenwich and have a proper old-fashioned fish and chip supper at that place we know.' Alf's, was it? Or Ted's. He remembered going there with her and drinking strong tea.

'This morning's delivery?' he asked, just to give himself the best possible chance of doing so.

Flora of the Flowers, a sturdy young woman in a white overall who had been up at four to go to New Covent Garden to choose her flowers, looked out of the window to the kerb where her smart red and white van was parked. 'Straight off,' she said. 'The delivery man's just arrived. St Luke's, oh, that's not far. Miss Pinero, oh, we know her, of course. Sent her some freesias only yesterday.'

Not quite so good, that, but so what, if he wasn't the only person who sent her flowers. He suppressed the twinge of jealousy. Enough of that, he told himself.

It was still early morning, just after eight, but the commuters were pouring into Spinnergate Tube Station. He drove past, then swung towards the new Headquarters Building. On a day like this it was hard to accept a world in which girls like Amy Dean were murdered and women like Betsy Coleridge were beaten up by their upright, hardworking, police officer husbands.

144

Josephine, Amy, Angela, they were there all right, in his world and in his mind, edging out Stella. He tried to hang on to his image of Stella Pinero but it was beginning to get misty.

He hoped to hear from her soon. Thanks for the flowers. She was good at delivering thanks. A giver herself, she welcomed another generous heart. Which he did not always have; he forced himself to recognize that unpleasing fact about himself.

Meanwhile, work had to go on. One of his secretaries always came in very early, they settled the rota between them, so the messages, letters and reports were already arranged on his desk in neat rows. That meant Fiona, she was the tidy one, not Lysette, but otherwise they were interchangeable. Efficient, quiet, and neutral. But he had a strong suspicion they had active social lives and what he saw was just one face.

'Don't put anyone through,' he said, sorting through his papers and arranging them in order of priorities. He could see by Fiona's face that his priorities did not accord with those which she had already awarded them. Why, for instance, was he pushing the letter from the Bishop of Billericay to the bottom of the file and moving upwards the letter from the Spinnergate Garden Club who wanted him to speak to them? (The reason being that he knew Bishop Bill would not mind waiting for an answer, whereas the Chairperson of the Garden Club was Mimsie Marker, who would.) In the middle went the great mass of official material which he would deal with or ignore as seemed politic.

'Don't put through any calls.'

Fiona nodded. She would do what she thought right, she felt she made better judgements on these matters sometimes than he did.

'Except Miss Pinero.' Fiona certainly knew about his own troubles, the communication network within the Force was swift and secret, but officially she knew nothing and would not refer to it even obliquely. 'I'll talk to her.'

Fiona gave the small secret smile she reserved for

145

worktimes when she knew something the boss didn't.
'Lovely photograph of Miss Pinero in the *Mail* yesterday.'

'I didn't see it.' All newspapers were delivered to his
office and he read as much as possible. Part of the job.

'I cut it out.'

Fiona put a clipping in front of him. There was Stella,
radiant, smiling, her professional face, and there with her
was the new young American star of the TV series in which
she still had her part. They looked on extremely good terms.

'He's lovely too, isn't he?' said Fiona.

'Yes,' agreed Coffin, mentally awarding Fiona a star for
neat bitchiness. He hadn't realized she disliked him so
much. Another little bit of the happiness he had started the
day with peeled away.

The morning passed, the telephone rang, messages came
in, and Fiona dealt with them. Stella did not ring.

Fiona brought in coffee and sandwiches, closing the door
quietly on him eating his solitary working lunch. He heard
her laughing with someone in the room beyond.

He continued going through his papers, making notes
and dictating letters on a tape. Lysette took over after
lunch, the two girls worked their shifts as it suited them.
Lysette was gentler than Fiona and not so compulsively
efficient. She was married, although she never spoke of her
husband, so that Coffin, who was incurious when he could
be (so much of his life having compelled him to asking
questions), had decided he must be a sailor or a long-
distance lorry-driver.

He was surprised by a voice outside and the door opening
with a thrust.

He looked up. 'Oh, you. How did you get in?'

'Yes, me. Not so much of a surprise, am I?' James Dean
looked thinner and greyer since their last meeting. His shirt
and tie did not match as well as before, his suit looked
creased. Grief could do things like that to you.

There were numerous checks and barriers, some electronic, others men wearing uniform, that should have
stopped Dean coming through without permission, but
clearly they hadn't functioned. Another sign, Coffin

146

thought, that Dean knew his way only too well into Coffin's world.

'You think you're protected? Not as well as could be.'

'I'm learning, thank you for alerting me. I shall do something about it.' He would find out who had let Dean through and why and for what price, because there would be one and it might not be money.

'Did you think I wouldn't be in? Did you think I'd quietly step aside while you let Martin Blackhall get away with it?'

'He hasn't got away with anything . . . Just at the moment he isn't charged with anything. There is no evidence to charge anyone.'

'I know all that.'

'I expect you do.' Paul Lane, no doubt, is your source. Coffin too had been making his inquiries and had discovered that Lane and Dean met regularly at the same Golf Club. Harry Coleridge could be another informer and glad to be, no doubt.

'I hold that boy responsible for my daughter's death.'

'I believe you do,' said Coffin, respecting the conviction in Dean's voice. 'But it's not enough. You know that.'

'He buried her.'

'I don't think he did.'

Dean looked at him. 'Does that mean you know who did?'

'No, it doesn't. I'm just telling you what I believe to be true. The boy did not bury Amy. He may have killed her, but he did not bury her.'

Dean frowned. 'I don't understand. What do you mean?'

'Think about it. I don't believe one person could have got Amy into that box.' He saw Dean flinch at the word. 'And then buried her in it. Or not alone. More than one person must have been involved.'

'That doesn't clear the boy of the killing,' said Dean quickly and almost sulkily. Sullen, Coffin thought.

'It complicates the picture immensely, though, doesn't it?' said Coffin with sympathy. 'There are more people involved than we thought at first. Whoever they were. Or are.'

147

He could smell that Dean had been drinking. 'How's business?' he said.

Dean's face sharpened. 'It's fine, fine. The recession's hitting me, but it's touching us all. I'll come through, and if I don't, well . . .' He shrugged. 'Who cares? Without Amy, I've got enough for my needs, she was the future. But I'll get that bastard Blackhall. And you too, if I have to.'

He was out of control and not caring who knew it.

Coffin went to the window to look out. If he wasn't careful, he would hit Dean. Or Dean would hit him. Either way, it would be disaster. 'I think you've already had a go at that, haven't you?'

'Rubbish.' Dean slumped down in a chair. 'If you're still going back to the time down by the docks . . . You thought it was me, I've always known that. Sold us down the river. What did I get for it? A pound of silver and a shot in the guts?'

'If I did think that, and you did do it, I'll never prove it now.'

'Quite right.'

'But I was thinking of something more up to date.' He could see Dean's hand behind his present crisis. If he hadn't started it, then he had helped it along.

Outside he could hear Lysette on the telephone. Coffin touched the button that would bring her in.

'Like what?' Dean laughed. 'You're paranoid, you are.' He added: 'Oh yes, I've heard about your little muddle.'

And helped it along, thought Coffin sourly. The jibe about paranoia, so closely echoing Stella, stung.

'Can I have a drink?' Dean asked.

'I can give you water.' There was mineral water on his desk, he pushed the bottle across.

'I'll take it. Give you time to ring that little bell of yours again.'

'I've done that already,' said Coffin.

'You should train her better. My girls jump when I say jump. They like it that way and so do I. I choose the ones that like to jump and I know how to choose.' He leaned across the desk so that Coffin could smell the whisky on his breath. 'I know what you're thinking about me this minute, I could always read you and I can do it now. You think I'm a mucky jock, smelling of drink and sweat. Well, I'll tell you: I shall go home, have a shower and change my clothes and take the chair at the board of one of my companies and see me then.'

Coffin was silent. The putdown rankled. He knew that he commanded many more men than worked for Dean, that he was the executive head of a larger and more complex concern than any Dean handled. But Dean was a rich man and he was poor and Dean's money was shouting.

Dean took another swig from his glass. 'Tastes bitter. You haven't put arsenic in my drink?'

'No. Just insecticide.'

'Oh clever, clever. I'd kill you if I could, and I believe you would me.'

'Maybe.'

'Maybe yes.' Dean gave another laugh, he stood up and patted his old colleague on the shoulder. 'The difference between you and me is that you are a decent chap and I'm not.'

Lysette came in, carrying a pad as if ready for dictation. She was good with her props and knew how to make them convincing.

Dean waved her back. 'Just a sec, darling.'

He turned to Coffin. 'You know Tom Blackhall's the son of a butcher? Of course you do, everyone does, and he's a butcher himself, his wife's first husband killed himself, his fault. Did you know that too?'

'I've heard something.'

'To me that makes him a killer, a killer by acquaintance. He's handed the gift on to his son. Nice little inheritance there.'

'You really are a swine, Dean.'

'That's what I said.' He went to the door. 'You can come in now, darling.' He pushed past her and was gone.

I wonder whom he hates most, Coffin asked himself, me or the Blackhalls? And what have we ever done to him? He nearly got me killed all those years ago. There was some

golden handshake there, I swear; he didn't leave the Force
for the reasons he said. I wish the bullet had killed him.

But his memory told him that Dean had pushed him
down even though he tried to deny the memory.

'Any calls of importance?' he asked Lysette.

'Oh yes, one. A woman.' She looked down at her pad.
'A Miss Farley. Edith Farley. She is an assistant librarian
in the university and she has something she wants to tell
you. She will ring back unless you telephone first.'

But not Stella, Stella had not sent any message.

'Call her for me.' Better get Miss Farley over first, then
he could think about Stella.

Edith Farley was sitting by her desk, hoping he would
ring. She answered promptly and with satisfaction. I knew
he wouldn't let me down, she told herself. Some people
never ring back, I knew he would.

She heard his voice with pleasure. It was as agreeable as
she had thought it would be. How nice of him to ring back
to little, unimportant old me. But there were ways of being
important, and she thought she had found one. Besides
which, it would get even with that shitty pair of students.
This was not an adjective you said aloud (so mother said),
but it had great power in private. Especially if said twice.
Shitty pair. Not like fuck, a word she had never used and
never would, not even in the darkest recesses of the night
when anything could be done and said.

'You have something to tell me?'

'Yes,' she breathed. 'I'm sorry to bother you but it
seemed important.' Truly, she was loving every moment
and Coffin could tell this but she told him succinctly, not
wasting words, which made him think that what she had
to say must be of value.

She named names: two students, Rebecca North and
Michael Frost, nicknamed Beenie and Mick. 'They were
talking about the murdered girl Amy Dean and their friend
Angela. I don't know her surname.'

But I do, Coffin responded silently.

'They knew something about Amy's death, and from
what they said Angela knows more. You ought to talk to

150

them. They really know. They thought I couldn't hear, wasn't listening.' A non-person, that's what she was to them; for a moment her grievance rumbled away inside her like indigestion. 'Of course I could hear, the acoustics are that good in the stacks, you wouldn't think so with the books deadening the sound but it is so. And of course it's dead quiet down there . . .'

And very boring, thought Coffin.

'Have you spoken to Chief Inspector Young?'

'No, I thought of it, but decided he would not listen and that you would . . . There's something else . . .' She paused, hanging on, waiting for him to make a response.

'Go on.'

'As they left, the girl Rebecca, Beenie, they call her, whispered to the other one, Angela was mad. Mad and might do anything. That's an accusation, isn't it?'

The conversation ended there. It had been taped. You shouldn't listen to hearsay, Coffin told himself, but something inside him told him that however wrong she might have got it, what Miss Farley had handed over was gold.

But how to handle it? Lane and Young must interview the two students, but they must be sent on their road tactfully.

In the end, he did it the straight way. He told Chief Superintendent Paul Lane about the telephone call and suggested he interview the two students. Ordered, really. It would not make him any friends but it would get the job done.

He remembered then that Josephine had wanted to talk to him about Angela. Stella had told him so. There had been no message from Stella as yet. She was working, she was busy. Why should she telephone? He would telephone her.

He put a call through to Star Court House and asked for Josephine.

Maisie answered that she hadn't seen Josephine all day. She sounded worried. And as to Angela, she had not been at Star Court House, she was not expected, and never had been expected. Whatever Angela was doing with her life, whatever lies she had told, Star Court was not responsible for them. Sometimes things go very fast and sometimes they move slowly; as he talked to Maisie, he had the sensation that although the conversation seemed to creep, getting nowhere, yet things were really moving very fast indeed.

If he was a real detective still, he would go out and do something about it, but as it is, it is time to go home. He signed a few more letters, then collected himself together.

Lysette came through the door with a letter. A letter in a stiff white envelope, the look of which he did not like.

'This came by messenger.'

Since it had come by messenger, he knew it was important. The letter was from the Chairman of the Police Committee summoning him, no other word for it, to an informal meeting of the committee. There would be an agenda.

And a hidden one.

How had he got to this point? It seemed a moment to look back.

He unlocked the bottom drawer in his desk and drew out an envelope from which he took several pages which he had typed himself.

His curriculum vitæ. His CV in common parlance.

Born . . . a post Big Depression baby which made him no baby now . . . Born South London. Exact address not known to him, owing to the wayward habits of his mother, but his birth had been registered by his aunt, for that was the given address. Father was a blank. Not unknown to his aunt, he suspected. Later, his mother's memoirs had provided different and no doubt equally false stories.

'Worked for a bookmaker, dear,' his aunt had said, 'and then in the Docks. Then we think he went to sea.' That was her story, while Mother, in her dubious memoirs, had called his father 'a romantic adventurer who loved and left'.

A disappearing man, at all events.

Coffin ran his eye down the page.

Educated The Roan Boys' School. No university. He had done his National Service, though, without much distinction but with no trouble.

Joined the Metropolitan Police Force and started as a constable in Greenwich, South London. Transferred to the CID.

Part of the investigation team dealing with a nasty series of murders in Greenwich at that time.

Coffin went to the window and looked out. A time to think of with a mixture of pleasure and pain, for it was at this time he had met Stella Pinero. He got promotion: Sergeant, Inspector, was moved to a difficult division. Got shot at once or twice, stabbed once, drugged on another. A bad time, as he remembered when he drank too much and a marriage sank.

A brilliant career with black spots on it. He had made friends and lovers, and made enemies.

It was a jungle out there, he had moved through it, was still walking through it, and someone, a friend turned enemy, a disappointed colleague, a former lover, wanted him down like a caught pigeon.

The name of his enemy and friend would be there stuck in his history; it was up to him to recognize it.

He got a driver to take him home, not trusting himself to drive. He walked in through the arched entrance to the quadrangle. Across the way, he could see Stella's door, and draped across the step, a big bunch of pink and white roses.

Neglected, unloved, delivered but never taken indoors, special roses. His roses.

He resisted a temptation to pick them up and throw the lot into the road. Let Stella find the flowers, whenever, dried out and faded. Sod Stella.

He let himself into his own front door and walked up the stairs.

153

CHAPTER 11

The day goes on

In a state of crisis depression (it's a special mood, deeper than the average depression, fiercer than anxiety, although of its nature it can be transient), you do one of several things: you can take a drink, a strong one, and repeat it indefinitely; you can have a hot shower and forget it; or you can kick the cat.

Tiddles did indeed appear, presenting a broad tabby form, but this option was not open to John Coffin. He considered the whisky, but he had gone that way once before, so he took the shower and played some music. No highbrow, he liked Verdi and was in the mood for *Nabucco*.

The music travelled in to the shower, rising over the top of the splashing water and drove right into his mind. That was what music was all about: an entrance, an opening up.

Sometimes it opened up more than you cared for. On his way home he had heard music and voices from the Theatre Workshop, now used for rehearsals. Still thinking of Stella, he had walked across and stood at the back as a full rehearsal, choir, orchestra, and soloists, of the last part of the extracts from *The Ring* was taking part. The music rose above him and tore into him, pain and pleasure all at once.

He knew the plot of this part of *The Ring*: Wotan, King of the Old Gods, had imprisoned his Valkyrie-daughter, Brunnhilde, inside a ring of fire, from which she was rescued by Siegfried's kiss. Later, through the machinations of Gunther, Siegfried betrays her. He is killed and Valhalla and the Gods go up in flames.

Love, betrayal, death, all organized by a malicious intelligence with greed the motive. Love does not prevail, evil does. That was how Wagner saw the world.

There was more hope in Verdi; now he reached out a hand and turned the volume up. The Israelites were just

154

sitting down by the Euphrates and raising their voices in vibrant threnody.

Coffin liked that chorus to be played loudly, very loudly. Tiddles, sitting outside, withdrew, his ears flicking.

Coffin emerged, wet, clean, and if not relaxed, at least in a marginally better mood. His mind was working.

Outside, all the police machines were operating. The pathologist, as Coffin knew from past experience, would not have finished with the body of Amy Dean, but would have handed over various organs for examination by his assistants. (Jim Dean knew this too and possibly this was what was causing him such anxiety that he was expressing it in rage.) The forensic experts, the crystallographers and those the police nicknamed 'the scrap merchants', would be going over the skin, hair, hands and nails, as well as every item of clothing that Amy had worn. Other scientists would be concentrating on the wood of the casket, and still others examining specimens of the soil and leaf mould in which that casket had been buried.

As well as all this activity, other men would be trudging around the area, talking to possible witnesses, questioning them and taking statements. Very often this process led to other contacts being discovered, who must be questioned in their turn.

There would be men at the bus station again, trying for what they could get. The passengers on that bus would be questioned again. There was still thought to be one more, the one they called Coney, whom they had not flushed out yet. Perhaps never would do. It made a maddening hole which took up valuable time while they tried to fill it.

Careful scientists, methodical detectives, it all took time.

No doubt other interviews were taking place of which he knew nothing. Every so often, Joe Public joined in with mad telephone calls offering information, or sensible telephone calls with something relevant, or just bored people seeking diversion. There had been the usual number in the case of Amy Dean, all of which had to be followed up. People like the librarian to whom he had spoken himself.

155

This was just one call that had got through to him, unusual in itself.

Martin Blackhall's involvement in the Spinnergate robbery complicated things too.

Coffin towelled his hair and admitted to himself that he had a strong desire to interview Martin himself.

Archie Young and Paul Lane would be making notes, reading other people's notes, studying the computer screens. Talking, always talking. Searching out other witnesses, other contacts.

Coffin made a list of crucial sites:

The University of the Second City.

The St Luke's and Fisher Dock Hospital where Victoria Blackhall worked.

Mimsie Marker down at the Spinnergate Tube Station. (He knew from experience that Mimsie was always valuable as an informant.)

The bus station. Yes, that missing passenger worried him.

They were still looking for the wood which had made the casket.

As always, the job was made up of waiting and looking.

Waiting for Our General to confess that she had beaten up and nearly killed Martin Blackhall, and not only because she thought he was attacking the girl in the shop, but because she didn't like men and wanted some of her own back.

Only she wasn't going to confess. They might have to make her.

Waiting for that vital bit of information, as yet unguessed at, which so often brought an investigation success.

Waiting . . . a hard game to play.

Coming out of the shower, he knew all these things. He also knew that Josephine was important, and that he should not have left the matter undealt with. Time mattered.

And all the while, the fear. The fear that what had happened so far was nothing to what might be going to happen.

This was an irrational fear, founded on nothing that he

156

could point a finger at, or tell Lane or Young. Lane for one dealt in logic and hard evidence, not intuition.

He dressed in the silk pyjamas and dressing-gown from Charvet that his sister had given him for Christmas because she wanted something out of him and thought they would be a bribe. In the kitchen he looked about for food. Mrs Fergus, at present on holiday, had arranged for her sister to do some cooking for him. The sister was kind but unpredictable, she moved his possessions around according to rules of her own. Hid things, he thought crossly. She was a good and tasty cook but you had to accept what she offered, no choice about it. Tonight she had prepared an evening meal for him to put in the oven.

She too was a vegetarian; he could have anything he wanted for supper provided it was made of vegetable matter.

Tonight it was one of her cheese and potato concoctions. With possibly a touch of basil. She was great on basil which she grew for him in his kitchen. He was probably the only policeman in the Second City with a pot of basil in his kitchen.

Coffin put the casserole in the oven, gave Tiddles some more food (Tiddles was allowed even by his cook to be a meat-eater), and went back to his sitting-room to telephone Star Court House.

'Maisie?' He had promoted himself to calling her Maisie, nor did she seem to object. 'Is Josephine there yet?'

'I don't know what you mean by yet . . . I never said she'd be here at all. She doesn't live here, you know.'

Pretty well, he thought. Also thinking that if Maisie Rolt was so irritated, then she was probably worried.

'No, I haven't seen her.'

'Give me her address, then.'

Maisie Rolt hesitated; life had so instructed her that she was wary of passing on any woman's current address to any man. Like Brunnhilde, she would have slept in a ring of fire if she could.

'Well, I don't know . . .'

'I can get it from Stella Pinero.'

157

'A man like you always knows how to get an address, just pick up the right telephone.'

'I'm not an enemy, Maisie,' he said.

'Sorry.' Her voice was weary. 'It's been a rotten day. Betsy Coleridge has gone. He came round with a car and took her home. She just went. I tried to persuade her . . . Give it a day, I said. But she went. He'll kill her one day.'

'I'll do what I can, keep a lookout,' he promised.

'Yes. Thanks. Well, Jo lives at George Eliot House. It's that big block behind the swimming pool on the Irene Iddesleigh Road. You'll see her number by the lift, which doesn't work, so don't try.' She hesitated again. 'I hope she'll be herself.'

'And what might she not be herself on?' he inquired, ungrammatically but pointedly. Drugs? Drink?

'Not sure. What she could get locally . . . She sometimes is, when she's not here,' said Maisie, not very coherently but perfectly to be understood. She didn't like Jo taking drugs but she did when the mood was on her and couldn't be stopped. Her mood had been bad lately.

'Does Rosa get it for her?'

'Rosa? No, that's not her style. All for clean living and tough muscles is Rosa. You don't get those on drugs. No, Rosa gets whacky when Jo does drugs. She might take the odd cigarette, but that's it.'

'Is she likely to be with Josephine now?'

'No, Rosa was in a mood after Betsy went off. We won't see her for a bit . . . Rosa can look after herself but I wouldn't like you to bother Jo.'

He could tell by Maisie Rolt's voice that she was not happy. 'I won't make a fuss. I only want to talk to her.'

'I suppose I mustn't ask? No.'

I have a whiff of death in my nose, thought Coffin, as he put the telephone down and it won't go away.

The death of Amy Dean occupied more and more of his thoughts. His mind went back continually to the huge collection of material that had built up in the weeks since her death. Paul Lane and Archie Young were in control, but he felt they were at a dead end.

158

By the time he got back to the kitchen, the potato and cheese casserole was burned black. He shovelled it into the waste bin, then put the dish to soak. He made himself a cheese sandwich instead. He wasn't hungry now.

He slumped in his big chair by the window, stroking Tiddles who lay across his chest, purring noisily. Tiddles was asleep first. It was a long while indeed since Tiddles, who had watched a murder in his youth, had worried about life.

In his sleep, Coffin found himself dreaming about Rosa Maundy, silent and tough in her black leather gear. She wheeled her bike at him, with no smile on her face.

Our General had called a meeting of her closest lieutenants; two of them, Commander A and Commander B. Under each was deployed a section of her supporters whose number varied with the strength of her gang. Numbers had been falling lately, not that this worried her greatly, although she liked a good turnout. Numbers did rise and fall.

What Rosa liked best of all was the whole outfit lined up on their bikes in the yard of her father's firm. Then she would walk down the lines inspecting the troops. She was generous with spares and petrol from her father's supplies, and if he protested, then she hit him. He had hit her in her youth, now it was her turn.

'It's not Betsy Coleridge I'm worried about. Maisie thinks it is, but it isn't, nothing to be done about her, she's a lost cause, you can just tell, one day he'll break her skull and that'll be it.' It might be that it would be given to Rosa to then break his skull, sometimes she had such dreams, but she would have to wait and see. It might also be that she, Rosa Maundy, would live out her life in peaceful respectability; that also had to be considered.

'So?' said Commander A whose turn it was to speak.

'It's Josie. We've got to save her.'

'Is she in danger?'

'No, it's inside her.'

'What do you want us to do, General?' Commander B's

turn. 'The A team are out there waiting to go on a run, and B are almost ready.' She glanced out of the window to the yard where bikes were already throbbing away. It was the joy of their life to race around the streets in formation, alarming motorists and pedestrians alike, and annoying the police patrols.

'I want you to come with me.'

'Both of us?' A glance passed between A, who was nick-named Dutchy, and B, who was called Jill, because it was not usual for Our General to call upon them both at once. She believed in splitting the command, there was no unity except in her. Dutchy had known Our General all her life, Jill for about a year; neither of them felt they truly knew her.

'Yes. A, dismiss your squad, no action tonight. We'll tour the Burlington Estate tomorrow. B, tell your squad to finish cleaning up and then dismiss. Burlingham tomorrow. Rendezvous here.' The Burlingham Estate, northwards of Spinnergate had been reported as having a gang in embryo. Our General meant to find and if possible crush any future rivals. But that could wait.

'Right.' They jumped to their feet and saluted. They enjoyed saluting.

The friendship between Rosa and Josephine was not one that her cohorts understood, any more than they understood what drove Our General, but they accepted it and were swept along by her energies.

What they appreciated without putting it into conscious thought was the order she imposed on their lives. They enjoyed the uniforms, the smartness, the glitter of their machines as they all lined up. The regimentation carried a thrill with it that was better than sex. Some of the girls had boyfriends, others had girlfriends, but sex was not impor-tant; being part of Our General's team was.

They were all of high manual skills but with no book-learning interests at all. Most were wage-earners in reason-ably good jobs, because gang life was not cheap, and one and all kept quiet when at home about life with Our General. The majority lived in the family home and were neat and tidy about the house.

The average age was under twenty, Our General herself was the eldest by a few years. Most of the girls knew in their depths that they could not go on with the gang as they grew older. But this was for now. The future was nothing, they might never get there.

One irritated member of the Second City Force had complained that they were as alike as two pins and there was a lot of truth in this. Identity did not count.

The three of them mounted their bikes and wheeled off, three abreast, then dropping into a file, one behind the other. Our General rode in the middle: the position of power.

Outside George Eliot House they slowed to a stop. It was a large block, pale in colour and marked with dark runnels where the rain had dripped down. A hopeful artist had painted an abstract mural in dark blue. Graffiti workers had pencilled their lewd comments.

Rosa looked up to the floor where Josephine lived and where there were lighted windows. But Josephine's window was dark.

'Doesn't look as though she's home,' said Dutchy, a girl who made up her mind quickly.

'I'm going up,' said Rosa.

The lift worked for once, although it smelt of vomit and urine as usual, but Rosa did not make her usual sharp comment about the muck. She hurried along the covered pathway.

Josephine's neighbour had the TV on loud behind curtained windows. Josephine's windows were uncurtained yet there seemed to be a flickering light within the rooms.

Rosa rang the bell. No response came, she tried again, then used her fist to bang. 'Josie, are you in?'

Still no answer. The nextdoor neighbour came to the door. She was a short, stout, curious-eyed woman. 'Think she's out. Haven't seen her all day.'

'Told you no one was there,' said Dutchy.

161

Jill had her face against the window. 'There's a light at the back,' she said.

Rosa looked for herself. Then she lifted the letter-box to stare through it.

'I say, is that—' began Phil, her voice excited.

'Shut up,' said Rosa. 'I'm going in.' She lifted her gauntleted hand, made a fist and drove it through the glass of the door.

A half-circle of fire surrounded Josephine where she lay in her bath. Reflected in the looking-glass on the wall and the white tiles about the bath, the circle completed itself. Josephine had her eyes closed. Like Brunnhilde, she seemed to sleep, ready to wake.

John Coffin and the cat were both roused by the doorbell ringing. Coffin woke up with a start and the impression that the bell had been ringing for some time. It gave one last despairing peal and then fell silent.

He stumbled down the stairs behind the cat, and opened the door.

It was Stella on the doorstep, with her arms full of roses.

'Just found them. I was out,' she said huskily. 'Can I come in?'

'Yes, please do.'

They both knew there was no need to say anything more. He held the door open wider and Stella came in.

CHAPTER 12

On the same day

Josephine lay in her bath which was still fragrant with verbena bath salts. Her head was resting on a rolled-up towel, her hair, freed from the turban of scarves which hid it, flowed over her shoulders and into the water. She was quite grey. But she had masked herself with a plastic bag

162

so that her features were obscured. Now she was naked you could see that she had put on weight but was still shapely. Her toenails were trimmed and shaped but unpainted, as were the nails on her hands.

She had arranged a crescent of rolled-up newspaper and bits of burnable rubbish about her bath and put a match to them. They had been slow to burn but were well away and the carpet had caught fire and there was a smell of smouldering wool and wood by the time Our General arrived. As the girls burst in, the draught caught the fire which sprang up with eager life. Suddenly it was everywhere, darting around the bathroom and then out towards the living-room.

Inside her circle of fire, Josephine lay in the still warm water as if asleep, but the water was a thin red.

She had cut her wrists in the classic style of suicide and let the blood drain out of her veins. From the bottles found beside her, she had also taken a sleeping tablet and some whisky.

The fire had taken hold, and was already too much for the three young women to put out. Rosa telephoned the fire brigade and the police in that order.

The fire engines arrived first, speedily and in number, because standing orders laid down that a fire in a block of flats like the George Eliot should always be a treated as a potential major conflagration. The police patrol car came hard after, followed very quickly by a CID sergeant and the police surgeon. 'Suspicious circumstances', was the word.

Rosa did not cry, tears came painfully to that iron heart, but she sat slumped against the walkway wall, waiting. The other two, with the street wisdom of their kind, had melted away. Rosa too would have disappeared, but she knew the neighbour had seen her face. In any case, she felt an obligation to Josephine.

Rosa was so used to being aggressive and positive that she hardly recognized misery when she felt it, but she was aware of a tight, cold feeling in her diaphragm, something physical and painful.

163

'It was you sent the alarm out, young lady?' asked the chief fireman. He did not know Our General, he was new to the district.

Rosa stood up, and gave a brief assent.

'Hello, Rosa,' said the CID sergeant, who certainly did know her. 'Didn't expect to see you. Friend of the deceased, were you?'

'Yes,' said Rosa. Her expression said: And what's that to you?

'Looks as though she killed herself. Do you know of any reason?'

'No reason,' said Rosa.

'Was she depressed? Spoke of suicide, of ending it all?'

'Is there a note?' asked Rosa.

'There may be,' said the sergeant. 'Haven't found it yet.'

'She didn't say anything to me,' said Rosa.

He gave her a long, sceptical look. 'I don't think you're telling me all you know. What made you come here this evening?'

'I wanted to see her.'

'Hang around, Rosa, I shall want to talk to you.' He turned away to where the police surgeon was preparing to leave.

'What are you doing?'

'Just looking, gotta do that, you know it, Rosa.'

'Mind her things,' said Rosa sharply.

He swung round. 'What's it to you, Miss Maundy?'

'I'm her executor.'

'Really? That's interesting. Shouldn't have thought she had much to leave.'

A first quick survey had shown him that Josephine had only a few clothes, which hung in a sad row in the wall cupboard, their flutters and feathers looking limp without Josephine inside them. Certainly he had seen no jewellery, and the furniture wasn't much, either. Not a well-stocked kitchen: some bread, a few tins of soup, coffee and tea, with a pot of organic peanut butter and vegetarian cheese in the refrigerator. He doubted if she ate at home much, probably always down at Star Court House, he had learnt that much about her. All the signs of someone who lived close to the bone.

'I'm her literary executor,' said Rosa again. 'So watch it.'

'Literary executor? Now what does that mean?'

'It means I have control of all her papers,' said Rosa.

'Now that does interest me,' said the sergeant. 'It does indeed. As I said, stay put. We'll talk about this later.'

Me and my big mouth, muttered Rosa to herself. Why couldn't I keep quiet?

'I'm not promising,' she called after him. But she knew she would stay and accompany Josephine's body as far as she could, riding behind the ambulance on her bike if she had to, as if she was following a funeral bier. You deserve it, Jo, she thought.

The sergeant took himself back, intending, when the SOCO and the photographers should have completed their business, to conduct an industrious search for Josephine's papers. His reasoning was simple: if Rosa was after them, then they must be important. He wanted to be the first to know.

But there were no papers: Josephine had kept not a scrap. She had pencils and pens but she had no letters, no diaries, no scribbled little messages to herself. Nothing.

CHAPTER 13

That same night

The roses were sweet and reconciliation after a breach even sweeter. Neither of them spoke of what had passed, for the moment it was buried. Both of them knew that this was not the wisest way to go on, some issues should not be buried. Coffin was ashamed of the violence that he had felt welling up inside him, while Stella was ashamed of having noticed it and of finding a black hole in a man whom she admired and loved. Loved perhaps more than he loved her: that was another fact she did not wish to face. She had sat in on a rehearsal of the Wagner last night, caught up Brunnhilde's passion of betrayal, and thought how well Wagner understood it.

The murder motif. You heard it in music, you felt it in life.

It's bloody loving, she thought, hardly worth it but you can't stop yourself.

But tonight they were happy cowards.

The roses revived in water, and Stella said she would take them home with her when she left. 'I'll stay to breakfast,' she said, flicking an eyelash at him. 'Because we ought to start taking ourselves seriously.' Her hands were busy with the flowers in the sink.

'I suppose I could start with apologizing.'

She swung round and put a wet hand over his mouth. 'Not now, no apologies now.'

'Well, one apology I will give: Miss Pinero, I've been a surly beggar, bad-tempered, rough to you and not willing to admit it. Forgive me, Stella.'

'Of course I've always known you hate to admit you're in the wrong,' said Stella. 'It's part of you. I've accepted that, ages ago.'

'Women really are nicer than men.'

'Of course.' She took off her shoes, curled up on his sofa, and made herself comfortable. 'And to prove it I am going to tell you what a much more attractive man you are now than when I first knew you. You've matured well, you know.'

'Thanks.' He didn't know whether to kiss her or to hit her. Both impulses welled up inside him.

'Oh, come on, don't be cross. When I first knew you, well, you didn't know how to dress, you could be awkward in company, you had no idea how to decorate a room.' She looked around her. 'But now . . . this room is lovely. And you did it by yourself.'

'I was young, Stella, that's what you're saying. And so were you. Do you want me to tell you how you were?'

166

'You might as well.' She settled herself against a cushion. 'Hit me with it.'

'You were over-ambitious, occasionally strident, sometimes a liar, and not nearly as good an actress as you thought you were.'

Stella nodded. 'I guess that's about right.'

'And you were lovely to look at, marvellous to make love to, a virgin longer than you ever admitted . . .'

'Well, that's true.'

'And I adored you.'

Stella gave a small secret smile. 'I was pretty bowled over by you, but too cunning to admit it.'

'Why did we quarrel all those times?' Bitterly and as it had seemed at the time irretrievably.

'I did the quarrelling,' said Stella.

'Not quite true, not always, but why?'

'Because I didn't want to depend on you. I wanted to be myself. I knew that you could swallow me up.'

'I didn't know . . . It would have been unconscious.'

'Of course. The worst way.'

'Do you know, underneath, I think I felt the same. I feared you. Still do, I think. You're very powerful, Stella, in all the ways you don't know about.' All the secret hidden ways she could control him, push him to anger, to love. The way she smelt, the way she moved, the deeper tones in her voice when she used them. Her jokes, her very bad jokes, and her good ones too. All part of it.

They were being very aggressive with each other and it wasn't hurting. No, not quite true, Coffin thought, it hurt, but it didn't seem to matter.

'Then there were the middle years when our paths crossed occasionally. We even stayed together for a bit . . . You were whiney then. Self-pity.' Now she was telling him.

'I was miserable.'

'So you said.'

'And you were too sharp, too overtly ambitious, shouting.'

'I was going through a bad patch, the work wasn't coming in.'

It was a war, blows were being exchanged, but they were not bleeding. It was a just war.

'You know, you are my hold on normality . . . It's very destructive, the work I do. Tears you apart if you let it, makes you hard if you don't.'

'You're not hard.'

'In a way, Stella . . . I hide a lot from you. But you keep in touch with the gentle things.' He stroked her cheek. 'You know that old line: "Grow old along with me, the best is yet to be"? It isn't true, of course.'

'Never believed it for a minute,' she said lightly.

I must be careful, Coffin thought, not push. Later on, she'll hear about the inquiry and think that I wanted our relationship tidied up for that reason. That would be fatal.

'Be worth a try?'

Stella hesitated. 'I'm never one to rush into things,' she said.

He looked into her eyes and saw that she had heard, and did know, God knew how, but what he couldn't read there was how she judged him.

He felt himself go white. The blood seemed to drain away from his heart and deposit itself somewhere else, his feet probably, they felt heavy and his hands hot.

He heard himself say: 'There's something I haven't been telling you.'

She nodded. 'Wasn't there always?'

For a moment there was silence. Then the telephone rang in the quiet room.

With a sigh, Coffin picked it up, he listened, not saying very much. 'Right, thank you for the message.'

Stella looked at him. 'Work?'

'Yes,' he said. 'A big fire in a warehouse on the Arrow Centre in Swinehouse.' This was the new industrial complex, just completed, but Swinehouse had never been an easy area to police and was getting nastier by the day.

'That's bad?'

'Bad enough. Looks like arson and three dead bodies inside,' he said briefly.

Stella was relieved. 'Nothing to do with . . .'

168

'No, nothing to do with Amy Dean.' Probably nastier. He did not inform her what had been done to the three corpses before they had died, but it was a case they would solve. Gangland killings usually came with name tags. Nor did he tell her that it was not on account of the three dead men he had been informed, he wouldn't have been bothered for that, the usual morning brief would do, but because there was gang violence in the streets around the Arrow Centre and one policeman had already been hurt.

Before he could come back to her, the phone rang again. Coffin hesitated.

'Answer it,' Stella said.

He moved to the end of the room with the portable telephone; some instinct told him to get further from Stella. 'Hello? Mrs Rolt?'

Stella listened. His part seemed to consist of saying Yes and No.

'What was all that about?' she said when he had finished.

'I'm not sure. Ostensibly to tell me she had had a phone call from Angela to say she was staying with friends and was all right . . . But yesterday she claimed to neither know nor care about Angela.'

'I distrust that phrase "all right",' said Stella. 'It nearly always means the opposite.'

'You could be on the ball there.' He sounded troubled. 'So?'

'Earlier, she claimed to have no interest in Angela. I think what she was really trying to pass were anxieties and fears that she couldn't find a name for. Or didn't want to. She's worried.'

'Who is she most likely to worry about?'

'God knows. You tell me. All the inhabitants of Star Court House, Rosa Maundy, Angela, Josephine, herself.'

'I don't think she worries about herself. Not from what Josephine has said.'

'All right: Josephine, then. She worries about her. What do you know about Josephine?'

'Anything I know, you are right there with me.'

'What does that mean?'

169

'It means I've told you all I know. I have no secrets.'

'I don't believe that.'

Stella was silent, studying her hands. 'I must get a manicure.'

'Stella?'

'All I know is that when Josephine was at her very lowest, drugs, drink, living in obscurity and poverty, there was a tragedy in her life.'

'Is that all you know?'

Stella nodded.

'Who knows more?'

'Yes, I thought you'd ask that. If you really want to know about Josie, then you had better talk to Maisie Rolt. If Josie has talked to anyone, then it will be Maisie.'

He considered what she had said, watching her face which could express so much, while covering up so much more. 'I think you do know more, or you guess or have heard it, but don't want to say.'

'Why ask, then?'

'Because I must, because it may be part of this murder investigation.'

'Do you know where you are going?'

Coffin hesitated. 'In the case, you mean? Or in life?'

Stella laughed. 'That says something about your mood. I wasn't asking a philosophical question. I meant, do you have any idea about the killer?'

He picked up her hand, studying it carefully. 'Yes, you do need a manicure . . . Try a darker colour red, your hands can stand it.'

'Thank you.' She knew he was right, but she withdrew her hand.

'And about your question . . . I suppose, yes, I do know where I'm going. The answer is: on the way. So now, what about a bit of confidence from you in return? About Josephine.'

'The story is that in that dark time in Josie's life when she was really at the bottom, there was some violent episode, a death, that Josie was involved in. A girl died.'

'It will be in the records.' Why hadn't someone dug this

170

up? A little whip of anger moved inside him . . . He tried to push it back in case it touched Stella.

'Yes, I'm sure. But Josie was probably using her own real name. It would just have been an obscure episode somewhere.'

She did know a little bit more, but it didn't seem fair to Josephine to tell. And after all, he was a policeman: he would find out.

The telephone call and the conversation did not break their mood, a half-smile passed between them.

Coffin felt at ease: we really have turned a corner. He took her hand and pulled her up from the chair. 'Come on. I want you.'

In the night, the moon shone on his face and woke him. Stella was lying across one corner of the bed, pink and flushed in sleep. She looked young. Where the moonlight touched her hair, it looked so soft and pretty.

He drew the blanket over her and tucked it round her. Gently. He felt gentle. Other feelings might burn inside him, but for Stella it must be gentleness.

He went to the window and looked out. To the west was the area of the university, the centre of so much of the investigation about Amy Dean. I must speak to those two students, he told himself, remembering the call from the librarian, or see that someone does. Like to do it myself.

South of it lay the hospital: the Blackhall boy had left the hospital but the victim of the robbery still lay there. Her recovery looked good, though. You could take a breath of relief there.

A car ride away from the hospital was Star Court House.

Beyond his horizon was the Essex woodland where Amy Dean's body had been found.

A procession of characters marched across his mind. Sir Thomas and his wife, James Dean, Rosa Maundy, Josephine, the strange girl, Angela. The flying Valkyries.

And there was the burning city at the end of *The Ring*. But this city, his Second City, must not burn, if he could prevent it. Yet he knew how thin was the dividing line between peace and violence. Not since Queen Victoria had

171

feared the Chartist mobs had there been such a real chance of civil disorder on a grand scale. He knew that somewhere in that city, as well as the fire of which he knew, there would have been several robberies, a clutch of car thefts, domestic violence, marital rape, and the usual variety of beatings and stabbings without which a night in the Second City could not pass. Even Christmas night was celebrated so. Only on the night of the Great Wind, when the hurricane had swept across a London more used to subtler bad weather, had there been little crime and virtually no violence. He couldn't answer for the other City of London, but that was how it had been in his Second City. The world out there was violent and virtuous, sad and sweet at the same time. Full of oddities like Our General, who might be a very good person, a saint of the pavements, or a very evil person, only time would tell how she would turn out. What she did or what her life forced her to do would shape her. She wasn't the only one. Thousands like her.

He got himself a drink and sat by the window. Tiddles leapt on his lap and demanded to be stroked. Coffin obliged, tracing the spine down Tiddles's back with a gentle finger. Tiddles looked up trustfully, eyes shining in the half light. Good old Tiddles, easily made happy, he thought. At that moment, he did not regard himself highly. The innocence of his youth had turned into something a little more shabby.

As a lad, he had never been sure if sex was something shining and splendid, or sordid and hasty, or a bit of a joke. It wasn't one that he had been able to laugh at very often, which was a shame, because he might have been the better for it. He ran his mind over it all: relationships before his marriage, then his marriage and his wife's death, their child's death (pain and guilt there for him to bear for ever), some brief relationships afterwards, and through it all, Stella. The only, truly important love. With her there was happiness. He might be content in making her content.

Then he laughed. Anyone less peaceful and content than his vibrant Stella who would never give up a battle was not to be imagined.

He finished his drink, then went down the winding stair-

172

case to let out Tiddles whose day began early, before dawn, ready for those early rising mice and other eatable wanderers.

There was a piece of paper pushed under his front door. It was folded over to make a kind of envelope and addressed to him.

Handwritten with a pale blue ballpoint on cheap but unlined paper. Probably not letter paper at all, but torn off a block of rough jotting paper. He made all these observations automatically. It said:

You let Josie down. We'll get you for that.

Short and sweet. Unsigned.

It smelt of smoke. He lifted it to his nose. Yes, smoke. Not cigarette smoke or pipe smoke, the smell of which you can pick up easily if you have the nose for it, but the scent of burning wood. Other stuff too, maybe, but fire somewhere there.

He closed the door carefully behind Tiddles. He found he was trembling with anger.

This was happening far too often: this angry reaction to stress or any threat. He forced himself to walk up the stairs slowly. He placed himself carefully in his chair; he must separate himself from Stella until he was calmer.

He closed his eyes and willed himself to sleep. I won't let myself think of what might be my violence. Let it go.

Yet the subject would not lie down. As they parted in the morning, Coffin said: 'Stella . . . if I ever hit you, really hurt you, violently, what would you do?'

'I don't know. I'd like to think that I would walk away and never see you again. However much you said you were sorry and it would never happen again. But I might not.'

'Yes, I would say I was sorry.'

'I might not be brave enough to go. It does require courage to admit someone you have loved is terrible.' She saw Coffin flinch. 'I would probably find it easier to blame myself. To think that somehow or the other it was my fault. Accept the guilt.'

173

'I don't like the sound of that.'

'Does it matter to you so much?'

'Yes, it does. It matters.'

Stella collected her belongings. 'I have to go: I have an important interview and the manicurist first.'

They did not kiss, but he saw her down the staircase to the door. She went out and Tiddles came in.

Up the staircase, the telephone started to ring.

His day had begun.

CHAPTER 14

Coffin's day continues

The news about Josephine was arrowed at Coffin from all quarters. It certainly felt like a weapon with a sharp point on it. He was pierced. Maisie Rolt was the first, hers was the telephone call which had started his day. Then Stella, alerted by Maisie, rang him from the Tube station on her way to London.

And then an item about Josephine appeared on the usual index of overnight crimes and major incidents that was always waiting for his attention when he got to his office. Fiona had it planted on his desk. As an unimportant incident. To her mind, the big dockland fire was the main item. Josephine earned just a few lines: her name, the nature of her death, and her address.

But come to think of it, his first intimation had been contained in the anonymous note pushed through his door.

Because he had failed to make contact with Josephine as she had asked, because he felt that he had indeed let her down in life, Coffin knew he had to interest himself in her death.

Not much information there, he thought, as he studied the few bleak sentences on his schedule of the night's events. Josephine jostled for attention with the major fire and a botched raid on a local bank and the attempted kidnapping of the bank's manager and his family.

Stella had had more to tell.

'Maisie says Josephine has killed herself,' she had announced over the telephone, her voice almost drowned by the sound of voices and the roar of the double escalators at the Spinnergate Tube station.

'She didn't tell me that, she was crying, I think.'

'I expect she blamed herself.'

I blame myself, thought Coffin. I ought to have done more, pushed myself that inch further on. Josephine needed an audience and it ought to have been me. 'Any idea of why she did it?' he asked Stella.

'No, she had no idea. I suppose Jo may have had worries we knew nothing about . . . illness, money. Just depression. She had been depressed. Can you find out?'

'Do what I can.' If there was a rational motive. People like Josephine, with her life, sometimes just killed themselves, as if they were unable to bear the weight of their history any longer. And he didn't blame them. You could drag only so much of your past around with you before you wanted to cut yourself away.

Just once or twice, he had felt like that himself. He surprised himself by admitting it.

And no, Maisie Rolt did not blame herself. She blamed him, and that was why she telephoned. So he could feel the blame. She might not know herself that was why she'd done it, but: 'The toad beneath the harrow knows . . .' He was the toad.

They didn't like men down at Star Court House.

As Fiona adjusted the papers in front of him with that assertive way of hers (it was Fiona's spell of duty) he knew what she thought the important news of the day: the attempted kidnapping. It was the sort of news she enjoyed. She would never comment, she was too professional, but he could see it in her eyes. Fiona's face was more revealing than she knew, it was Lysette who had the real poker face. The death of a woman in a council flat was not important.

Josephine was not important.

175

'It hasn't anything to do with the death of the girl, has it?' Stella had asked.

'No, I don't think so.'

'It may have worried her.'

'You can't tell,' he said in a neutral voice. 'She may have left a letter.'

But he judged that Josephine's death was one of those sad coincidences, of no significance to any larger scheme of things.

'Look, I must go. Find out what you can, will you?'

'I will.'

Stella was still there, he could hear the voices of other commuters, a child calling out, the sound of feet passing. 'Don't let it get to you. Not your fault . . . I can tell from your voice how you feel. You have a very expressive voice. Know that?'

Violence, one way and another, could come between them. Casual violence, professional violence, suicidal violence. 'Don't worry, Stella.'

She needed reassuring too. 'Last night was good, wasn't it?'

'Yes. You know it. Bless you, Stella.' He wondered what it would be like to have an orthodox, straightforward married life. If there was such a thing. But he wasn't that sort of man, and neither was Stella that sort of woman. They had both tried it with other partners and it hadn't worked. Their lives had changed and shaped them out of true. Anyway, he could not ask her now with this inquiry hanging over him, which she would get to hear of and conclude that was why he had asked her to marry him.

Perhaps it would have been.

He had to clear his own soul first. He had never used that word of himself before. To have it come up now was interesting. Policemen did have souls to save, but they were hard to uncover.

'I love you, Stella,' he said. But she had gone, the line was dead, and his words floated out to the empty air.

Fiona was standing waiting for orders and his personal assistant, a plain clothes inspector, Andrew Fletcher, seconded to his office from his normal duties, was at work at a table across the room. The position was a new one, Andrew Fletcher had only been on the job a few months, they were just getting to know each other, but Coffin had observed that between Andrew and Fiona there was a steady quiet rivalry and jockeying for position. It was not going to make his life any easier.

He handed Fiona a tape of notes and replies to letters to type. 'Here you are. Not too much there, but let me have them back by lunch-time. Oh, and ring up Mr Chambers's office and settle an appointment for me to meet him. You have my diary?' And if my meeting with the Chairman of the Police Committee goes badly, then you might not have to worry about me for much longer.

He saw Andrew give him a quick look. So he knew too, and was probably wondering where it left him. Doesn't do to get touched by a falling star. Failure rubs off.

I'll give you something else to think about, my lad, Coffin thought. He studied the Information List which sometimes seemed to him to have a resemblance to the Court Circular. 'Have you got anything new on the suspected suicide and arson in George Eliot House?'

'Nothing you won't have, sir.'

'Who's handling it?'

Andrew Fletcher drew a supplementary paper from a file. 'It's in Spinnergate North Division. The CID Inspector there is Charley Bates, but he's away sick at the moment so it will be his deputy, Amesbury. Ted Amesbury.'

Yes, he knew the man. Or anyway, remembered his face. Plumpish, with merry blue eyes.

'It's a good unit down there,' he said absently. And of course they could always ask for assistance from the Serious Crime Group, headed by Paul Lane, which he had set up at his headquarters, but Paul had plenty going on there, what with the Dean investigation and the new big arson inquiry starting up. 'I want you to find out at what stage they are and what they've got so far.'

'Certainly.' Andrew rose to his feet briskly. Coffin got down to the work on his desk. Even as he attended to the business of the day, a dream was forming inside his head. He would resign from his position, let someone else carry on what he had started (and he had created well), and he and Stella would marry, or not marry according to how they felt, but they would move out of London. To the country perhaps, find a house near enough to London for Stella to work on the stage and do TV work, while he would cultivate his garden. No, he hated gardening. But there would be Tiddles and Bob, so a garden there must be. But he might take a degree from the Open University.

But definitely he would not write his memoirs (although he had had some newsworthy cases), he had had enough trying to edit the life-history of his itinerant mother. For all his early life he had thought of himself as an orphan soul, with no blood relations left in the world. Then, suddenly, life had presented him with a half-sister, Letty Bingham, and a half-brother in Edinburgh, a Writer to the Signet, no less.

He loved Letty, a beautiful and clever woman, brother William he cared for a little less (distinctly less, if he was honest); both of them were richer than he was. There would be some money for him and Stella. Letty, now divorced again and embarked on a career of feminist independence (how like she was to their mother, after all), had offered to employ him in her theatre. But that had been a joke.

Too old to go on the stage, but he could collect the tickets at the door. He started to laugh.

Fiona put her head round the door. 'Mr Chambers is away until the weekend. So I have settled for Monday of next week. In his office, but he'd like to meet you for a drink first. At the Rackets Club.'

Nearly a week before execution day, then. And the condemned man will be given a strong whisky first.

He nodded at Fiona. 'Accepted.'

As she withdrew, Andrew Fletcher reappeared. He was breathless as if he had been hurrying.

'No need to run,' said Coffin mildly.

'Thought you wanted to know.'

'So I do. So?'

178

'The first SOCO examination and photographs completed.'

'Nothing else?'

'The Fire Service wanted to carry out certain checks to see if the floor was safe. Also to confirm arson. Although it sounds as if it must have been a deliberate fire.'

'And the body?'

'Taken away to the police mortuary for the usual, sir.'

Coffin nodded. 'Ask Ted Amesbury to meet me there.'

'Now, sir?'

'Now.'

He passed Fiona on his way out, enjoying the faint air of disapproval on her face. He felt like someone escaping. But even as he walked by her desk he noticed Fiona's eyes give a quick flick at the inner door. He had observed her taking an interest in Andrew. He also knew her nickname: Fickle Fiona, only the word used when he was not around was not fickle.

She might or might not get anywhere with Andrew, but now was a chance. Take your time, Fiona, I shall be gone some time. And cheer up, I might soon be gone for ever.

The air outside was cool and fresh, it had rained in the night, and the streets of his Second City smelt fresher than usual. But it was no time for walking.

Nor for driving himself. He sat behind the hunched back of his official driver, wearing his own official face. Ted Amesbury would expect to be treated with due formality, and in any case, by now all systems would have been alerted to what he was doing. He was not an anonymous man.

As they drove through the streets he realized what pain it would give him to leave this city in someone else's hands. It was his place. He hadn't created it: many centuries and many hands, from Bronze Age immigrants through to the Roman, Saxon and Norman invaders, had done that, setting up wharves and docks to be inherited by their descendants. He had taken over their territory and their law. He was just one in a long line. But he valued it.

He knew already that the fire in the shopping complex had been dealt with; that the attempted kidnapping linked

179

with the robbery of a local bank was nearly wound up—
the kidnappers had been caught; but he also knew that at
any moment the car radio might inform him of another
crisis. They had a royal visit coming up (unless Sir Thomas
had asked for a postponement because of his own crisis)
and that usually provoked some action somewhere.

But it was a quiet ride, the driver the silent sort. Coffin
had never been to George Eliot House before but the driver
knew the address and the sight of the uniformed constable
standing on the third floor walkway told him where he had
to go. It was not a very tall block, and there were lifts,
which sometimes worked, but it was more pleasant if you
walked up the stairs. They smelt slightly fresher. Amesbury
was there before him. A woman poked her head out of a
door three places away, but the doors on either side of
where Josephine had lived were quiet.

'We had to move the neighbours on either side out,' said
Amesbury, 'just in case, but the fire didn't spread. Both
families will be back this morning. May be a bit smoky but
nothing else.'

Inside Josephine's flat, the windows of the sitting-room
had been broken by the firemen, the room was damp and
smelt of burning. The furniture, what there was of it, had
been pushed to one side.

Coffin stood in the middle of the room.

'The worst damage is in the bathroom,' said Amesbury.
'That's where it started.'

Coffin nodded. 'I'll have a look in there.' He was moving
round the room. 'What's the judgement on the fire? They've
finished, have they?'

'Yes, it's all ours now. The Fire Service people say it's
certainly arson. Looks as though she started it herself.
That's what they think and they usually get it right.'

The room did not yield much information to Coffin. As
a case goes on, a detective has to think himself into other
minds. In his life, Coffin had been inside many skins, he
had been a swindler, a rapist, a murderer, several times
over. He had tried them all on for size, noted where they
fitted and where they pinched. It was disconcerting to find

180

how the skin of the most depraved fitted you at some points.

But you need a little material to get the imagination going. Josephine had not left him a lot. A few sticks of furniture, no books, no papers, no photographs. A ballpoint pen on the table to show that she could write but no evidence that she ever had. Even the pen might have been left behind by someone else.

'Not much to see here.'

'I don't think she had much. It was the way she lived. But even so, it looks as though she cleared things out before she died.'

'How do you know?'

'One neighbour reports seeing her carry bags of something down to the waste bin the day she died.' Before Coffin could say anything, Amesbury went on: 'Of course we've checked, but the bins were emptied that day and already on the way to the tip.'

Coffin understood the implication: if this had been a major murder inquiry, then the bins would have been traced; for a routine, straightforward investigation to an unimportant, if nasty, suicide case it wasn't worth it. A dirty business which might bring no returns.

'I think it might be an idea to see what can be salvaged at the tip,' he said. 'You never know.'

'I'll get someone down there.'

Coffin knew what Amesbury really wanted to say: What are you doing down here? Why are you bothering about this unimportant case?

He walked to the bathroom door and looked inside. 'Some interesting aspects though,' he said, answering the question that had not been asked. 'The fire, for instance.'

'It happens. Suicides do funny things.'

'No note?'

Amesbury shook his head. 'Not as far as we've discovered. She may have said something. We shall be asking her friends and neighbours.'

'So what would be the motive for killing herself?'

'I think she was at the end of her tether . . . There's hardly any food here, she didn't have much of anything.

181

Nowhere to go, sir. That's often when people take this way out.'

And they do it without warning, Coffin knew this as well as anyone.

The fire had burned fiercely in the bathroom, the lavatory pan and the handbasin were cracked with heat and smoky brown. The bath itself was less touched. The floor looked dangerous.

'We photographed everything before we let the Fire Squad have their turn,' said Amesbury, on the defensive.

Josephine was gone, but the bath was still half full of bloody water. Pinkish, rather than deep red. Coffin studied it.

'Cut her wrists, did she?'

'Yes. But she did more than that. She took some whisky, and put her head in a plastic bag. She may have taken sleeping tablets, we're waiting for the PM to see about that.'

Coffin withdrew silently into the living-room.

'Have you got the photographs?'

'I'll send a set round, sir.'

The room was chill and very damp. Probably someone else would try to make a home here when it had all been repaired and repainted. Would someone tell them what happened here? Of course they would. Stories like that were always handed on. It might not even be the first death here. George Eliot House was ten years old, Josephine was unlikely to have been the first tenant.

'I know some of her friends,' he said, half to himself, 'I knew her. Slightly.'

'Thought you might have done, sir,' said Amesbury, who was beginning to sweat. Somehow, although the room was cold, he felt hot. There was unacknowledged tension here.

'Nasty business.' Coffin handed out the platitude to stop himself thinking. The presence of Josephine was strong in this room.

'The damage could have been worse, a lot worse, the Maundy girl got here before the water was cold in the bath.' He knew all about Rosa, all the police units did; he did not like her, but regretfully he had to decide she had done

182

nothing but good here. Also, she had been crying, which surprised him.

'Oh, she was here?' This was the first intimation Coffin had had of the presence of Rosa Maundy.

'Yes, with one of her girls.'

'How did she get in?'

'Broke in. Close to the dead woman, apparently. Says she's her executor, whatever that means. Not what it usually means, I shouldn't think.'

'Did she say why she came?'

'I don't think it was just a social call. She said she was worried about Miss Josephine—that's what she was always called round here. Her real name was Day. Peggy Day. Miss. She wasn't married.' But everyone was allowed to change their name if they wanted.

'You got on to that fast,' said Coffin approvingly.

'No secret about it, that's how she appears on the list of Council tenants. And the DHSS confirm it.'

'Yes. Still, you got it.'

'They don't know anything more about her. She wasn't in debt. Her rent was paid up to date. But she didn't have much money, her handbag survived the fire, just a few pounds in it.'

Once again, Coffin wondered what Josephine had lived on.

'No pension book, not yet of age,' said Amesbury, confirming that he too had wondered. 'I think it might have been money worries. I got her NHS number and located her GP. Haven't seen him yet, though.'

'I think you've done a lot in a very short time.'

Amesbury looked pleased and suddenly felt a whole lot cooler.

'Let me have the photographs and Rosa Maundy's statement, will you?'

'Fastest, sir,' said Amesbury. He escorted Coffin to his car with relief, and, now it was over, with a good feeling that he had made contact with the Chief Commander, not let himself down and made a good score. Life was not all bad, after all.

Before he got into the car, Coffin paused and looked up at the windows on the top floor of George Eliot House. Several faces were now staring down at him, his visit had not gone unrecorded.

'What did she burn? How did she start the fire?'

'Rolled-up newspapers. And a bit of paraffin.'

'Well, it's one way to start a fire. You could always use firelighters, of course.'

'She had it planned, sir, must have had.'

Coffin nodded. He was driven off as Amesbury watched, and was thoughtful.

From the upstairs windows came a shout: 'Bloody murderers.' Something soft and squashy came down, missing the Chief Commander's car which had gathered speed away but landing on Amesbury's left shoe. He lifted his foot and shook it like an angry cat, he felt like raising his fist and swearing, but revolutions have been started that way and he was not about to start one now.

The police were not popular in George Eliot House.

The photographs and Rosa's statement arrived on Coffin's desk before the end of the morning. He was on his own, Andrew and Fiona had both taken an early lunch. Together?

He spread the pictures of the flat out on his desk. The one to which his eyes were drawn pictured the body in the bath. It was in colour. How long had police photographs been in colour? Certainly not when he had been one of the youngest and newest Scene of Crime Officers in South London.

Josephine was lying back in the bath, her arms limp in the pinkish water, her features looking filmy and indistinct behind the plastic bag as if the process of decomposition had already started. She was a chrysalis, getting ready to turn into something else.

He read the statement that Rosa Maundy had made. She had said little, long practised in not giving anything away to the police. She had wanted to call on Josephine, she had seen the light of the fire, and had found her friend. Yes,

184

Josephine was her friend. She was proud to be her friend and her literary executor.

He supposed that it was the literary executor, or one of her girls, who had put the note through his door.

He put the papers aside and dialled the number of Stella's hairdresser. He knew the place, having collected her there once or twice. He might just catch her.

He could hear voices from the salon and the music that was always flooding through the rooms. It sounded gentle and Italian today, which was unusual.

He could visualize the telephone being carried past the washbasins and up to the table where Stella would be unobtrusively studying what was being done to her hair, while pretending to read a magazine. Or she might be having her nails manicured. A darker, brighter red perhaps?

'Hello?' Stella sounded alarmed. 'What is it? You never ring me here?'

'I wanted to tell you that I took a look at George Eliot House myself. The first judgement is that it was suicide. Josephine did kill herself. It looks a very deliberate, planned affair. I don't think I could have stopped her. She may just have wanted to see me to tell me what she planned to do.'

'You would have tried to stop her,' said Stella swiftly.

'Yes, of course. And perhaps she did want to be persuaded to live . . . that's something I shall have to live with.'

'Was it—' Stella hesitated—'an easy death?'

Coffin chose his words, the picture still vivid in his mind: the face in the caul, the naked body slumped in the discoloured water. 'I don't think she suffered.'

He could hear her saying something to another person, then she came back to him. 'Sorry, I was talking to my stylist . . . he was cutting too much, my neck can't stand it, you see.'

'Stella, have you any idea why Josephine did it?' In spite of what he had said to Stella, there was a sense of self-mutilation about the death, almost of punishment.

Again Stella hesitated. 'There must have been many times in Josephine's life when it could have happened.'

185

'Yes, you're probably right.' And some event, possibly trivial, just tilted her spirit so that this was the day.

'So sad,' Stella's gentle voice carried across to him her grief. 'She was a lovely woman. But there was a blackness in her, one knew that. The work at Star Court House can't have helped, nor the murder.'

Yes, an accident of life, he thought. Sad for Josephine. She had collided with a horrible event and she had cracked. She had got caught up in the tragedy of Amy Dean which had nothing to do with her and it had killed her. 'I'll see you tonight, Stella. That is, I'd like to. Can we?'

She muttered something soft, but it sounded like a yes, and was certainly affectionate.

He would tell her tonight what hung over him.

No lunch. He worked on. Andrew and Fiona reappeared, not together, a tactful interval between their arrivals. He felt like shaking his head at both of them, but he contented himself with giving Fiona the look she well understood. He knew he ought to speak to her about the way she went on, but a man who lived in a glass house . . . There you were. Perhaps he should resign before he was pushed.

He considered telephoning Maisie Rolt but decided to leave it until the evening when he and Stella could do it together. She probably knew already all that she ought to know and maybe some more that she would be happier without. Our General had been there in the room, had seen it, and would pass it on. In the end, someone would tell Stella too, but it wasn't going to be him. I can be a coward too, he told himself. And for some reason that satisfied him.

The afternoon had passed, Fiona murmured her good-byes (it would be Lysette tomorrow), and Andrew had departed soon after.

He looked in his diary at the entry next week for the crucial interview. It seemed to innocuous: just the time and the name and the place.

A breath of air was what he needed. He went to the window to open it. Across the inner court, he saw a group of five: Beenie, Mick, Archie Young, one of his sergeants, and a WDC he did not recognize.

Josephine's death had pushed other matters to the edge of his mind. Temporarily, only temporarily.

There was something about Archie Young's back and the way he was walking that expressed anger. The experience that angered the Chief Inspector most was not getting answers when he wanted them.

Coffin drew back into his room. Rebecca and Michael were not being cooperative. Whatever they had been overheard to say in the library, they were not yet willing to talk about it.

From Archie Young's gait, and the head-up, I-will-not-be-beaten attitude of both young people, he could guess how the conversation had gone.

Students enjoyed obstructing the police and talking about civil liberties. But he thought he could trust Archie Young to get what he wanted. It might take time, not today, perhaps not tomorrow, but he would get there.

But you had to wonder what those two were hanging on to that was so sensitive.

There was only one piece of information that could be so hard to handle: they knew who had killed Amy. Or thought they knew.

But they claimed that they had loved Amy. Then why not speak? Who was so important in their lives that they would keep silent.

Martin Blackhall?

His father? Yes, certainly, a very powerful figure in their world.

He sat there, considering. They would come across with whatever they knew in the end, he had a lot of confidence in Archie Young. Or he might move in himself. They might trust him.

He switched back to his own interview with them. Angela's name had figured. That girl, he'd almost forgotten her. But she was there all right, embedded in the case like a fly in amber. In the amber the fly was dead. Angela very much alive.

187

The pile of work did not seem to have become much less in spite of the day's labours; he put his back into work (and so, to do them justice, did Andrew, Fiona, and Lysette), but fresh material always piled in. There was too much to attend to in too little time; pay, working conditions, the relation between his police authority and the central government, new British and European legislation on a multitude of matters. Everything landed up on his desk.

Would he mind so much, giving up?

He tidied things up, because Lysette who would be on tomorrow liked a tidy desk, locked his drawers and made ready to move. WALKER was going home.

He had got his overcoat on when the telephone rang. He looked at it, considering: the call had come through on his private line. Very few people had that number.

'Stella told me this number,' said Maisie Rolt. Her voice was husky. 'I didn't want to speak to a secretary.'

Coffin waited.

'I've heard now how Josephine died. Worse than I thought.' Maisie's voice was sad; death was a visitor in her own house, but she was not going out to meet it.

He answered it the best way he knew. 'I don't think she suffered.'

'But before, when she made it all ready . . . What must have been in her mind then?'

'Yes, that's always the hard part to take.' He was wondering what she wanted. Not just sympathy.

'I've been questioned.'

Getting there, he thought.

'One of your men, nice young man called Amesbury. He thought I might have had a note from Josephine, a suicide note. I hadn't, of course. He had a look round, perhaps there was a note somewhere . . . There wasn't anything. Or not much. A case of clothes, but he didn't bother with that. Josephine had a locker here and there was a diary in it, I doubt if there's much in it, I think it was a Christmas present and she never used it, but he asked to take it away. I said yes, but Rosa—'

Ah, here it comes.

188

'She was there?'

'Came in. She refused to let your man have it. Said she was Josephine's literary executor . . . Bit of a scene.'

'Where is Rosa now?'

'She's here.' Possibly within earshot.

'Did you know about this?'

'No, no idea.'

'But you're not surprised? You don't sound surprised.'

'Not at the way Rosa reacted, she'd always gone for Josephine and they have been very close lately. As if they shared something.' So Rosa was not listening.

Coffin thought about it. 'And Josephine? How was she?'

'Off the record?'

'Off the record.'

'She had been in a very strange state for some time.'

'And you think Rosa knows?'

Maisie chose her words carefully. 'I think whatever it was that troubled Josephine, Rosa probably knows and may be part of. I don't understand what being literary executor to Josephine in the context of Josephine's life can signify, but it seems to mean a lot to Rosa.'

'Well, thanks for telling me.' A question had to follow, he could feel Maisie waiting for his next move. 'What do you want me to do?'

'What you can to protect Rosa. She may need it. She says the police are after her for something else. They think she was the attacker of Martin Blackhall. They've got a witness.'

Some irony here, he thought, considering how Rosa and Co. felt about him.

'I can't interfere.'

'Stella said . . .' She did not finish the sentence, but she didn't have to: Stella said you could.

Thank you, Stella.

But of course, he did interfere: a silent, accusing procession of Paul Lane, Archie Young, and the hardworking Amesbury (among others) lined up to remind him of this fact. He interfered all the time, always had and probably always would.

Anyway, this case was personal. He had James Dean to thank for that.

'She's loaded with something. And I think it has something to do with Josephine and the girl Amy, but what I don't know. You may get it out of her.' There was a pause. 'I have a lot of time for Rosa. She was abused as a child. Probably by her father, or some older man in the family circle. She hates all men.' Maisie retained her sense of humour. 'You've probably noticed.'

She's going to hate me more, Coffin thought, when I ask some of the questions I am going to ask.

'Keep her there. I'll be round.' He paused. Someone was at the door. 'Wait a minute.' He turned away from the telephone. At his door, Sir Thomas had appeared. After him came two uniformed officers. He looked as though he had battled his way through them and could do so again, if he had to. Coffin turned again to Maisie. 'Don't go away. I'll be there as soon as I can.'

Sir Thomas said: 'I want your help.' His voice said he demanded it. 'Two of my students are here being questioned. I should have been told. I should be here.' He was pale and angry. He would defend his own to the last.

'They aren't juveniles, you know, but yes, I agree that as a courtesy you should have been told.' Not asked to sit in on the interview, however.

'Yes, yes, I was told, but I didn't know they were going to be taken in for questioning.'

Coffin took up his coat. 'I'm going that way, let's see what is happening. I can give it about five minutes.'

The death of Amy Dean was right back with them and top of the list.

Ten impatient minutes later, he was talking to Chief Inspector Archie Young. 'So what did they say?' If they had said anything, by the look on the Chief Inspector's face, he had not got far. Beenie and Mick looked flushed, harassed and unhappy. Young gave them a baleful look.

'They have said that Amy was under the influence of someone older.'

190

'Who?'

'We're stuck there.' He shrugged. 'But Star Court House comes into it.'

'Ah. So you think they are lying? Or is that all they know?'

'They are being what I might call oblique. Giving us something at an angle.'

Mick said: 'We've both of us told all we can. Amy had someone. That's all either of us knows.' Mick, usually such an ebullient lad, looked at Coffin with the expression in his eyes that he had seen in Bob's, dog's eyes saying: I've done all I can, it's up to you. Help me.

Coffin was careful to give nothing back in return. 'Let's leave it there for a moment, even if you've got nothing.' Something or nothing?

'No, it's not nothing. And I'll get it from them. I shall have to let them go for now, Sir Thomas is with them, but I'll be back for more of the same.'

Coffin believed him. Star Court House had a meaning in the context of this case, but as yet he could not tell what. Perhaps Maisie Rolt and Our General could enlighten him.

Star Court House in the rain, grey and damp, did not look welcoming, but it was home to the women and children who needed it. Someone had been tidying the garden and a big clump of yellow chrysanthemums had been tied up to a stake, where they looked uneasy as if the hands that had tethered them were new to the job.

He rang the doorbell twice before the door was opened by Maisie Rolt. She looked tired and thin, as if the disease she had been resisting for so long was suddenly gaining on her.

'Sorry to be slow. I was on the telephone.'

The hall was warm and quiet. Coffin had half expected to be greeted by the child he had met before. No sound of voices or noises either.

'Very quiet,' he said.

Maisie gave a half smile. 'We're a bit empty just now. It happens sometimes.'

191

'What's become of the boy I saw last time?'

'Teddy, was that? No, it must have been Darren.'

'Could have been. His mother seemed to act a kind of watchdog.' She had watched him, certainly.

'Oh, they've moved on. We've been able to find her a place to live. A kind of halfway house, you know, a safe house where she can stay for a bit until she gets something more permanent.'

'Where's Rosa?'

'In my sitting-room. She's been helping me in the garden, good therapy although she's not got what you could call green fingers . . . It's along here.' Maisie led the way down the corridor, then up a short staircase. For the first time, he noticed that she was moving awkwardly as if in pain. 'Here we are.'

He had not been to her sitting-room before and it was a mark of how far he was getting into the secrets of Star Court that he should see it now.

'You could do with a lift,' he said.

Maisie gave a hoot of laughter. 'Do with a lot of things. A new leg for me wouldn't come amiss.' She pushed open a door. 'Here we are.'

Her room was small, overheated and full of furniture. Rosa was standing by the window as if she was preparing to jump out of it.

'Here we are, Rosa,' said Maisie. 'I told you he'd come.'

The announcement did not seem welcome.

'I didn't want to see you. It was Maisie's idea. I'm only doing it to please her.'

'Come on now, Rosa,' said Maisie. 'You're doing it for yourself. You don't want to go to prison.'

'I'll manage.'

'I can always leave,' said Coffin obligingly, although in fact he would have been loath to leave this sight of Rosa rampant.

'I won't go to prison, get off with a fine. Might even get a medal. Commendation for bravery, that's what you pigs get, isn't it? I thought I was saving her, I didn't know he

192

was the dear, innocent prince who was defending her. That's my defence, and that's what I shall say.'

'You nearly killed him,' said Coffin.

A small smile flicked across Rosa's mouth before she returned to being stonefaced. 'So what?'

Coffin turned to Maisie Rolt. 'I don't know what I'm doing here. I'm afraid Miss Maundy doesn't like me very much.'

'Too right,' said Rosa.

'Shut up, Rosa,' said Maisie in an equable, matter-of-fact voice, no anger towards any one, and perhaps not much emotion either. 'In spite of what she says, Rosa did agree to meet you and does wish to speak to you.'

'Only for Josephine's sake,' said Rosa fiercely. 'Not that you did her much good. Dead, isn't she? You ought to be satisfied with that.'

Coffin was silent. Got me there, he thought.

'Josephine left a diary. It's a notebook, anyroad. You lot want it. I want it. I want it. I own it. I'm her literary executor.'

'At the moment, it counts as evidence.'

'I have to protect Josie, no one else will.' She was swelling with emotion like a toad. 'Maisie said you'd help.'

Coffin blinked. 'But you didn't believe it? What's in the diary?' Nothing much, Amesbury had said.

'It's not the diary—' began Rosa. 'She didn't put much in that, not the sort to pour her heart out—' Then she stopped, and flushed.

'So what?'

'Josie trusted me ... I am her literary executor, no papers should be looked at or touched except by me. And I don't give permission.'

Coffin looked interested. 'Did she have some papers to leave?'

'Is it that box?' said Maisie. 'The one in my safe? The one you gave me, Rosa? It's wrapped up and perfectly all right, you should have asked.'

Coffin said: 'I'd like to see this box.'

In a fury, Rosa turned upon Maisie. 'Damn you!'

Coffin, looking in Maisie Rolt's eyes, saw that she had known all along about the box and had always meant him to see it. She had not long to go and meant to preserve that truth.

CHAPTER 15

Towards the end of that day

Maisie Rolt's safe was in the wall of her sitting-room behind a picture. It's protective powers were symbolic rather than real, Coffin decided as he looked at the ancient structure.

'I don't keep much in it,' said Maisie. She reached inside and removed what she wanted. 'Here you are.'

She had attached a label. Jo's PROPERTY HELD FOR SAFE-KEEPING. 'I put that on to make sure. You never know, I might not be here.'

Josephine's parcel was wrapped in brown paper fastened with string. Underneath was a further wrapping of tissue paper.

Coffin undid it slowly, watched by Rosa, protective and fierce at the same time. She ran her fingers through her dark brown hair which she wore in a square bob. It was the most feminine gesture Coffin had seen her make, but he observed that her hands, although short and powerful, were well kept, the nails trim and clean. Rosa had her vanities, then.

She took the box from him. 'Let me, this is my job.' She hung on to it for a moment. 'I'm not sure if Josie would have wanted this.'

For a moment Rosa did nothing. As patiently as he could manage, Coffin said: 'Unless Josie made a will naming you as her literary executor, then it means nothing. Even then, the will would have to be proved. Is there such a will?' He looked at Maisie, who shrugged.

'Josie said it to me,' said Rosa. 'Gave me charge of her papers. Verbal contract, that means something.'

194

'It's got to be opened. Come on, open it.'

Rosa unpeeled the tissue paper which was yellowed and brittle as if years had passed since Josephine had wrapped up the box.

Inside was a tin, the sort of tin that biscuits are packed in to keep them crisp. The edges were sealed down with sticky tape.

Rosa looked at Coffin, her eyes doubtful. 'It's private.'

'Open it.'

Rosa peeled away the last of the wrappings. She still hesitated.

'Now the lid,' said Coffin.

Inside several pages of newspaper were folded. A stuffy dry smell floated out. Coffin took the box to the table by the window. With careful fingers he took out the newspapers and laid them on the table. They were as brown and friable as autumn leaves.

Underneath the dried-out pages were the flattened remains of a moth, wings tight about its body. A pinpoint head could just be made out. Coffin left it where it lay. The shape of its body was marked on the underside of the bottom piece of newsprint, and oddly, it looked stronger and darker than the moth itself. In its way it was a certification of the years that had passed.

He found there were pages from three different newspapers. Two local, the *Easthythe News*, and the *North Thames Times*, and one London evening newspaper: the old *Star*. None of them existed any longer.

Josephine, or whoever had collected the newspapers, had cut round one story, nipping through advertisements for cough cures and headache remedies and double glazing for windows.

THE BODY OF A GIRL DISCOVERED IN WOOD-LAND. This was the Easthythe paper. The other local paper had gone for a grimmer headline: STRANGLED BODY FOUND IN LOCAL LOVERS' WOOD.

The London paper had simply said: BODY IN THE WOOD.

But in each case it was the same story. A girl's body had

195

been found in the woods, named in the two local papers as Pickerskill Wood.

He heard Maisie draw in a sharp breath as she leaned over to read. Rosa said nothing, but stared down at the table, her lips moving as she read.

Not that there was much to read. Not one of the newspapers had much to report. The body of a young girl had been found lying in Pickerskill Wood. It had been there some time before being discovered by a couple. Lightly covered with leaves, there had been no real attempt to hide the body. She had been strangled. But before her death she had been roughly treated, for there were bruises on her arms and face. Some bruises were old, some new.

The newspapers were all dated within the same week in May, 1970.

Moth and girl had been dead for over twenty years.

'Do you know anything about this?' he asked Rosa.

She shook her head. 'No, not me. 1970? I couldn't read then.'

'What about you, Maisie? Heard of it? And of any connection with Josephine?'

'I knew there had been a tragedy in Josephine's life,' said Maisie reluctantly. 'It was part of the myth about her: that something terrible had happened.'

'Myth?'

'I suppose I mean I never quite believed it,' said Maisie reluctantly. 'I thought Josie liked to cloak herself in a bit of drama.' She studied the newspaper cuttings but without touching them. 'What this girl meant to her, I don't know.'

Daughter, niece, cousin, neighbour? Coffin asked himself. But he could find out. The case would have left some records somewhere.

'Have these papers been packed up all that time?' Maisie asked Coffin.

'Some years, but not necessarily that long,' he said absently. 'Modern paper yellows quickly . . . Pickerskill Wood?' he said. 'Know where that is?'

There was a long pause before Rosa said: 'I think it's the name of the wood where Amy Dean was found.'

So she knew, Coffin thought, I have made a connection at last. The links are joining up.

'Let's put the newspaper cuttings back in the box,' said Maisie. 'I don't think I want to see them any longer.'

Coffin picked up the tin. 'I shall have to take them away.'

'Josie didn't mean you should see them. No one should have seen,' said Rosa. 'Bloody men. Always poking in where they're not wanted.'

'Be quiet, Rosa,' said Maisie in a weary voice. 'You're in enough trouble as it is. You need all your friends.'

Coffin picked up the papers. A white sheet fluttered from the folds of the *Easthythe Times*. He picked it up.

'A letter?' asked Maisie.

Coffin read it. 'Not exactly.' He held it out for her to read.

Three lines of poetry, handwritten in pale ink, ran across the middle of the page.

Regions of sorrow, desolate shades, where peace
And rest can never dwell, hope never comes
That comes to all: but torment without end.

'It's a quotation. Might be from Milton, sounds like Milton,' said Maisie.

'If you say so.'

'But what does it mean?'

Coffin said slowly: 'It reads to me like a confession of guilt.' He looked at Rosa, whose face was set and grim.

'I'm not saying anything.' The words came out like hard pebbles dropped in a pool. 'I'm not saying anything.' Her mouth shut tight.

You might have been a pretty girl once, Coffin found himself thinking, but something inside you reached out and twisted your features. We make our own face, Rosa, and you made yours hard.

He got home at last to his dark, empty tower rooms. Even Tiddles was absent. It would be good to have a proper home. You get what you really want, and perhaps this was the first time he had felt a strong, true need of a settled home.

He was his mother's son, after all. She had been a wanderer and a mystery and he saw now that he had been essentially rootless and was a mystery to himself.

CHAPTER 16

The next day

In the morning, he pushed a note through Stella's door, a formal invitation to dinner that evening. No telephoning at the last minute, no dropping in at Max's Deli, this was going to be a big evening. He would be delivering a statement, no not a statement exactly, he would be both telling and asking. A declaration perhaps?

But at the end of the handwritten note, he added, because she had to know: *Josephine left a box of mysteries. Ask Maisie Rolt.*

She'll hate me for putting it like that, but last night's disclosure was a kind of confidence.

'Tell you more when we meet,' he muttered as he popped the letter in at her door. She was home, probably bathing, he could smell the strong scent of the rose geranium and jasmine essence she used floating through the letter-box. Tiddles and Bob were there with her. He could hear a snuffling which was must be Bob, and Tiddles's presence could be deduced from his absence anywhere else.

Six days now to the interview which would be so crucial.

What was private as yet from Stella was not private from Paul Lane and Archie Young to whom the documents had already been delivered. By hand, by the Chief Commander himself, late last night. He had already spoken to them both on the telephone before sealing the note to Stella.

There was no meeting, but a quadruple-link telephone call was set up. Faxes were also busy flipping reports and

198

messages on to various desks. Four different police units were now involved in what was a multiple investigation.

The Met group investigating Amy Dean's car had handed over its reports and was more or less out of the picture. 'Reports meagre,' was what Chief Superintendent Paul Lane had summed up. Traces of the girl, James Dean and Martin Blackhall were all found. The car itself was sealed, covered and under lock and key. But the general feeling was that there was nothing more to be gained from it.

At this point, Paul Lane pointed out that an examination of Martin's hands had confirmed that the scratches were likely to have been made as he climbed out of the river. It was not clear how he came to be in the river, but it was likely he was drunk when he fell in. He had been seen drinking in the riverside pub called the Waterman.

The mainstream investigation into Amy's death was still the centre of everything, but it had now drawn into it the death of the woman called Josephine who had built a ring of fire about herself like Brunnhilde.

The earlier discovery of a dead girl in Pickerskill Wood brought in a new element. Coincidence?

Or had the killer known of the first discovery and used the place because of some curious kicks of his own?

Or was the killer of the first girl also the killer of Amy?

Chief Superintendent Paul Lane was for coincidence. 'And I don't believe we will ever discover who killed Amy Dean.' He was not one of those who soon became on familiar terms with the victim, he liked to keep his distance.

'Or who buried her?' queried Coffin sharply.

'Or who buried her. The case will stay on the files.' They wouldn't give up just yet, he meant, but slowly activity would quieten down. 'I think you are wrong in reading too much into the newspaper cuttings. Of course we'll go into it. The old North Thames Division, it would have been then. That was before we were reorganized.' He still resented that reorganization, even though he personally had profited from it with an accelerated promotion. (But

199

deserved, he told himself.) 'Probably discover that they got the killer and put him away.'

'And he might now be out and killing again,' said Coffin.

'If we know his name, then we'll know where to go and get him. But I'm betting on no connection between the cases. Nothing in the poetry, sir, not to my mind.' Lane was experienced and sharp, his instincts finely honed by years of murder cases which usually ran to a pattern. He was mostly right and sometimes wrong. He passed over the wrong times in his mind.

CI Archie Young took an opposing view. Unlike Paul Lane, he was responsive to poetry and could feel the force of the lines from *Paradise Lost*, he had even read it. 'There is something in it, I think, sir. Could be. Those lines do tell of guilt. And handing the box over like that when she knew she was going to die. I think that does constitute a confession.'

He was speaking from the Incident Room set up to deal with Amy Dean's death and perhaps was the more influenced by that. It was how they felt in that room, a consensus which he had learnt to trust. 'I believe in the papers found in the box belonging to the woman Josephine.' He made her name sound like a disease, he had met and feared her; women like Josephine menaced men like Archie. 'I believe they show interest and knowledge. She collected those papers and preserved them for some reason.'

He felt he was being listened to, and with respect. 'And her death, sir, yes, that's definitely a message.'

His wife was an educated woman, and although he didn't think she would ever kill herself, if she did he could imagine her setting up a suicide scene in that way. Some women would.

Archie Young, having got his voice into the telephoning queue, was having his say. 'And then it's confirmed by what the students said. They connect the death of Amy Dean with Star Court House. They didn't put it directly like that but it was in their mind.' It was in his, anyway, 'And that brings us back to the woman Josephine. She's in there somewhere.'

200

'But no evidence,' said Paul Lane.

'We'll get it. When you know where to look, then you get evidence.' He spoke with conviction, he felt able to open his mind freely because he could not see the faces of his superiors.

All this time, Ted Amesbury had been silent, outgunned by the ranks of those in this conversation. The fact that he could not see their faces was no help to him, since of the three he knew only John Coffin by sight. Rather the reverse in fact, since judging by their voices the Chief Superintendent was a tartar and Chief Inspector Young was too sharp by half. His not to argue with men such as these.

But he had to make his point. 'We haven't got the PM results on Miss Day,' he said. No more. He knew better than to overdo it.

'Get me all the newspaper reports from two local newspapers. I presume they were microfilmed before they closed down?'

Archie Young agreed. 'In the archives, but they may not have much.'

'And of course, all that is on the police files. Where are they now?'

Lane and Young consulted. 'In the Met's Central Collection. Should be.'

'Get them.'

The material was on his desk by evening. He had to go down to the basement of the building where he worked to read the microfilms. She had not won a lot of space, this dead girl. At first she was not named, and all he read was a description of the finding of the body.

Two young people had driven to the spot, their names were not revealed either, and parked their car. The headlights had outlined a foot, then a shape covered with leaves. They had got out to look, and then telephoned the police. An investigation had been started, but the affair was sparsely reported, fuelling Coffin's suspicions that no great interest had been taken. The big story at the time was the disappearance of a local lawyer with a great deal of money

201

that was not his own. He had been traced to Spain. His photograph was prominent, Coffin studied it with interest, but he had never seen the face.

Never would now, he discovered as he moved the film on: the absconding solicitor had died of a heart attack before he could be arrested.

The microfilm was hard to read, so that he had to concentrate. The next few weeks had produced only one small paragraph in one of the papers (the other had apparently lost interest entirely), but this paragraph identified the girl as Noreen Day, aged eighteen.

He leaned back: the probability seemed strong that this was Josephine's child. Noreen could have been a sister, niece or cousin, but Coffin did not take this seriously. Nor did he admit coincidence. Josephine had treasured (or at any rate, had kept) the newspaper cuttings, the connection had to be close. Very close.

He walked across to the dispenser in the corner to get a beaker of coffee which he drank while he stretched his legs. He could hear voices in the corridor outside, but no one disturbed him.

His eyes soon picked up the short account of the inquest. The girl had been strangled, there were recent bruises on her body. Her mother had identified her. Josephine?

A few bleak extra sentences said the girl's mother had been detained and questioned by the police but then released.

Coffin wound the microfilm machine on but there was no more to come. The case seemed to have ended there. The police records would have vital information on it and he would read them next, but one conclusion seemed inescapable: a strong whiff of suspicion of causing her daughter's death had hung over Josephine.

He hurried back to his room to see what the police records had turned up. Surprisingly and disappointingly little. The police team seemed to have taken up the case, come to a brisk conclusion as to the killer but been unable to bring in a proof.

Yes, they had suspected Josephine, but how and why

they had arrived at this conclusion were hardly brought out. It almost seemed as if they had satisfied themselves in private discussion and resolved to leave it there. He sensed that Josephine had been disliked.

Coffin sat back, unsatisfied. The investigation appeared to him to have been hasty and short. A handwritten note was attached to one page. It said: *Miss Day has left the country.*

Taking with her, he had to assume, a box with newspaper cuttings and her private despairing cry of guilt.

Coffin paced round the room. He was restless. One way and another there was a lot of guilt swirling around this affair, his own included.

What did he have here? Was it tin or gold?

He had received, by messenger, a formal acceptance of his invitation from Stella. Did he detect a slight amusement? He did. The messenger was a lad from the St Luke's Theatre Company, dressed for the occasion as a 'thirties' telegram boy and wearing a large smile. He recognized the suit as coming from a successful production of *You Can't Take It With You.* But Stella was playing his game, and would come.

Lysette, her day on, had booked a table at the Dreadnought, the new and vastly expensive Docklands restaurant. It was an occasion to be expensive, money had to be spent and be seen to be spent. They would meet there.

He was early, she was late.

Stella had turned herself out platinum hard and diamond bright. She was playing his game, but using her own rules. He felt scruffy by comparison, dimmed.

Which was probably what she had aimed at.

'That dress . . . ?' He took her wrap, a gauzy shawl, and stood to attention, they were doing it all the right way.

She laughed. 'Not really Lacroix.'

And the scent was new. He kissed her cheek. He might get to kiss her on the lips but he would have to graduate.

'Those earrings?'

'Ah well, I have to admit those are real.' She did not

attempt to explain how she came by them, two carat diamonds in each ear, and his not to ask.

'Are they insured?' He pulled out her chair.

'Don't be so professional.' She seated herself, and looked hopefully at the wine glasses. Two of them, and one for champagne. Good.

He sat down himself and nodded to the waiter who was hovering with a bottle. He asked again what Stella knew of his own special predicament. More than he wished, no doubt. She had her own sources of intelligence.

But a smile in her eyes, and no one could produce such a smile better than Stella, gave him confidence.

'A drink first, then we'll talk.'

'Champagne,' said Stella happily.

'Stella, I want to tell you—'

She stopped him, putting her hand over his on the table. 'No. Let me tell you.' The smile in her eyes was real. 'I know, I know what's been going on, what's hanging over you.'

'Not in detail you can't, because I don't know myself,' said Coffin thoughtfully. 'My sister's property transactions, and the fact that I bought my flat from her. I thought I paid a fair price, but I dare say they could do something with that. I'm said to be dictatorial and at the same time too free with my Force. I do interfere and I hope I'll go on doing so. And then there's you.'

'I'm not anything.'

'You're everything to me.' Hackneyed words but meant. 'I can't bear to think that you should be a part of this.'

Stella drank some wine, sat up straight and said: 'Let me be a clear and definite part, then.' She opened the slim, silver envelope that was her new handbag, and pulled out a diary. 'Now let me see, I have Friday free from rehearsal this week and I could have the weekend as well . . . What about your diary? That way, we would be married before your meeting. You could manage that?'

He drew a breath, he hadn't told her about Josephine's daughter nor the strong suspicion of Josephine's guilt, but he thought she could have told him things. Nor must he wonder what on earth he was doing on Friday, this was no time to hesitate. He let the breath out. 'I don't need a diary.'

She pencilled a note in her diary. 'Good. I'll make the arrangements . . . I've always wanted to propose and be accepted. I take it that was an acceptance? . . . No, don't answer. You might spoil it, you did it beautifully just now.'

She went on: 'In case you were wondering, Tony and I got a divorce over a year ago. No fuss, no publicity. Suited us both that way.'

They looked at each other and began to laugh. 'You get the special licence and I'll arrange for the flowers,' he said.

'Right. Let's start as we mean to go on.'

The restaurant had become crowded, but they had a table by the window from which they could look down on the river. The water moved oily and dark but lights shone from boats in the marina and from the big apartment houses that now lined the river bank. A string of coloured lights stretched along the river's edge so that emerald and ruby flashed and glittered in the water as it moved. A wind was getting up, pointing up waves.

As they drank coffee, he told her what had come up about Josephine. The box, the newspaper cuttings, the dark thoughts.

'But I think you knew this already?'

'Not the details . . . a general idea.'

Coffin sat looking at the water. If you stare too long at the darkness and the moving water, you begin to think dark thoughts. Monsters stir from out of the deep and surface, grinning and grimacing. He turned to Stella, determined to speak out. 'Stella—'

But before he could go on, he was interrupted by the head waiter. 'A telephone call for you, sir. I can bring the telephone to the table.'

'No, I'll come.' He stood up. 'They always know where to find me,' he said apologetically. 'Have to.'

At the desk in the manager's office, all new wood and soft leather, he stood for a moment before picking up the

205

phone. This had been quite a night, quite a day. 'Yes?'

He was not surprised to hear Archie Young's voice, he was always first with the contact if he could manage it. 'I thought you ought to know that we've taken in Rosa Maundy.'

'For the attack on Martin Blackhall?' How far away that seemed now, so many other crises piling in on top.

'No, although that's still there. She's not charged, but we will be questioning her regarding the murder of Amy Dean. The forensics have finally come through with a match on the wood: it came from her father's workshop. And we have a palm print on the coffin. Hers.'

He added: 'She didn't do it alone though, sir.'

So Josie was guilty after all of Amy's death?

He went back to Stella. 'I have to go. I'll put you in a taxi.'

Stella looked thoughtful, but she stood up and assembled herself for departure.

There was a taxi outside and she let herself be put inside it. Coffin held the door, and kissed her gently on the lips. 'Sorry, but that's the way it has to be. Start as we mean to go on, eh Stella?'

CHAPTER 17

The same night

They always knew where he was, everyone always seemed to know where he was. Had to, they said. Must know what WALKER is up to.

He drove fast. He felt as though bells were ringing all around his head, each one striking a different note. It was raining, the raindrops were making a pattern which he observed while he was thinking of Stella. Our marriage might fall apart, and if it does we will both be dished. He wondered what the chances were: equal each way, he thought, but already his thoughts had moved on. Rosa Maundy.

Rain had begun to fall even more heavily, making the roads slippery so that he had to concentrate on his driving. Ahead lay a short but difficult journey. The new Thamesway Tunnel, opened last year by the Prince of Wales, was just beyond the traffic lights. He stopped on the red, glad of the pause. By day this road and the tunnel would be heavy with traffic; tonight it was empty except for the odd taxi and the over-large lorry speeding south to the Channel ports.

There was water sloshing around the entrance to the tunnel, more than there should be, he thought, but as he got further into the tunnel all became bright and shining and white. Wouldn't stay white long, the dirt would settle and the graffiti merchants would arrive, risking mutilation and death to pen their messages.

A car disappeared round a curve in the distance, a motorcyclist drew ahead, otherwise it was a quiet night. He had never known the tunnel so empty.

The cyclist was weaving across his path. Drunk? 'No, damn it, not drunk,' he said aloud. 'Doing it on purpose.'

In the rear mirror he could see the lights of other cyclists, four of them in a line. They too seemed to be performing a kind of dance, now they were coming up close behind him, their headlights at full glare, shining in his mirror and dazzling him.

Then they swung in a line beside him. One, two, three, and the fourth cycle drove in front, joining the other already there.

They edged closer and closer, swaying dangerously towards the car, then curving away again.

They were expert performers on their machines, he had to admit their skill even as he cursed them. They were weaving around him in a dangerous dance. Then they shot ahead in formation: one, then two and two.

Behind him four more cycles had come into view and were streaming forward.

All masked, all black-leather-jacketed, shining and sing-

207

ing. Swift and powerful. Damn them, he thought, the Ride of the Valkyries.

They were swinging closer, then moving away, unpredictable and dangerous, forcing him to concentrate on his driving. He knew what they were trying to do: push him towards the wall of the tunnel.

He slowed down, but they edged closer. Ahead the tunnel curved to the west so that the leading bikes momentarily disappeared. Behind him, no other cars had yet appeared. He wondered why, but he wouldn't have put it past this lot to have blocked the entrance in some way.

He could not decide if the game was just to frighten him or to force a crash.

It could go either way. He knew himself to be a competent, steady driver but not a brilliant one, whereas this troupe handled their machines like circus artists.

One rider had spun her way up on his left-hand side, waved and shot ahead. To avoid her, he swerved slightly to the right, only just avoiding the bike ahead of him on that side. He accelerated away. He could see the exit of the tunnel. The leading riders were there, straddling their bikes, waiting for him.

The bikes travelling with him began to swerve in a curving dance around. This hands were sweating on the wheel, his lips were dry. This was fear, not fear of killing himself (although he would prefer to live and Stella would grieve) but fear of killing one of them. Or even injuring one.

Apart from the death of a human being, his own career would be dead too. He could see the headlines, hear the comments.

He lost concentration for one brief minute, the car skidded in the water and hit the wall of the tunnel, bounced off it and on again and stopped. The windscreen shattered and as he jerked forward against the wheel, he felt a sliver of glass hit his cheek.

The riders sped away. 'Got you,' came the call. 'Got you!'

Happy that he was not dead, relieved that he had not killed

anyone, but with a bloody face, a damaged car, and an irritating interview with the traffic patrol team who had managed to be sympathetic, helpful, passionately interested and yet slightly amused all at the same time, he was ready to meet Rosa Maundy.

He was alive, bloodied and very, very angry. They had 'got' him, just as they had promised, but he had Our General. His anger was transformed into vibrant, crackling energy.

The interview room was full of people. Archie Young had a sergeant with him and a woman detective, both unknown to the Chief Commander. Paul Lane had come in with Coffin himself and there was a uniformed constable in the corner.

'Glad to see you, sir,' said Archie Young. 'That looks nasty. Shouldn't you have a stitch in it?'

'Nothing much,' said Coffin, dabbing his cheek. 'It's stopped bleeding.' It had, more or less. He was happily unaware of a streak of blood down one side of his face.

He had insisted on being breathalysed, determined to leave no loopholes for critics, deeply thankful that Stella had drunk most of the champagne.

Young felt the energy sparking from the Chief Commander and fell silent; it was alarming. He had heard that such cold explosions appeared occasionally with his boss, but in all their years of working together, this was the first time he had seen one close up. Perhaps you had to draw his blood to get one, he reflected.

He looked at Rosa. She didn't seem to know what was moving towards her. The Iceberg Man with Wotan's thunderbolts to hand.

'Hasn't admitted anything,' he murmured to the Chief Commander, 'won't talk.'

Rosa's dogged expression changed slightly as she observed John Coffin's. 'Took a dent' was how Archie Young put it to himself.

'Can I have a cigarette?' she said. Her first spoken words that night.

No one answered.

'Oh, sod you lot,' she said morosely. She had an empty cigarette pack in front of her.

Coffin sat down facing her. 'So you can speak, then, Rosa?' Her lips set, but she gave a grunt. 'There is evidence that the wood making the shell in which Amy Dean was buried came from your father's yard. I think you made it.'

'Prove it,' said Rosa.

'We shall. You will have left traces, Rosa, now we know what to look for.'

She shrugged, she picked up the cigarette pack and smelt it. 'This smells better than you,' she said.

Coffin ignored the comment. 'So if you buried her, then we have to look at the possibility that you killed her.'

'Didn't,' said Rosa. 'I would never kill a girl or a woman, never. Kill myself first.'

Coffin said softly: 'Oddly enough, I believe you, but I have to tell you that in the matter of Amy Dean, the opinion in this room is fifty-fifty. You did bury her, didn't you?'

'Supposing I say yes?'

'Then I shall say: who was with you? You didn't do the burying on your own. Perhaps you didn't do the killing on your own. Was Josephine there? What was her part? Did you initiate it or did she? We know now about the first girl, the very first one of all. Or was she the first? Did Josephine tell you of others?'

Noreen Day, Virginia Scott, Amy Dean, was that the procession? He wrote the names down on a piece of paper, then pushed it towards her. 'Read it.'

Rosa lowered her eyes. She shook her head, and then shook it again, as if his soft voice was cutting into her.

'You won't like prison, Rosa. You don't like being shut up, do you?' Valkyries liked freedom, needed it to survive.

'You're a devil,' said Rosa. 'Rough and mean as the rest of them. Do you beat that woman of yours?'

Coffin sat very still. She knew how to hit hard. Battle had been joined.

The long night went on. Coffin, then Archie Young, then Paul Lane, then Coffin again. Questioning, and questioning again. Sometimes she spoke, sometimes remained quiet.

As the night lightened into morning, Coffin said: 'Get some tea in.'

And then, as the mugs full of dark, hot liquid arrived and she was offered one, she pushed it away and broke. Tears began to roll down her cheeks.

They let her cry for a bit, and then asked their questions. How had it been? Who had done what, and when?

Josephine had come to her, told her there was a girl's body in the woods down by the estuary, and they must bury it. She had made the coffin at Josephine's request, and transported it in one of her father's trucks.

'Did she say she had killed the girl?'

'Didn't say.'

'Did you think she had done?'

'Yes, I did think so. I thought Josephine had killed her. She was a nice girl, a good kid, but Josephine knew something about her that I didn't.'

'Why do you say that?'

'I saw them talking. More than once. They were both angry. Very angry.'

Coffin sat back in his chair, his mood was not triumphant although he had won. A rotten battle, but all war was rotten. Worse, he had used a form of violence against a woman, and he knew it.

He drank some tea. The blood began to trickle from the wound on his face.

CHAPTER 18

Early morning

The three principals, John Coffin, Paul Lane and Archie Young, assembled again very shortly afterwards in the Chief Commander's own room. A tray of breakfast had been brought in and spread out on a table in the window by a silent Lysette. Coffee, soft, squashy, greasy bacon rolls, with buttered toast and marmalade.

211

The mood was a mixture of exhaustion and exhilaration, the buzz feeling that they were at the end of an investigation. It was over, they could start to think about other things. Paul Lane remembered that he had toothache and wondered what reception he would get if he smoked, while Archie Young found himself considering the holiday he had booked in Majorca. He might get there now; for a time it had looked in doubt.

Then, aware of the sombre presence of the Chief Commander who was not saying much, the mood went the other way. But was it the end? And if it was the end, could you call it a satisfactory end?

Still questions to be answered, but some questions were never answered, they all knew that for a fact. At the end of every case there were points left unresolved. Real life is never tidy.

Paul Lane drank a second cup of coffee and said: 'Do we accept that Margaret Josephine Day killed the girl?'

'She seems to have thought she did,' said Coffin thoughtfully.

In a confident voice Archie Lane said, over a mouthful of bacon roll: 'Yes. Kind of a self-confession in the box of papers. A two-time killer . . . A serialist.'

'Of a special kind,' said John Coffin.

'I agree with you there, sir. But even serial killers have their ways.'

Coffin gave him a wary look.

'We need some other evidence,' he said.

The feeling was that they would get it. Coffin would use any modern device and expected his CID to do so with skill, but in the end it came down to old-fashioned basics. Policework was talking, asking questions, using the feet. Writing out a record sheet, getting the details on the card index, collating it all. No substitute for the human perception; computers could only do what someone's intelligence had fed into them. He preferred to use his own brain.

'Things fall into place after a bit,' said Paul Lane, stating his philosophy. 'I'd better be off.' He could have done with a night's sleep, but there was no chance of rest. 'I'm going across to the Incident Room to see what's come in.' Something always had, sometimes initiating action, sometimes leading to a dead end. He hoped Rosa Maundy felt worse than he did.

Coffin went back to St Luke's Mansions, to his own apartment and took a bath. He telephoned Stella but got no response, not even from the answering machine, she had a tiresome trick of not leaving it operational.

He soon found out why: on his own answering machine was a message from her: *Have gone to see Maisie Rolt at Star Court House, great unhappiness there.*

He could imagine the unhappiness, he even sympathized, but he hoped Stella was not going to turn into the guru, the mother goddess of the wronged woman. She had enough to do being a successful actress and running the St Luke's Theatre.

Apart from which, he wanted her in his own life. She was always apt to take up a role and play it, he didn't want her turning into a mother goddess figure. They had enough with Josephine, who had cast herself as Brunnhilde with Rosa's girls as her Valkyries. No, that's your imagination, he told himself, but it was a small move then in his mind to Lydia Tulloch and her production. It was Lydia who had identified Rosa as the attacker of Martin Blackhall. Strange how things ran together, he had seen it before.

Back his thoughts circled to Rosa and Josephine. What a pair. Bad for each other, no doubt about that.

Later, Archie Young called in, standing at the open door, half way in and half way out, with an anxious Lysette hovering behind him.

'Come in or go out,' said Coffin. 'What's it about?'

'Something interesting about Josephine Day. It fits in. You wanted confirmation, you have it.'

'Go on.'

Archie Young said: 'We now have a vital witness. At last we have flushed out a passenger on the bus to Pickerskill Wood who remembers seeing a woman dressed in what he calls "bits and pieces" travelling on the bus. The chap Coney who seemed to have got lost, he's surfaced. What's

213

more, he says he saw her on that journey more than once. He lives out that way, and noticed.'

Coffin said: 'I wish I had known earlier. Why haven't we heard from this passenger before?'

'He was in hospital, emergency operation, says he never saw any newspapers and didn't know about the killing . . . When he went back to travelling on the bus, another passenger told him we'd been around asking questions. That's the why and how. One of those lucky things. And since he went right to the end of the road, he noticed she did. Each time. He never spoke to her and she never spoke to anyone else. Just got off the bus and walked towards the wood.'

'Pickerskill Wood meant something to her.'

'He thought she was a birdwatcher or a naturalist, but knowing what we know it sounds more like a check-up or a pilgrimage.'

Coffin made one of his black jokes. 'Instead, it was where she put her bodies.' He shook his head. 'I don't know. It's hard to make out. And what about the girl, Virginia?'

'If that was one of hers.'

'If one, then all three. That's how I feel about these killings . . . One killer.'

'Well then, there were special circumstances about that killing, something which ruled out Pickerskill Wood . . .'

'She had to get the girls to go there,' said Coffin. 'She had no car, couldn't transport them dead. They walked or went on the bus. The picture is getting stranger every minute. You must agree, Young?'

'A lot of killings are strange when you get down to it,' said Young doggedly.

'And the gap . . . Such a time between killings and then two relatively close together.'

'Two we know about. When we start looking we shall find more.'

'You think so?'

'I do. It's the way with serialists. Look at the Louisiana killer; once caught, he confessed to several others. Also the Morningside murderer, bodies or bits of them found buried all over Scotland when they knew where to look.'

'What about a motive?'

'Do we have to look for a motive for a serial killer?'

'We have to dig out something as a label. Even serial killers give themselves a meaning.'

What name had Josephine herself given it? He wondered what language Josephine used when she named it. It must be no ordinary language. Was there a word for love in it?

Young was muttering something about forensics. *Post hoc ergo propter hoc*, Coffin thought. We shall prove the case after we have decided upon the facts. It was like *Alice in Wonderland*. We can believe anything once we decide to believe.

Still, forensic evidence counted with judge and jury, and was held to represent detached truth, never mind if it was no more than expert opinion.

The rest of his day was consumed with other business, which included a visit to his solicitor for advice on his all-important meeting.

Finally that evening he crawled home, to find a message. *Dinner on me at Max's*. Stella would never cook if she could help it. *I'll be there waiting. Come on when you can.*

He fed Tiddles who seemed back in residence, brushed his hair and washed his hands, and feeling nursery clean walked the few yards to the Delicatessen.

It was crowded, the whole of the Choral Society seemed to have arrived in a large group, but Stella had a table in the window. She stood up when he came in and from that moment on he knew it was going to be a good evening. For him personally and for Stella, unhappiness all around for others, but they were home and safe. At least for the moment and he knew better than to ask for more.

Stella told him how miserable they were at Star Court House over Josephine and over Rosa.

'Rosa will be all right,' he said, without sympathy. 'But about Josephine now, that's different.' He told her the whole story, hardly edited at all. 'She did kill herself,' he said to Stella. 'That means something. And she buried the body, that too means something. She has to be guilty.'

'So it's all tied up and settled?' said Stella.

'Looks like it.'

They walked home together. He wondered why he felt so depressed when everything was going so well with him and Stella.

It was a bad sign.

CHAPTER 19

Another day, another vision

Just for a moment all was suspense and yet the picture held: Josephine had killed, not once, but twice, and possibly more often. John Coffin, Chief Superintendent Paul Lane and Chief Inspector Archie Young were all of this mind. It was how it had happened. Amazing, unpredictable, unlikely, but that was how it must be.

In a little while their critical faculties would revive and they would begin to pick holes in the story as outlined. Then they would fill in the holes with forensic evidence, the words of witnesses as to character, behaviour and movements. If they were lucky, then the picture would set and be varnished, ready to send off to the Crown Prosecutors. Who might, or might not, approve it.

It was hardly a triumph, their handling of this case, and there would certainly be criticisms from Jim Dean and Sir Thomas Blackhall. Rumblings had already reached them. In a way, the file on Amy Dean would never be closed.

Josephine was dead, of course, and not to be prosecuted, but they would get Rosa Maundy for something, and gradually the story would come out, a book would be written about it which would be serialized in a leading Sunday newspaper, and possibly turned into a television programme. A major film seemed unlikely.

But Josephine was certainly a character. Archie Young said to his wife: 'I don't think we will ever know what went on in her life, and as for her mind, how can you fathom a woman like that? I mean, women don't do things like that.' His wife said she didn't know whether to be shocked or pleased that he should separate women off in that manner. Then she added thoughtfully that it had started with Josephine's own child. 'What do you mean by that?' Archie had said sharply. She had answered that she did not know, but it was a point. It struck her as a woman. Young had the uneasy feeling that the first hole to be plugged was appearing. And when you thought about it, it was a worrying point. Perhaps she thought of them all as her daughter?

Science fiction land, he told himself. Stop thinking about it.

Paul Lane accepted the oddness of human behaviour. Long years of investigating what went on had almost deprived him of the ability to be surprised. He could be shocked, as about Josephine he had been, but he was hard put to know precisely what shocked him. Was it what she had done, or how she had died? Or something deeper? But there was an element deeply disturbing about this case. It reflected on the human race. 'Knew it from the beginning,' he told himself. 'Knew it would be a stinker even if I didn't say so. It's a fearsome business.' Like a hideous face staring at you out of the darkness. He was not an imaginative man, so he claimed, but he had the sensation of other faces queuing up behind to be seen in their turn. In spite of himself, his mind, slow-moving but methodical, became engaged with the problem. 'I just don't see it,' he said to himself, 'I just don't see it.'

John Coffin, for once the least imaginative, was the most grieved. He had liked what he had known of Josephine. She had seemed a woman of style. Such a woman was hard to accept as a serial killer.

Meanwhile, other issues pressed upon them all. An armed break-in at a small factory down by Lower Greendock Street involved Archie Young, while the Chief Superintendent was being briefed by a man from the Home Office on the impact of Chinese Triads on the local drug-dealers. Paul Lane kept nodding politely and looking out of the window. Two late nights did not suit him; also the civil servant was a bore. He could have written it all down and not bothered to call; he had written it all down, there was a report on the table and now he was relaying it again. He caught the eye of his uniformed colleague opposite, who was also being briefed, and a silent yawn passed between them.

And John Coffin was gearing himself up for his own crisis.

Stella Pinero had her problems too. She had achieved the miracle of bringing St Luke's Theatre and the related Workshop Theatre under control; she had just appointed a young female assistant which left her free to take on acting roles as she fancied. Money was tight, but they were managing, and she had hung on to the TV part.

And her private life was a pleasure. She smiled as she did her face before going out. This time they would manage and not savage each other emotionally at intervals.

But she was concerned about the Wagner production which was taking up valuable rehearsal rooms and, what was more, demanding use of the main auditorium. Politics came in here, as so many of those involved in the opera were strong supporters of St Luke's Theatre. They had given money and hard work and now wanted something back.

All right, Stella was willing, fair was fair, but they were impeding the work of the professional company and she was getting complaints. Her own office had been invaded by Lydia Tulloch, Philippa Darbyshire and Marcus Deit, the conductor, for what they called a conference but had sounded more like a quarrel. More, her telephone line had been tied up for an hour by Turnwall Taylor protesting to Philippa about his costume.

But this was not it. Her problem was a small suitcase which contained all the possessions of Josephine Day that she had stored in her locker in Star Court House, and which the police had not taken away.

Maisie Rolt had handed them over. 'I want you to keep them. They might not be safe here. You know how things

218

disappear, and there's a chance I might have to go off to hospital.' She knew it was more than a chance, and dicey whether she would ever come out. Stella knew this too. 'I suppose Rosa ought to have them as she claims to be Josie's executor, but I can't get at her. Just do what you can with them. I don't feel I can handle them.' Josephine had been a kind of icon, and if she was not what she had seemed but infinitely worse, then something had crumbled in Maisie's world. She would carry on at Star Court House as well as possible, but for the moment the lights were dimmed for her.

Stella understood her. It was all going to be a horrible business.

The suitcase sat on the table and she tried to ignore it.

'You know what?' she said aloud, suddenly surprising herself with the truth. 'I am troubled: I cannot believe any of this.'

What Stella Pinero, actress, sometimes film star, occasional TV performer, believed or disbelieved, might not have been important, but fate had given her a card to play.

She opened the suitcase to take a quick look inside. A few clothes, a pair of tights, some paper tissues, a sweet smell of iris and lavender all mixed, the powdery scent she associated with Josephine. It was all so personal, she could neither bury not lose the suitcase and its contents.

She would hand the suitcase over to John Coffin and he would know what to do with it.

That day, Professor Lincoln, the head of the Docklands Forensic and Pathology Institute, which was jointly funded by the Home Office and the university and which the Second City police had access to, recovered from the 'flu that had swept through his laboratories and decimated the staff, and came back to work. He would have been back before but his wife had been sicker than he was, and blamed it on him. 'All those nasty bugs you work with.' He had tried in vain to tell her of the precautions that were taken, but she had refused to hear and had hidden herself away behind her sneezes. He was glad to get back to his office.

He read through his letters and papers, he prided himself on keeping his eye on everything. That done and a cup of coffee drunk, he telephoned John Coffin. He knew the position he was in and intended to show support.

'What about lunch at my club?' He had recently joined the Athenæum, and although he called himself 'not a clubby man', he liked to pop in occasionally just to show them he was alive.

Coffin murmured something. It must have sounded like a Yes.

'Good, good, get your diary out and we'll fix a date.' Then he remembered what else he had to say. 'This'll interest you, but you may have had the report already: the beautiful Josephine . . . not suicide, after all. She was murdered . . . Signs of pressure on the neck and shoulders, and she was dead or moribund when the wrists were cut. She didn't do that herself.'

So that's why there was so little blood in the bath, thought Coffin, remembering the paleness of the water. I knew there was something wrong. He found himself nodding down the telephone as if Lincoln could see him doing it.

So he knew the worst when visited in a hurry by a perturbed Chief Inspector Archie Young. The news broke into their conviction that they knew who the killer of Amy Dean was, even if the motive was still a puzzler. They had a confession.

Or they had thought so. But now the sanctity of the confessional was broken. Nothing was quite what it seemed. Perhaps it never had been. For a man like Archie Young, strong in convictions, honest-minded if not subtle, this was hard to bear.

If Josephine was a murder victim herself, her death was no longer a confession.

The Chief Commander went back to St Luke's Mansions and waited for Stella to arrive. He had left a message for her; he guessed she would call as soon as she could.

She let herself in with own key and hurried up the stairs. She came in, bright-eyed and cheerful, the day had gone really well and her new make-up was pretty, and it was lovely to have a message from John and she was happy to be here, and then he told her the news. 'She was murdered.'

Stella took a deep breath and began to cry. Her tears were angry. 'Shouldn't have happened,' she muttered. 'I knew she was in a state, Maisie knew, you knew and we didn't help her.' She rounded on him: 'Who did it?'

Coffin shook his head without answering.

Stella banged on the table angrily. 'I need a drink. Whisky, I think.'

The Chief Commander said: 'If it's any comfort to you, I think she would have gone soon, anyway. If someone hadn't killed her, she would have taken her own life. There was much truth in what we thought. She was tired of life. And a little frightened, I think.'

'It's no comfort. Can I have that whisky?'

He got her one, not as strong as it might have been, he hated it when Stella drank, he knew what she could be like. He took nothing himself, he found no comfort in it these days.

'Aren't you having any?'

He told her why.

'No comfort in it. No comfort anywhere, by the way you look.'

'Except in you.'

'And not even me always?' She put down the drink. 'You're right. Doing no good at all. Will you get who did it?'

He put his arms round her and she rested herself against him. Warmth and comfort given and received.

'I promise, Stella, I promise to do my best.'

She remembered then. 'I've got something for you. Her case, Josie's case with a few things in it that she left at Star Court House. They were not taken by your people. Maisie handed the case over to me.'

'Where is it?'

221

'I left it in the hall. I was going to bring it over to you.'

'Josephine seems to have kept more of her possessions in Star Court House than in her own home.'

'It was a habit she'd got into after she was robbed twice. She thought it was safer. George Eliot House was always being vandalized or broken into. Especially before Rosa came on the scene.'

The case was sitting by the front door and Tiddles was sitting on it. Might be nothing in it that would help but you could hope. 'Hop it, Tiddles.'

Upstairs, he opened it. As Stella had said, it contained nothing but the sort of clothes you might need if you were staying overnight. Tights, underthings, a nightdress. The clothes were old but of good quality, silk and soft lace, carefully darned with mismatching cotton in clumsy stitches. Oddly, piercingly touching.

He felt like crying himself.

'Nothing much.'

'No.' Stella sat and watched. 'Nice bra and pants, but very old. *Mousseline de soie* . . . can't get that now, the silk-worms have gone on strike.'

Coffin slipped his hand into a pocket in the lid. Papers. He drew them out.

A few folded pages from a newspaper. One printed on good shiny paper. He unfolded it. The student newspaper from the university. Not an old copy but from last year.

On the front page was a large photograph of a university function: a ball following a meeting of the Senate and a Degree-giving.

Sir Thomas and his wife, his son Martin with a pretty girl. That must be Amy Dean, there she was in a low-cut dress, smiling. Behind her was her father, also smiling and holding a champagne glass. Angela was there too.

He studied the background figures. That surely was Harry Coleridge in a black tie and dinner jacket with his arm round his wife, gaunt and anxious in an over-fussy dress? And he couldn't be sure . . . but that pair looked like the pair of students, Beenie and Mick.

There they all were, all the star players.

222

CHAPTER 20

The last days

Stella stared over his shoulder. 'I went to that ball myself.'
'They asked me, I think,' said Coffin, abstracted by what
he saw. 'But I didn't go.'
'You wouldn't.' But she uttered the words kindly.
Now he wished he had. He stared thoughtfully at Harry
Coleridge's face. Wish I'd known he was there, I'll need to
talk to him.
'Whom did you go with?' he said to Stella.
'Perry Dalloway.'
'Ah.' That was all right. Everyone knew about Perry
Dalloway. 'Was Josephine there?'
Stella considered. 'Yes, I think she was.'
And Harry Coleridge. Stella wouldn't know him, of
course. Josephine would have known Betsy Coleridge.
'Do you know Mrs Coleridge?'
Knowledge flooded into her eyes. 'By name, poor lady
. . . You wouldn't think a policeman would do that, would
you?'
'In some ways,' he said, 'we must count among the most
violent of men. It's in our life and it must shape us.'
Stella stared at him as if she didn't understand.
'Never mind,' he said. He was moved by a strong sense
of urgency. He reckoned he had less than a day or two
now in which to see this complex web of interlocking cases
cleared up.
Or anyway set the investigation on the right course from
which it could not be deflected. After that, his own position
might be such that he had no power. He would be pushed
to the sideline by his own resignation.
True, he might then be heading for a happy private life
with Stella, but he would have no power. Possibly not much

223

money either. Perhaps he could work for sister Letty. And there were his mother's memoirs to edit.

'I'm going to act,' he said aloud.

'You usually do, don't you?' But she could see he was looking through her and not at her, and that he had not heard what she said.

She touched his arm gently. 'I'm here.'

Next day was wet and stormy, neatly echoing his mood. He cleared all the urgent matters on his desk, then ordered in every relevant file on the death of Amy Dean and Josephine Day. Also what there was on the earlier murder of Virginia Scott and what could be obtained on the even earlier death of Josephine's daughter. What they had, he said.

'Précised?' Fiona asked.

'No, the lot, in full.' He turned towards his young assistant. 'You can stay, Andrew, I will want your help.'

'Mine too, I should think,' said Fiona under her breath, having some idea of what was coming.

It took time to get all that he wanted, and he could imagine that some comment was passing around, not all of it friendly, especially from Paul Lane and Archie Young, the two most closely concerned.

And Harry Coleridge. But he let his mind pass over that name for the moment.

Not quite a roomful, he thought, as the trolleys of documentation arrived, but certainly several deskfuls.

And how many days' work? he asked himself. Well, he hadn't got the time. He would keep at it all night if he had to, and Andrew too. He handed out his instructions, and settled down.

He worked fast and efficiently, already he had seen a lot of the material and knew his way around it. There were certain facts he was looking for.

Noreen Day, Josephine's child, father unnamed. Was her birth and the absence of her father the first crisis trigger in Josephine's life? He had Noreen's picture and she had been bonny. Dark-haired, plump, and with an air of soft vulner-

224

ability that must have been very attractive to men. Perhaps Josephine had looked like that once, before she thinned herself down to become a model and before age, drugs and drink had taken their toll.

Noreen had been strangled and her body left in Pickers-kill Wood. Before this, she and her mother had been heard to quarrel violently. Josephine was already on the bottle and probably drugs as well, her behaviour had been erratic and unpredictable. Violence from her could not be ruled out. A neighbour, one Sergeant Harry Coleridge, had spoken of a fight between mother and daughter. About a man, he had thought, the girl had only just started work and was finding her feet in the world. Josephine seemed to have been unable to accept the girl's desire for freedom, hence the quarrels. They might have had a fight. Bruises on the girl could be related to this. But there had been no hard evidence. No fingerprints or body traces could be found. The killer had worn gloves, that much was clear, there was at least one mark on her throat which looked like a gloved hand. The case was left on the record. The investigating officers had been Inspector Tim Taylor and Sergeant Wendy Lotham.

Virginia Scott: a mass of forensic evidence that had got them nowhere. She had been strangled, her body left on the university campus, on a deserted area near to the car park but hidden from observation by a belt of trees and shrubs planted by the landscape gardener to hide the cars from the Senate and Library buildings. It was not over-looked. The girl's body had been found by the security guards and it was conjectured that the killer had been planning to move the body but had been hindered by workmen arriving to clear away a marquee used for a ball the night before. She had had old bruises on her arms and body. Her handbag was nearby, but it had no fingerprints on it except her own. A smudge of mud where the killer might have handled it with gloved hands. Students had been interviewed, the teaching and administrative staff gone over, but nothing definite had come out of it. Virginia had friends but was close to no one. She had worked hard, and done a variety of welfare work both on the campus and in the local community.

From her photograph, she too had had that air of soft attraction that Coffin was coming to see as the mark of this killer's victims. This killer liked them soft.

Her parents lived in France and had fled back there after the inquest released their daughter's body. An unsolved case, still open.

Amy Dean, the most complex case of the three. He knew all the details here, it was fresh in his head, but he ran a quick check. No helpful traces in the car, her blood, her father's fingerprints, some other smudges not identified.

CHAPTER 21

Towards Thursday and a certain Friday

He drank some coffee, and let Andrew go. It was past midnight, and he had the confused impression that he had spoken to several people on the telephone, and to Stella twice, without remembering what he had said.

The forensic evidence on Josephine Day was still not complete, he had a question he wanted to ask. He looked at the clock. Professor Lincoln worked late. Or if he didn't, he was going to.

Not in his office, he was tracked down at home, unsurprised and alert.

Coffin asked his question. 'Yes, strangled manually by soft, steady heavy pressure. Yes, gloved hands. No, not rubber or plastic, leather gloves, you could pick up the graining on the skin.'

'Thanks. You have given me what I wanted.'

'Think nothing of it. Can I go back to bed now?'

He went to bed himself. Hungry for confirmation of what he suspected. But before departing, he left a note for Fiona or Lysette (it was due to be Fiona but he was never sure

226

which face he would see) to make an appointment for Chief Inspector Coleridge to call on him.

He underlined it. No refusal, that meant. Lysette would understand. Out of courtesy he ought to let Lane and Young know what he was up to but he had no doubt they would have ways of knowing.

He got into his office early, but not before Lysette. She was doing more than her rota, could it be she was sorry for him? They met in his outer office where she was sorting his post.

'Surprised to see me so early?'

She smiled politely. Not surprised at anything you do, the smile said. But it was nicely said; with Fiona it would have had a sharper edge. Still, you need a Fiona in your life, he told himself again.

'I'm surprised to see you, though. Where's Fiona? Thought it was her day.'

'She has 'flu. She'll make up for me later.'

'Did you get through to Chief Inspector Coleridge?'

She nodded. 'He's there now, waiting for you.'

Coleridge was standing with his back to the door, looking out of the window. He swung round as the Chief Commander came into the room. His face looked pale and grim.

'You wanted to see me?'

'Yes, let's sit down.'

Coleridge still stood. 'If this is about anything personal . . . domestic . . .'

'Not at the moment. I wanted to ask you about the death of Josephine Day's daughter, the girl Noreen.'

Coffin watched the other man's face. I've surprised him, not what he expected.

Coleridge frowned. 'That was a long while ago.'

'I think it's relevant to a current investigation.' He saw Coleridge change. 'It was never cleared up, was it?'

'No.'

'But you were a neighbour, you knew them both.'

'Not well.'

'How well?'

Coleridge did not answer. Then he said: 'The mother

227

was not easy to know, even then. The daughter was only a youngster. On her first job. She wanted out, I reckoned, and her mother wouldn't have it. She didn't want the girl to go to work, wanted her to stay at school, go to college, Noreen didn't want that. Not all girls do. I helped her get the job, I knew the manager of a small haulage company, one of Jem Dean's.'

'I think you knew them both better than you are admitting. You knew they quarrelled? Actually fought?'

'It's the sort of thing neighbours do know . . . They were very physical, both of them.' He realized what he had said and started to walk around the room. 'Look, I don't like this. What is it you want?'

'Just to go on talking a bit.'

'There's something else for sure. You've got it in for me because of the business with Betsy.'

'I'm not concerning myself with that at this very minute. It seems you gave evidence to Inspector Taylor that a man was involved.'

'I don't remember that,' said Coleridge sourly. 'You'll have to ask Taylor.'

'He's dead, though, isn't he? And Wendy Lotham. Killed in the same car accident three years ago. But what you said is on the record. Were you that man?'

'If you are asking me if I was involved with either the girl or her mother, then the answer is no.'

'But you know who the man was?'

'No. Someone she met at work, probably.'

Coleridge sat waiting.

'That's all,' said Coffin. 'Thank you for coming.' He knew that he had left Coleridge in mid-air and he meant to do it.

Coleridge sat there for a moment without speaking. Then, still without speaking, he got up and went out.

Just at the door, Coffin caught his eye. Expression of a man who knows the hounds of hell are after him.

Lysette appeared at the door. Before she could speak, the Chief Commander said: 'Forget it, whatever you were going to say, I'm going out.'

'I was going to offer you a cup of coffee.'

'I'll wait for that.' Lysette's coffee was worth waiting for. 'But let no calls or visitors through while I drink it.'

He knew and Lysette knew that a queue would be forming. But he had long since learned how to walk past.

He drove himself to Josephine's flat in George Eliot House. It was a dark morning, still early, and few people were around. He had the key in his pocket and let himself in.

Empty. The traces of the fire had been tidied up. Something the investigators might regret now it was a case of murder. Otherwise nothing had been touched.

He walked round. He could see the signs of the earlier police inquiry, drawers opened and the contents turned over, cupboard doors not quite closed. A bit of white powder here and there as if a desultory attempt had been made to find fingerprints. Well, they would have to try harder. They might flush out a few fingerprints, but they would not be those of the killer for he had worn gloves. Other forensic traces would be difficult because the fire brigade had been here too. The fire had doubtless been started with the purpose of destroying evidence.

A sad, lonely dwelling place, he thought, as he went around, but there is hope here, I may find your killer, Josephine. Oh, Josephine, what were you up to? What stopped you behaving in a straightforward fashion instead of burying the girl?

Some terrible inner compulsion, compounded of what?

Did you know who killed your child? I think I know. And if I do, then I believe I will have the killer of those girls too. Could you have named him, Josephine, is that the guilt you bore?

He picked up the tablet of soap by the bath and studied it. There were some greasy marks by the kitchen sink which interested him too. Soap again, he thought. A muddy streak by the fireplace, and one on the door.

He was ready to leave when he heard a noise at the door.

Harry Coleridge stood there. His face was blotched with red, his eyes angry.

'I followed you round.'

'You shouldn't have done that.'

Coleridge swayed back and forth on his heels. 'You think you know everything.'

'I know I don't.'

'I hate you. I've disliked you for a long while, but now I hate you. I'd like to kill you.' Coleridge tried to push his way through the door.

Coffin held steady, he got the door closed behind him. 'There's enough of that already. Don't be a fool. Go home. Phone in that you're ill. Wait till I come to you.'

Coleridge hesitated, then turned and walked down the stairs. At the bottom, he turned round and looked up. Just once. Then he strode away.

God help his wife, thought Coffin. I shouldn't have told him to go home, I'd better do something about that quickly.

He went down to his car and picked up the telephone. 'Lysette . . . get hold of Chief Superintendent Lane and tell him to send someone round to Chief Inspector Coleridge's home and wait for him if he isn't there. Someone ought to stay with his wife, whether he comes there or not.'

It was all he could do for the moment.

'Sir . . .' Lysette had something to say. 'Mr James Dean telephoned. He would like to make an appointment. Soon, if possible.'

'Did he ask to speak to me?' I am thinking about this, Coffin told himself, I am definitely thinking. The interview with Coleridge had raised the level of his mood, it had been like pouring petrol on a fire. He was very nearly out of his own control.

'No. Just to make an appointment.'

'Right. Make an appointment for today as soon as he likes. Don't say I am out.'

He issued a few other directions and then started the car.

He drove past the university where Sir Thomas and Lady Blackhall were probably still at breakfast, with their own burden of death and guilt, the memory of which had shaped their marriage. They both had professional success, but the canker would always be there. Martin Blackhall seemed a

230

nice boy, if weak; now he too would have Amy Dean in his memory to brood about. Some families collected bad memories.

By now it was not so early and he had to decide which of two addresses he should go to. A telephone call would have settled it, but he wanted to arrive without warning. He had gambled.

The office would do it.

He knew the address and knew the building, one of the big new office blocks near the Tower of London.

James Dean had the whole of the first floor, and his logo, an interlocking JD, was so dominant that it felt as if he must own the whole building.

He pushed his way past the usual security and reception desks to Dean's own office. Through an outer office with another receptionist and a secretary ensconced in her own alcove, complete with flowers and flashing green screens; through another door to an ante-room leading to the holy of holies.

A familiar face stared at him from a desk here.

'Hello, Angela.' He was half surprised, but he had had some expectations of seeing her. 'What are you doing here?'

'Mr Dean gave me a job.'

'So he did. This is where you were running to when I saw you packing.' Coffin looked round at the thick white carpet, the grey suede chairs and banquette, her white desk with no sign of work on it. 'So you didn't go to Star Court House?'

'My mother knows,' she said defensively, 'and I've got a flat. Maisie Rolt didn't want me.'

She stood up, swaying slightly, with that air of sexual invitation and vulnerability that could be both exciting and damaging. She came from behind her desk, he could smell the scent of violets and a faint hint of sweat. She smelt like a woman.

'Nasty bruise on your arm. How did you get that?'

She looked down at one very white and rounded upper arm where a thick bruise was spread, and did not answer.

'Sit down,' he said, harsh in spite of himself. You had to

231

push Angie away from you, or you'd be moving towards her fast. He could feel the draw. 'I'm going through to see your boss . . .'

'Oh, but . . .'

'He wants to see me.'

Jem Dean appeared at the open door to his office. He looked from Coffin to the girl.

'Toddle off, Angie. Get yourself some coffee.' He held the door open for the Chief Commander. 'Come on in. Didn't expect you. I was going to see you.'

'So you're looking after Angela? Nasty bruise she's got there.'

'She must bruise easy,' said Dean in a comfortable voice. 'Walked into something, I expect.'

'Like a hand.'

'Sit down, won't you?' He sat down himself behind his desk and motioned Coffin to a chair on the other side. 'Not been here before, have you?'

'No.' Coffin looked around him, and thought of his own office. A soft cashmere coat was slung over a chair, briefcase and brown gloves thrown upon it. 'I'm impressed.' He was meant to be, of course. 'Has Harry Coleridge been on the telephone to you?'

'Harry Coleridge? Why should you think that?'

'Because you telephoned my office. I thought it might be cause and effect.'

'He might have.'

'He thinks I've got him marked for the murder of a girl, one you might have known. Noreen Day.'

'And have you?'

'I'll answer that later.'

Dean sat back in his chair. 'Bit early for a drink, or I'd offer you one. Still, it's there. Whisky?'

'No, thank you.'

'You'd have said yes fast enough, once.'

'Long past.'

'So what brings you down here?'

'I could turn that back on you and ask you why you wanted to see me.'

232

'News about Amy, of course. It's about time I heard something. You seem to forget what she was to me.'

'It wasn't because you had that call from Coleridge?'

'Why should you think that?'

'You and Harry are close enough, I think.'

'I hardly see the man.'

Coffin leaned forward. 'Perhaps I wasn't thinking of seeing . . . There are other ways of being close. Shared habits, tastes, opportunities.'

'What you are you getting at?'

'I'll answer in a different way: I never forget what Amy was to you and what you were to her.'

Dean frowned. 'You really are a bastard.' He got up and walked to the window. A carefully arranged courtyard was all he could see. 'I'm not sure if I like being banded with Coleridge. He's a brutal beast.'

'Glad to hear you say so. Yes, he does enjoy beating up women. He'd say it was his temper and maybe he'd had a drop too much, but I think he relishes it.'

'I'd be a fool if I didn't see what you were getting at with your remarks about Angela and her bruises.'

'Glad you see it.'

'But I might remind you that Amy was my daughter.'

Coffin was on his feet too now. 'Ah, but Amy was not your daughter, was she? I remember your blood group from way back and I know hers. You adopted her. There is no way she could be your natural daughter.'

'I won't remind you of how you know my blood group,' said Dean. 'Although you might think about it . . . I loved Amy. All right, she was our adopted daughter, but that doesn't rule out love. Far from it.'

'I know you saved my life. But frankly, I've also always believed you betrayed us that day. That's what I think about. No, don't draw up your fists, we're both too old for that sort of thing and I think I might be fitter than you are these days. I've kept in the job, you see, Jem.'

'So far.'

'Oh, I'm well aware that you've had a hand in stirring up that sort of trouble for me, Jem, it's your style. Once

233

false, always false. A false husband and a false father. Amy watched your violence towards her mother, and she must have found your attentions to herself difficult to handle. And yet she may have liked it too, you always went for the ones that liked it a little rough. But I guess it got to her. And Josephine had been talking to her, they were seen . . . Her friends knew the state of mind she was in, the pair Beenie and Mick knew. They knew about your sexual and bruising relationship with Amy, but they didn't feel free to talk about what Amy had hidden inside herself, she felt so guilty. But that's why she was drawn to Star Court House, it exorcised something inside her. Virginia started it and Amy carried on. She was looking for a pardon, a remission from her disease. Maisie Rolt sensed that she was looking for something out of Star Court House and knew it wasn't healthy. But it was your fault with Amy. She had guilt inside because of how she felt about you. But I think she was going to talk and that's why you killed her.'

'You've said too much.' There was violence in Dean's face. 'I'll see you lose your job over this.'

'I dare say you would if you could, but there might be some doubt about that. What you don't realize is that I don't care. That means I feel free to say what I like.'

'You accuse me of killing my own Amy. I won't stand for that.' He was angry but cool.

'Yes, you killed her, and put her body in Pickerskill Wood, dumped the car, her car, your car once, and dropped her sweater where it would be found. You tucked the bus ticket in her pocket . . . because I think you wanted her found. You're a devious bastard, Dean.'

Serialists got their kicks from strange pleasures and Pickerskill Wood and the exposed body could be his.

'You used Pickerskill Wood once before when you killed Josephine's daughter, and I think Josie knew it but was helpless to do anything about it. She was under suspicion herself.' She had been helpless then, that first time, but she had meant to make things right after the death of Amy Dean. 'She buried Amy for you. And I'm only guessing why, not to hide her, but to give her respect. And then she came to you. Or to Coleridge. Perhaps he was the go-between.' Coffin was guessing there again, but it was a good guess. These two men hunted as a pair.

'She was out of her mind.'

'A little bit, I think, but she was ready to go for you. You employed her daughter. Coleridge got her that job. Did he look for birds for the farmyard for you? That was what you called it, I believe.'

'I was good to that bloody Josephine. I gave her a pension. What do you think she lived on?'

So that was what had fuelled Josephine's guilt. She had taken money from her daughter's killer and kept quiet. Fact after fact was slotting into place.

Dean's voice was rising. 'And the other girl, Virginia, am I supposed to have killed her too? I suppose I couldn't get her body to Pickerskill Wood. Only three murders. I'm very abstemious, aren't I?'

The right girl, the right mood, he had to have those, and then there was the desire for death and violence. He was a periodic serial killer.

'Yes, you are fastidious, hard to satisfy in your specifications, but get them right and you do your job, Jem. You liked it, it was your pleasure.'

'You are playing with words, guessing. You'll never prove it.'

'No, I may not get you for those other murders, but I will get you for the murder of Josephine Day. Oh, you wore gloves, lovely soft leather gloves such as I see over there, and gloves leave a print too. You left prints.'

'There was a fire, I believe.'

'Yes, set up by you to burn any evidence that you might have let lie. But you know yourself that once we start looking, when we know where to look, we find things. That's what we are good at. And one thing leads to another. You'll stand trial, Jem.'

'You've already tried and convicted me.'

'Right, I have.'

'Very ethical. I'll get you for this.'

'Try it . . . Oh, and don't destroy the gloves, that would

235

be very silly. Oh, and another thing, I have asked Chief Superintendent Lane to meet me here. I shan't go till he arrives.' He sat back in his chair. 'And Angela won't be out there. I've asked for a policewoman to come and take her away.'

Dean started to fumble in a drawer low in his desk.

Coffin watched without moving. 'Go ahead, I won't stop you. Shoot yourself. It'll be a pleasure to watch you.'

'I'm not going to shoot myself, I'm getting a drink.' Dean planked down a bottle of whisky and a glass. 'I'll fight you on this.'

They sat staring at each other in bitter hostility until the deep tones of Chief Superintendent Paul Lane could be heard outside.

As he drove away, a kind of film of people, places and events was running through his mind. His city. He knew that somewhere in that city Angela was crying and nursing her bruises, and that Beenie and Mick were saying I told you so to each other. Josephine, Maisie Rolt, Sir Thomas and Victoria Blackhall, Stella, yes, always Stella. His own face was there somewhere.

The university. He slowed down as he passed its buildings, almost minded to stop and say to the security guard: And is it you who have been telephoning me with warnings about watching my back? Your daughter works on the switchboard and probably knows what you've been trying to do. It could have been her voice in the background. But he knew he wouldn't bother. Might take the man out for a drink one day and see what he had to say.

He wasn't going in the direction of Star Court House, and nowhere near Pickerskill Wood, but he wouldn't forget it.

He recalled his drive through the tunnel, struggling not to crash into one of Our General's riders. Her Valkyries.

But all the time underneath, he was thinking of that relationship between Dean and Coleridge.

Coleridge might never be punished. He'd get away with it, retire and grow roses and heaven help his wife.

236

He felt as though he had lived through his own *Götterdäm-merung*. He avoided his own headquarters, he didn't know what was going to happen to him professionally, nothing good probably.

He drove straight back to St Luke's Mansions. Too much to hope to see Stella, but he would find her somewhere.

But there she was, surrounded by the cheerful group of ladies from the Choral Society and the Friends of St Luke's. She greeted him.

'Tremendously good rehearsal for the chorus and soloists. Lovely stuff.'

'I want to speak to you. Come upstairs.'

'Of course, love to.' She let herself be led away.

For once they were on their own. No cat, no dog to disturb them. Both animals had been there, however. A letter was sticking out from under the mat, where Tiddles usually hid away his trophies. Goodness knows how long it had been there, Tiddles had chewed it and possibly Bob had sat on it. He put it on the table, he would read it later. Now he wanted to talk to Stella.

'I've really blown it. I shall probably resign. I let personal anger and animosity boil over.' He clenched his hands into fists. 'But I was right, I was right.'

'Calm down. Of course you were.' It was her turn to be the stronger, the comforter. She put her arms round him. 'You'll come through.'

'I might be a dead loss to you. I've still got that bloody Board of Inquiry hanging over me. I'm supposed to be seeing the chairman tomorrow.' Was that really tomorrow? He felt timeless. 'He'll probably suggest I resign quietly. I'm not sure you ought to take me on. I might be a walking disaster for you. You ought to steer clear.' He looked at her painfully. 'I have to admit that, inside me, I thought I was the one to choose and that you would be lucky marrying me. I wrapped it up, but it was that way. I know better now. Forgive me for being insufferable, Stella.'

Stella started to laugh. 'I will say for you that when you have a swing in mood, then you do it thoroughly. I love

237

you and you love me, whatever that means, and I mean to hang on to it. And cheer up, tomorrow's Friday.'

He stared at her: the day he had the interview with the chairman. What else?

'Friday, remember Friday. We're getting married.'

'Stella, dearest Stella.' She had cracked some hard carapace inside him, releasing him. He started to laugh. One way or another, Friday was going to be his **Big Day**.

His eye fell upon the letter which Tiddles had chewed and which Bob had sat upon. How long had it been under the rug in the hall? No stamp, it had been delivered by hand. His eyes still on Stella, he opened it. 'Let me just read this, love, then I'll be with you again.'

It was from Josephine, she had signed it clearly and boldly, dated it the day of her death. He read:

When I saw you that first day I had already buried Amy. But I wanted her found and I knew you would find her. I could not leave her where she was. A rat had begun to gnaw her face. I am a little mad on this issue, I know. Why did I not go to the police? Quite simple. I was frightened. I had come very close to being accused of murder before. I had found this body. I knew how the police mind worked. I would be their first suspect. There was so much to incriminate me. I knew her, I had worked with her, I had found her.

Then such guilt swept over me, I decided to confess after all, tell all that I knew about my own child, her life and her death, most of all tell of her relationship with Dean, tell everything I could. I shall let Dean know. You might call this suicidal, perhaps I desire a death. I write this to you, just in case. I judge you an honest man. Help me if you can.

'What is it?'

'Read it for yourself.' He handed the letter over. 'I didn't help her, I didn't help her.'

238

The telephone began to ring. He picked up the telephone, listened, then turned towards Stella, her head bent over the letter.

'Betsy Coleridge stuck a knife into her husband this morning.' He took a deep breath. 'He died on the way to hospital.'